FATES ILLUMINATED

CALL OF THE NORNS
BOOK 1

AIMEE VANCE

REVEL BOOKS

Revel Books
ISBN: 979-8-9863649-7-1

www.aimeevancebooks.com

This book is for you, whoever you are. I am so unbelievably grateful you've even picked up my book, and I hope that you, too, can remember that the sun is still shining even on the cloudiest of days.

I'm so proud of you for being you.

PROLOGUE

On the edge of a forest deep in the wilderness sat a space untouched by time. Mist rose off a lake, fog settling in after dusk. A small hut of rough-cut wood was perched along the water's edge. Smoke curled out of the chimney, rising into the night sky as green and purple wisps floated overhead.

Nothing truly spectacular could be noted about the setting, the scene not uncommon across the stunning land-scape of Scandinavia. However, the same could not be said of the residents of that hut — three women who were anything but common.

Stories had been passed down of the legendary trio, weaving fates throughout the ages. Each day, the women gathered, casting runes and foretelling the fates of mortals and gods alike as they'd done for millennia.

A short woman, hunched with age, rocked back and forth slowly on the small porch, eyes fogged to match the mist rising off the lake. Her long, white hair was pulled back into a loose braid, flowing over her elbow. She sat like this often, silently watching the passing of time. Her chair creaked to match the sound of the wind through the trees.

Suddenly, she stopped. The wind seemed to pause, waves on the lake settling, as everything went still, posed, and listened.

"Stop," she muttered, her voice husky with age. The sky lit suddenly, greens swirling overhead in streaks, almost resembling the roots of a tree as fate bent to her words.

Inside the hut, a woman — younger but not young, taller but not tall — was perched on a seat in front of a large loom. Her long, brown hair, greying at her temples, swayed as she worked, delicately handling each thread. The only thing tying together the sisters in looks was their pale, almost glowing skin.

At hearing her sister's voice, the woman paused, and her hands fell to her sides. She gently placed the thread in her hand on the edge of the loom as she stood. Her movements were so fluid that she seemed to float as she emerged from the hut and stopped at her sister's side.

"What do you see, Urd?" she asked her sister, leaning closer.

"The missing thread," Urd answered in a hush.

The younger sister's brow scrunched, but she said nothing. She was used to Urd's whims and statements after all these years.

Turning to her sister, Urd's fogged eyes cleared for a moment as her voice filled with urgency. "The thread that was in your hand doesn't belong there, Verandi. Her time is not now but long ago. The Promised."

If the tone Urd's voice had taken on hadn't piqued Verandi's interest, the mention of a Promised would have. It had been a long time since anyone had mentioned the sisters' followers and friends. But how could a thread be missing?

Verandi cocked her head to the side in thought before responding. "Tell me what must be done."

Leaning down, Verandi took Urd's hand, helping her rise to her feet. They shuffled inside, light dim as the fire glowed from the hearth. Verandi's hand flicked towards the fire, and it roared to life. The room was cast in a warm, bright glow, highlighting the tapestry in front of them.

They stopped at the foot of the loom, admiring their work. The tapestry was massive, easily stretching the length of the hut and impossibly beyond. Every inch was full of tiny images and details. Threads of every color imaginable, and even some that weren't, came together to paint the picture of time.

However, the threads lay still, unmoving. Once, long ago, some of the threads had glowed, magic imbuing the very lives of those chosen by the dragons. That seemed so long ago, though. It was hard to remember what was fact and what was only fireside stories.

Verandi dropped her sister's arm, easing her gently onto the stool she'd vacated earlier. She hesitated for a moment but then stepped closer to the tapestry. No light shone from the weave as it had in the past, the only light in the room coming from the fire in the hearth.

"Go back," Urd instructed. Verandi nodded, scanning the weave in front of her. She walked along the edge of the tapestry, eyes searching for any imperfections, even though she was confident there were none. Fate didn't make mistakes.

There, far back, was a snag, just as her sister said.

Verandi gasped, reaching for the fabric. She ran her fingers over it, feeling the tiny dimple in the weave. Her lips turned down as a memory from long ago surfaced. "This has never happened before. Do you think —"

"Find Skuld," Urd interrupted. "It will take all three of us to fix this."

Verandi paused, standing stock still. "You know the rules of time, sister."

She nodded. "I know."

"Who could be worthy of such a risk, knowing the effect we could have if we change this? There is a reason we foretell each Fate at birth. To change it after could be catastrophic in ways we cannot yet see."

As if listening to the conversation, a large, dark head peeled itself above the calm waters of the mist-covered lake. Small waves were sent across the surface, lapping against the shore. The thread resting along the edge of the loom, waiting to be intertwined with the fates around it, glowed for a moment. It let off a subtle light but dimmed again before the sisters noticed.

"Not one fate, but all," Urd declared on a nod, her eyes having now returned to their foggy state. "It's the only way."

"You know how dangerous this is," Verandi's tone was now full of concern, urging her sister to see reason. But Urd said nothing; her unseeing gaze now turned to the fire.

Verandi sighed, accepting there was no changing Urd's mind once it was set. After all, she was the Past. Decisions were already behind her.

"Find Skuld," Urd instructed her again quietly.

With that, Verandi walked out of the hut. She stood on the porch staring over the lake, lost in thought. It was still once more, only the sound of the trees rustling overhead filling her mind.

"I hope you're right," she said, glancing back at her sister, now sitting at the loom. Then, she stepped off the porch and into the mist.

Usually, the sound of the birthday song filled me with joy. Each repeated verse forced my smile a little wider, ending in a finale of happiness gushing from head to toe. After all, I was the self-proclaimed queen of birthdays.

Any excuse to throw a party, you could count me in. In college, this was a handy skill to have. No one could pull together a theme party quite as I could, and I wasn't talking about your run-of-the-mill luau or Athletes and Mathletes. I could pull together that too, of course, but I liked to be different, original, one of a kind.

The usefulness of this skill set followed me into adulthood. But now, I was cornered by my young nieces at holiday gatherings to brainstorm very elaborately themed parties months prior to their actual birthdays. Themes were now based on cartoon characters, movies, animals you name it, I'd done it.

I was the master of balloon arches, a crepe paper whiz,

and the inventor of new and ridiculous party games for kids. It was my own brand of magic, weaving together a party sure to leave everyone in the room smiling.

I still loved parties, but the high of seeing everyone around me happy and enjoying themselves wasn't the same anymore.

Today, the birthday song was for me. I glanced around my best friend's adorable suburban kitchen at the banner, the kid-decorated cake, and the giant number "31" balloons. Combine that with three of my favorite people in the entire world — my best friend Sabrina and her two little daughters, Annie and Jasmine — were singing their hearts out at max volume, and this easily should have been my favorite day of the year.

I forced a broad smile, as that was what they expected, and finished the song with them, harmonizing the end the way my mother always did growing up. Leaning forward, I exaggeratedly blew out the obscene number of candles covering every square inch of available space on the top of the cake.

"I put all 31 candles on, Aunt Shelbie!" Annie squealed in delight, clapping. That much was evident from the flames licking off the cake, ready to take off an eyebrow or two.

"No lo toques!" Sabrina cried, too late, as Jasmine ripped a large chunk from the side of the cake. "I'm so sorry. We had her hearing checked and everything. It turns out she is truly a terrible listener and doesn't give two shits about anything we say," she said in an exasperated sigh.

Now covered in icing, Jasmine climbed into my lap and shoved her toddler fingers in my mouth. I chuckled, leaned into her poufy black pigtails, and kissed her head. It was impossible to resist loving on this cute little hellion my best friend was raising.

"That's okay," I replied, licking Jasmine's sticky brown fingers now covered in white icing. Her giggle floated through the room, warming me from head to toe. "Annie, did you decorate this for me?"

"Yes!" she cried excitedly. "Do you love the sprinkles?"

"I sure do. Especially the way you put them on only the left side." I tried not to laugh while I eyed Sabrina. I knew how much it must have driven my perfectionist best friend nuts not to fix it. "Thank you for my wonderful party, girls. I feel so loved!"

Sabrina handed me a slice of funfetti cake, arguably the best flavor, and gave me a side hug. She rounded the table to sit with her little girls. "This is going to be your year, Shelbie. I can feel it."

After I helped Sabrina get her girls in the tub and ready for bed, I grabbed my bag to head home.

"I love you. You know that, right?" Sabrina said as she walked me to the door.

"I sure do." I leaned in and kissed her cheek. "That cake was something. I can't believe you didn't fix it. You've loosened up a little, it seems."

She punched my shoulder, and I mock-rubbed the sore from my arm. "Did you hear Annie give me the blow-by-blow of each part of the box-mix funfetti cake?

She was ready to present her show stopper to the judges."

Sabrina laughed, shaking her head as her silky brown hair swayed with the motion. "She does that with everything now. That kid took it a bit too literal when she was named after you. Shelbie *Ann*. You'd think I would have been more prepared for her extra behavior and the massive mop of curls." At that, I got one of her signature eye-rolls. I earned many of those from her over the years with my 'extra' behavior.

Annie's hair, though, that was all André. I refused to be blamed for that. Any genetic traits that Sabrina had brought to the table with her shiny, straight brown hair had been overridden completely. Both of her girls had pretty black textured hair, like their dad, and it had been an uphill battle for Sabrina to learn to deal with it. Curl care was no joke.

I laughed as I hugged her again. "How did I get so lucky to land you sixteen years ago?"

"If I remember correctly, you decided we'd be friends and then wouldn't stop talking until I answered," she reminded me with a sarcastic tone. The memory caused her to bubble out a laugh, no matter how much she tried to stay serious.

She was right, though. I happened to love introverts. Once you put in the time to make them comfortable, they made the best, most loyal companions.

"I'm the greatest thing that happened to you other than André and those two little girls, whether you admit it or not.

I knew I was just what you needed before you could even see it."

"That I can't argue with. You're the over-the-top extroverted yin to my 'leave me alone' yang." She nudged my shoulder, and I leaned in for another hug. I loved this woman fiercely. "Drive safe, okay? Give Thor some extra pets for me tonight."

Even though we lived only a thirty-minute drive apart, I always hated leaving Sabrina. She was the best friend that every girl dreamed they'd have one day — the balance in my life.

This late in the day, her usually perfect bob haircut was a little messy. Even still, it showcased the face lit with a now tired smile after a long day spent with her kids.

We were the opposite in every way physically. She had a petite frame that I towered at just under six feet, and I had the bone structure to match. Her deep tan tone and chocolate eyes sharply contrasted my pale, freckly skin and ice-blue gaze.

But really, I always felt like her sleek brown hair, compared to my frizzy, wild mane of golden curls, was the perfect depiction of our personalities; organized and orderly, practically perfect in every way, versus… me? Not so much. More like Hot Mess Express.

I waved as I headed down the front path to my Jeep parked on the street and hopped in. Who knew that the quiet, new girl I met on the first day of ninth grade would change my life for good? Sabrina was always supportive and wanted me to be happy. At the same time, she wasn't afraid to tell me her honest opinions on the many questionable decisions I'd made in my twenties, particularly in my choice of men.

I turned over the ignition and waited for the air conditioner to kick in. It was late, but the heat of the day still permeated the inside of the car. As I was buckling my seatbelt, my phone rang.

"Hi, Mom," I answered.

"Happy birthday, Bee!" she proclaimed in her high-pitched voice. "Hang on; your dad is here too. STEVE!! DID YOU FIND MY GLASSES? I CAN'T SEE MY PHONE!"

"Honey, you're *talking* on the phone, not FaceTiming her. There's nothing to see, Janet," my dad said in the background. I had heard this same conversation so many times in my life. My parents were more than a little technologically challenged.

"Thanks, guys," I said, shaking my head with a smile at their side conversation. "I'm leaving Sabrina's house from a little birthday party the girls threw me and headed home. I can FaceTime you after I take Thor out, though."

"Oh, that's okay," Mom answered. "We just wanted to make sure your day was as wonderful as you are, sugar. Dad and I always love to reminisce on the day you were born. My perfect, plump little girl. Nothing like your brother who came out with a big cone head, right, Steve? As a first-time mom, I felt so bad that I didn't think my baby was the cutest one I'd ever seen, but man, Jacob was funky. You, though, darling, were my angel baby."

I listened to her ramble the way she did every year on my birthday. I smiled as she went on about how my big, macho football player dad had adored *Steel Magnolias*, hence my name Shelbie. But since "Smith" was such a boring name, she had to spice it up with the "ie" on the end. That was my mom's definition of spicy.

She always told me how much she'd dreamt of having a girl and the years she'd spent trying, to which I could only cringe. My parents *trying* was not an image I needed in my head.

"It's dark, so I think I'm going to hang up and concentrate on driving home," I interrupted her monologue, which is what this always turned into. "I love you both. Thanks for calling!"

"Make sure you check your oil levels in your car, honey," Dad added before I disconnected. He was always looking out for me in whatever way he could.

How fortunate was I to have such loving friends and family around me? Deep in my bones, I knew that I had so much in my life. And yet, today, of all days, I couldn't escape this empty, sinking feeling.

Today, I was 31. Not even 30 anymore. I was now *in* my 30s. For some reason, that fact hit me differently.

At this point in my life, most of my friends were either living the suburban dream with kids and a husband or on some big career path with their plans laid out before them. Me? I was just getting by.

The highlight of my days was my dog, Thor. Not that there's anything wrong with being obsessed with your dog, but even I could recognize his and my bond was borderline overboard. What could I say, though? I was a sucker for the big dude.

My car rolled to a stop at a red light, and I leaned my elbow on the window's edge, resting my head in my hand as my thoughts swirled. I wasn't depressed, but I didn't have much I was looking forward to in my life, either.

A tap on my car window had me jumping to attention. I spun to see a young woman panhandling at the light. Immediately, my heart hurt to see someone so young, with so much life ahead of her, already in this position. She had a folding chair set up in the median with a suitcase of her belongings and a cardboard sign propped next to it. I turned, grabbed my purse off the passenger's seat, and pulled out what cash I had.

As I rolled down my window, I smiled genuinely at her, hoping that kindness emanated through my eyes and my gesture as I handed the money across.

"Oh, bless you," the young, blonde woman proclaimed as she leaned towards my car. She was wearing an oversized dress hanging from her tall frame, and her long hair hung loose down her back. I couldn't help but notice that she'd be stunning with a shower and clean clothes, standing tall and straight.

"Of course!" My heart warmed, happy I could be of help. I was rolling up my window when she spoke again.

"Much change is coming your way if only you open yourself to it, Shelbie. So many have been waiting for you, Promised."

My head whipped up as my eyes expanded in shock. How did this woman know my name? Did I know her? I didn't think so.

And what the hell was a *Promised?* The way she had used

it, it sounded like a title. The word sent a jolt of electricity through my body, spine straightening. I leaned back in my seat and took a second look at her.

She had changed. The dirty, homeless woman of before was no more. Instead, I saw exquisite, clean, long platinum hair curled in waves. Her clear, white-grey eyes blended into her pale, almost glowing skin.

A horn honked at me, jostling me out of the odd moment as I stepped on the gas and drove through the light. I glanced in my rearview mirror as I searched for an explanation for whatever had just happened.

But she wasn't there. The woman was gone, her bags and sign nowhere to be seen. Goosebumps broke out over my arms as I drove the rest of the way home. I cranked my music up, blasting 90's grunge rock to distract myself from the odd encounter.

I parked my car at my apartment, waving at my neighbor Sandra as she walked her tiny Pomeranian before bed. These apartments were fine, but nothing special. Three stories rose above me, with a long hallway and stairs running between the units. I was on the first floor, which I preferred with Thor.

I would have loved to own a house like Sabrina's that I could make my own, but that seemed pretty far-off in today's real estate market. Especially on one income.

As I walked down the hallway, I could already hear the thundering bark coming from my apartment.

"Thor, I'm right here!" I announced, putting my key in the lock as I talked through the door. "I see you've decided that a bark collar is useless, huh? I'll have to apologize to the neighbors again, I guess. I hope you haven't been doing this all day at every passing squirrel and falling leaf." His bark turned to a growl at my comment, and I chuckled. "I'm coming, bud. Ready for your walk?"

I turned the knob and was greeted by his hulking frame pushing through the door, ready to cover me in furry kisses.

Thor was huge. He was some kind of mutt, but he was entirely too large to be just a black lab like the rescue shelter had advertised when I brought home a puppy eight years ago. His hair was long and fluffy, silky like a black fox pelt along his shoulder blades, and his tail curled slightly up at the back.

I grabbed his leash off the wall, and he shoved past me once I had it clipped onto his collar. We headed down the hall, across the parking lot, and around the apartment complex to a walking trail nearby.

It was mostly empty this time of evening, which was excellent considering Thor loved to growl at other passing dogs for no reason. He'd never actually done anything other than growl. Even still, combining his deep rumble with his hulking size, I'd received more than a few complaints from the property management company.

I didn't care, though. This apartment was short-term, and Thor was a lifer. This pup was made for me, and I adored him, surly personality and all.

July in Denver meant that I could still feel the heat radiating off the concrete, even this late in the evening. Thor, of course, managed to find the one puddle left from yesterday's summer storm to run in, drenching his paws.

The fact that he could still maintain his scowl while

splashing in a puddle like a toddler had me laughing at the sight. I let him play for a minute, wandering around the trail and sniffing everything.

"Come on, boy." I tugged on his leash after a while, leading him home. "I'm hot, and I want a glass of wine for my birthday. Let's go inside."

Fortunately, he turned to follow me. I wasn't sure I had the arm strength to force him to do anything. We headed inside, and Thor walked over to his bed in the corner of my living room. I was glad I had the foresight not to let him on the furniture. The tiny couch in my little apartment would certainly not be big enough for us both.

My apartment was small enough as it was — tiny living room, tinier kitchen. My queen-sized bed hardly fit through the bedroom door, the space just big enough to squeeze it in with a dog bed next to it.

I'd been living here for two years but hadn't done much to the space. A few pictures hung on the walls of Sabrina and my family, but nothing of any true meaning to me.

I had told myself this was a temporary stop until I figured out where I might like to be long-term. But two years had gone by. I still had no idea where I'd rather be, and this apartment certainly wasn't home. I didn't know where that was yet.

Making my way into the kitchen, I opened a cabinet overhead, grabbing a wine glass and the bottle of wine Sabrina had given me for my birthday. It was a pinot noir, my favorite, and a much more expensive brand than I would have purchased myself. "Thanks, Sabrina," I said as I gave myself a heavy pour.

Glass in hand, I walked into my bedroom to change into pajamas. Last year for my birthday, Sabrina gave me matching pajama sets. Plural. She was convinced that a thirty-year-old (now thirty-one) shouldn't still be sleeping in free party t-shirts I'd gotten in college. I happened to like the memories of an era gone, thinking fondly of the many days I'd spent planning those elaborate parties for our friends.

Plus, I'd been alone for so long that I didn't see the purpose of upgrading my old college tees and oversized shorts. Thor had never seemed to mind what I slept in. Considering he was the only one who was ever-present here at bedtime, I didn't know why I bothered to listen to her.

I slipped into a blue and white short set that made me feel like a ritzy mom of three from New England waiting for my butler to bring me breakfast. "Breakfast, James, please," I said aloud in a nasally voice, a terrible impression of a life I could hardly imagine.

I ran my hands over the silky cotton and couldn't deny they were comfortable. I just wasn't sure I'd ever actually admit that to Sabrina.

Grabbing my wine off my nightstand, I headed to the living room and plopped down on the couch. I dug around for a minute in search of my remote, finally locating it stuck between two cushions. Some stale popcorn and a Swedish Fish that I didn't recall even eating recently were also jammed in there, but that was beside the point. I tried to keep my house tidy for the most part, but my life was a far cry from being neat and organized.

Vacuum under the couch cushions next time, I added to a mental checklist.

Remote in hand, I flipped on the TV to the newest home improvement show and curled my feet under me. Several minutes had gone by while I sipped on my wine, mindlessly watching them renovate a house I could never afford, even if it was in semi-rural Waco, Texas.

"Shiplap is overrated, don't you think?" I muttered, apparently to Thor.

He and I often did this. I talked aloud and waited for him to answer. If this were one of my favorite fantasy novels, he totally would. That was my most recurring dream: talking to dragons. Who wouldn't want that?

I purposefully chose not to think too heavily about why I talked aloud to a dog or dreamt of talking dragons. Instead, I flipped channels to find something more interesting. Thirty minutes had passed, and nothing had caught my attention. I finally turned the TV off and grabbed my phone from where I'd tossed it onto the couch earlier.

"Maybe I'll download a new book," I said again to Thor. He looked up at me in annoyance for interrupting his nap. Swiping to unlock my phone, I noticed several new notifications. All were warm wishes left on the cute social media post Sabrina had added of the girls and me posing with my cake. Most were from people I hadn't talked to in years, but it was nice to read through them, even if they were shallow, generic responses.

Swiping further, I scanned through the rest of the app. The next thing I knew, I'd been scrolling for an hour, mindlessly flipping from one pointless video to the next.

A low groan escaped me as I dropped my phone down at my side. I *hated* when I did this. There were so many other, better things to do with my time. Why on earth was I watching stupid videos of moms dancing badly? Or humorous extreme sporting accidents my brother Jacob loved to send me? I didn't know.

Taking a large sip of wine, I picked up my phone again. It was my birthday, so today I'd give myself a pass. I scrolled some more, stopping at a beautiful mountain scene.

I grew up in the mountains, so maybe that's what drew me in right away. Whatever the reasoning, I watched, mesmerized, as green and purple wisps danced through the night sky above the mountains.

The Northern Lights.

They were heavenly, weaving across a star-painted sky. The video had looped several times before I was jogged out of my focus at the sound of Thor yawning loudly next to me. Rubbing my foot through his fur, I clicked on the profile of this video. Something was calling to me, and I needed more. The next swipe landed me on a video of the hottest man I had ever seen.

"Oh," I turned the phone for Thor to see and took another sip. "Now, *this* is what I need. Someone should have found him for my birthday, don't you think?"

Thor picked his head up from his bed and shook it at me. Did that mean no? Or was he adjusting his collar? I sighed and took another sip, not drunk enough to think my dog was talking back to me yet.

I glanced down at my phone as the video looped. This

delectable man was riding bareback on a horse along the edge of a forest. Everything about it was captivating, from the snow-tipped evergreens to the sun streaming through the branches. Even the horse was magnificent, tall, black, and shining coat as it galloped so smoothly it seemed to fly. The man, though, looked straight off the cover of a romance novel. He had dark hair, and his beard ruffled in the wind. I was spellbound.

"He looks like he might be named Thor, too."

I'd gone too far as, this time, a growl came from deep in Thor's throat. I chuckled as I leaned forward to pet his head. "Don't worry. You're the only one for me."

Scrolling again, I looked for more of this man because yum. I needed more. Sipping my wine, I read through the profile of a travel page detailing trips to Scandinavia.

"Oh, look! He's a modern-day Viking! Now, do you like him?" Thor huffed, more than likely over the fact that I kept talking and interrupting his nap.

I had traveled through Europe some in college, determined to use my French minor at least once, but knew nothing about the Scandinavian countries. Diving head-first down a rabbit hole, I clicked on the link to read through the company's webpage.

Nordic Riders, the page said. I topped off my glass of wine as I read through their information on an all-inclusive two-week vacation in the Swedish countryside.

That could be fun.

"Think Thor will be on the trip, too?" I asked, disrupting my pup. This was apparently the last straw for him. He got up and walked into the bedroom, done with my one-sided conversation. Thor could pretend he didn't love me, but I knew it wasn't true.

Downloading a new book was forgotten as I spent the next hour sipping wine in a Swedish trance.

Mountains, lakes, beaches… this all sounds spectacular!

Views of the Northern Lights? That's always been on my bucket list.

I used to ride horses as a kid and grew up in the mountains of Colorado. A two-week trip of hiking, camping, and horseback riding would be no big deal.

I wonder what it means by "expert riders only." Surely, that's to warn travelers that this was not a trail ride.

Somehow, before I knew what had happened, I was on the payment page and mindlessly entered my credit card information to book the trip.

Maybe it was the wine. Perhaps it was my melancholy feeling over my birthday; I didn't know. Something felt *right* about this.

Screw it. I was going to Sweden.

An ear-splitting chime jolted me awake, and my head flew off the pillow at the sound. The sudden movement was the exact opposite of what my body needed. The room spun, and a moan escaped me as I slumped down on my pillow.

Eyes still closed, my hand fumbled across the bed. There, on my nightstand, I eventually found my phone to turn off the incessant sound. Sun was streaming in between the slats of my blinds in the window, but I was not ready to be awake no matter what time it was.

There was truly nothing worse than the sound of an alarm the morning after you overindulged. Against every rule I'd ever heard about drinking, I had done it alone. And from the way my head was swimming, I'd over-served myself.

Has my alarm always been this loud, or are hangovers this much worse in your thirties? How much wine did I even drink?

My mind whirled, sloshing around in my brain, as I

tried to muster the strength to do... *anything*. I moaned again, squeezing my eyes shut, trying to doze back off.

It didn't help that I'd been having the most vivid dream of a bewitching lake surrounded by mountains and trees. However, the clearest part of the dream had been an island in the lake's center. A massive tree took up most of the island, its roots exposed, clawing towards the water's edge. Whispers had filled the air but said nothing I could understand. The setting felt *right* in a way I couldn't describe. I wanted to go back there, not be forced into this awful reality.

My phone buzzed again, drawing me further into this wretched morning and away from the dream. I peeled my eyes open, a physical struggle at that moment, and glanced down at my phone to check the time.

Several notifications lit up my phone, and I quickly scanned through them. A message from my bank alerted me of a charge exceeding $1,000 was the first to catch my eye.

My brow creased in confusion, trying to recall what I'd purchased. Everything was groggy until it suddenly clicked. I groaned, throwing my arm over my eyes.

I had booked that trip to Sweden.

Why?

I knew *nothing* about Sweden; its history, geography, politics, language. None of it.

Wasn't it a horseback riding trip? My butt hurt just thinking about it.

I hadn't camped since I was ten, and I wanted to go camping for two weeks? There was no man on earth hot enough to make me go two weeks without indoor plumbing, not even that Viking man. No matter how foggy my brain was, I remembered him.

It's too early to deal with this.

I threw my phone across the bed and smashed a pillow over my head. I was going to call in sick.

However, before I could fall asleep again, I heard the sounds of Thor stretching on the floor beside me. I knew what came next as I scooted more towards the middle of the bed.

"Ugh, *gross*," I whined as Thor licked my elbow, the only part of my body not covered by the blankets. At least I'd moved far enough onto the bed that he couldn't reach my face. Dog slobber in your ear first thing in the morning is not a pleasant experience — trust me, I knew.

"*Fine*, I'll get up," I sighed, knowing he'd start whining soon if I didn't. Good thing I'd worn those matching pajamas last night because I was in no mood to change.

I glanced in the mirror and cringed. My curls had mashed in a way that there was no saving. Black rings graced my face with what was left of last night's mascara. Thirty-one was off to a glorious start.

I shuffled across the room to put on my shoes and sunglasses, grabbing Thor's leash as he pranced around my apartment.

"If you pee on my floor right now after you just made me get up, I will take you right back to the shelter," I glared at him. He glared right back, calling my bluff. Thankfully, though, he sat, and I attached his leash.

"Good morning, Shelbie!" I heard as I opened the door.

I jumped at the sound, seeing Sandra standing there with her tiny dog. They were already returning from their morning walk and far too chipper for how I felt.

Thor's growl mirrored my own emotions, but I forced a smile that I knew looked fake. The rumble coming from deep in my dog's chest sent Sandra's Pomeranian into a fit of shaking as she stooped to pick her up.

"I don't know why he always does that when he sees my sweet Gracie. She's the most precious puppy," her eyes looked at me accusingly and then down at Thor. "What kind of dog did you say he is again?"

"He's a lab mix," I answered in a voice that hardly sounded my own. I fully realized that was a bogus claim. Thor looked far more wolf than lab most days, but here we were. "I ordered one of those DNA tests on him to see what else he's mixed with, so we'll see soon enough."

Sandra eyed Thor as she tiptoed by us. Even though her apartment was around the corner from mine, she hurried in the other direction. My smile became much more genuine as I bent to pet Thor's head. Sometimes his dog aggression was handy. He excelled at sending annoying neighbors fleeing.

I hurried him along, ready to lay back down now that I'd officially talked myself into calling in sick. It would be my post-birthday gift to myself. I never took time off anyway, so I deserved it.

We stopped at my mailbox on the way home. I pulled out the little Doggie DNA envelope mixed with several pieces of junk mail. Those I dropped directly into the recycling bin nearby.

"Want to know who your ancestors were, bud?" I waved the envelope excitedly in Thor's face, to which he huffed.

We went back to my apartment. I hung up Thor's leash, filled his food and water bowls, and kicked off my shoes, heading straight back to bed.

Today, I was doing nothing. I was going to lay around, read a new book, and that was it. I shot off my email to my boss informing him of my sick day before I downloaded the latest fantasy novel my book subscription recommended. It was another fantasy retelling of Hades and Persephone. I'd only read about five of those lately. What was one more?

Thirty minutes later, I quit.

That Persephone was awful. Why was she so *whiny*? I hated whiny female characters; they made women collectively look bad. Sure, this Hades sounded lovely, but that wouldn't carry me through an entire book. Plus, I was sick and tired of main characters barely out of their teens. No one knew what they wanted from life at 22. I *still* didn't know what I wanted from life, and I was 31.

I dropped my tablet down on the bed, frustrated to have my plans of nothing ruined already. My mind wandered as I stared at the ceiling. The fan whirred overhead, but it wasn't enough to drown out the sound of Thor knocking around his now empty food bowl in the kitchen.

The moment my brain thought of food, even *dog* food, my stomach growled in response. I laid there for a moment more, torn between refusing to move and the hunger pangs now racking me that I desperately tried to ignore.

Finally dropping my feet off the side of the bed, I shuffled into my tiny galley kitchen as I piled my hair up into a messy bun. I squeezed by Thor, forced to walk sideways past his big, fluffy body. He easily blocked half of the kitchen, and I bumped him with my hip as I reached down to grab a pan.

An omelette and some coffee might soak up the last of the wine in my system and get me out of this slump. I turned the knob on the stove and waited for the pan to heat as I grabbed eggs, bacon, cheese, and some mushrooms from the fridge. Whisking the eggs together, I reached for Thor's DNA results I'd thrown on the counter. I slid my finger through the envelope flap and unfolded the paper as I quickly scanned the document.

Labrador retriever, the shelter got correct. But what on earth was an Elkhound? I'd never even heard of that breed. I threw the mushrooms and bacon in the pan to brown and grabbed my phone, opening a search bar for Elkhounds.

"Thor!" I gasped as my eyes scanned the search results. "You're a Viking! Well, I guess I did a good job naming you after all, huh, buddy?"

I poured my eggs into the pan and clicked on the link to read more.

"The Norwegian Elkhound breed is a medium- to a large-sized dog with a loyal demeanor. This breed is one of the oldest in Europe, dating back to the medieval ages. Known as the Vikings' companion, the Norwegian Elkhound has a thick, dark grey coat with a tail that curls up over its back."

I peeked down at Thor. His coat was jet black, but he did have the curled tail, and his coat was thicker than the shorter-haired labs I'd grown up with.

"Dogs tend to be hardy in stature with a thick, muscular chest and

thighs. While affectionate with their family, this breed can be dog-aggressive and is not recommended around small children."

A laugh bubbled out of me, and I kept reading, flipping my omelette.

"Elkhounds can make wonderful guard dogs as their bark is loud, and they are likely to alert you to strange sounds, be it a leaf or a neighbor. They can be reserved and aggressive when first meeting new people. Once acquainted, they make steadfast companions."

"Okay, well. You are most certainly an Elkhound, bud. It turns out your grumpy nature is genetic." He glared up at me at my words, and I chuckled. "Think, though. Now I can tell people that you're a Viking, and that's why I named you Thor. Everyone assumes I love Chris Hemsworth. Which yes, sure, who doesn't? But really, I picked a name to explain your hammer of a tail."

He turned to walk by me and slapped me with his hammer tail as if responding to my comment.

Leaning over to the stove, I turned it off and dropped the cheese on my omelette. Then, I slid it out of the pan and folded it over on my plate. I poured myself a cup of iced coffee and popped two ibuprofen in my mouth.

By the time I'd circled the counter and headed to the couch with my breakfast in hand, my mind had returned to the trip to Sweden.

How odd that Vikings had come up twice in two days, first that video and again with Thor's results. I hadn't thought about Vikings ever, really, except the day I named Thor.

He was a tiny(ish) puppy with a thunderous tail set on doing damage to shins and coffee table contents alike. The moment I'd seen him at the shelter, a feeling of peace had washed over me. I knew from that moment that he was meant for me.

Smiling at the thought of puppy Thor, I cut off a piece of my omelette. It was delicious. Savory and cheesy — the way I liked it. I was a terrible cook, but somehow I'd mastered the art of omelettes. Baking, though, was a different story. I could make a mean cheesecake. Frequently arriving with a tray of cookies in hand had made me the office favorite.

I took another bite and then reached for my phone. It was time to quit avoiding this.

Scrolling through my emails, I finally landed on one from Nordic Riders. A bright, breathtaking picture of a Swedish forest popped up when I opened the email. No matter how superb the scenery was, I knew this was a mistake.

I didn't make impulsive decisions like this. Ever. What had I been thinking?

If I was being frank, I didn't even really like the outdoors.

Yes, I lived in Denver.

Yes, I realized I was surrounded by awe-inspiring nature every single day here. But did I seek it out? Did I enjoy it?

No.

I didn't.

I enjoyed air conditioning and a good book.

Flicking my finger across my screen, I scrolled through the email. My eyes scanned through the details I definitely had not looked at last night until my phone rang.

"Hey, Sabrina," I answered absentmindedly. "What's up?"

"Not too much, just checking on you. You seemed like you were in a funk when you left last night," she responded. She was always so in tune with my emotions.

At that, I chuckled. "You know me too well. Oh. Speaking of, you'll never believe what I did last night."

"Picked up the clothes on your floor?"

"Let's not get our hopes up, Sabrina Inez Montoya-Williams."

"*Que serio,* full name. What did you do?"

"I was watching this video advertising trips through the Swedish countryside. I was drinking that wine you gave me and decided, what the hell. I booked a two-week trip to Sweden. I'm going camping, hiking, and horseback riding, but mostly to see the Northern Lights. I can check that off my bucket list."

A long silence filled the phone line before Sabrina said anything in return. "That's… a little random. Are you really going to go?"

"Well, I don't know. I haven't thought about it enough yet," I paused. "Why? You think I shouldn't go?"

"I won't say *no*, but I'm not sure it's a great idea. The last time you went hiking, you broke out in hives."

"Yeah, that's because I was wearing shorts. We later found out I'm allergic to grass. I promise I will not wear shorts in Sweden."

I could hear her laughing through the phone. "You're allergic to everything. I'm sure there's lots of grass in Sweden, too. When is this trip?"

"The Winter Nights Festival, so that's the end of winter. At least I did that part right. The Northern Lights will be perfect."

"Can't you see the Northern Lights from somewhere like Oslo? That might be a better idea than a camping trip."

"You think I shouldn't go then."

"I don't know; I'm just thinking. You know I'll support whatever you decide. What will your mom say about this idea?"

I groaned, thinking about how that conversation would go. "I'm sure she'll have lots of mostly sensible reasons to guilt-trip me into changing my mind," I sighed. "I don't know. I feel like I'm in such a rut lately. Maybe I need to do something out there to shake it up."

"Well, let me know what you decide. I have to run and get Jasmine to preschool. Keep me posted, okay? *Te amo*."

"Love you, too," I said, but she'd already hung up.

Watching Sabrina be a mom to those two precious little girls had been such a joy. She was made for it. Nevertheless, some days I missed our friendship before kids and husbands.

André was wonderful, aside from the traveling for work part. It left Sabrina home alone with both kids most of the week, but I was so happy she had him.

That didn't mean I didn't miss our days together, however. She would have been all-in on a semi-spontaneous trip to Europe with me a decade ago.

I shoved aside the anxiety about our changing friendship and glanced at this email, reading through the instructions attached.

Experienced riders only.

You could have called me experienced at one point in my life. But decades, *plural,* had now passed since the last time I'd ridden regularly. However, the thought of picking riding up again was not an unpleasant one. It could be kind of fun to ride again.

I'd need to learn some basic Swedish since I doubted translator apps worked well in the remote bogs and forests of the countryside.

My hiking boots had been in the purge pile in my last move, so I'd have to replace those, too.

Before I knew it, I made a mental checklist of all I'd need to prepare for this trip. Was I going to do this?

A few days had passed since my Mental Health Day, and thoughts of Swedish vacations were gone as I got lost in the routine of everyday life.

Client meetings were timed just right one day to give me a long lunch break, so I grabbed my bag and walked to the park across from my office.

I snacked on veggies with dip, crackers, meat, and cheese — anything easy to avoid cooking — as I pulled out my notepad. If I was going to make this trip happen, I needed to get organized. I had six months to plan, so a list wouldn't hurt to keep me on track.

TO DO:
- Renew passport
- Learn Swedish
- Buy gear
- Break in hiking boots - don't be a rookie
- Take riding lessons

- Buy a plane ticket
- Ask Sabrina to pet-sit Thor

I was sure I'd think of more things to add to the list, but seeing it all written down made this trip seem less intimidating. A few of these I could even make progress on today.

My fingers took on a mind of their own as I started scrolling my phone, searching for software to teach me Swedish. I'd need to learn some basics to get by, but that shouldn't be too hard. I was good with languages.

Living in Denver would make acquiring all of the hiking and outdoor gear easy. Plus, there were tons of places around town and towards my parents' house in the mountains to practice. There was even a sporting goods store on my way home. I could stop by tonight for some new boots, and Thor and I could hike the next time I went to see my parents.

Nodding to myself, I was happy with my new course of action. I packed up my lunch and walked back into the office, ready to finish out my day writing press releases about things I cared much less about than planning this trip.

Daydreams of international adventures filled my head through my afternoon meetings until I realized it was time to leave. I grabbed my bag and made for my Jeep. As I put the car in reverse, my phone rang.

"Hey, Mom," I said, wondering if she had somehow heard of my new plans.

"Hi, honey. How was your day at work?"

"It was a regular day, no major fires to put out. Fortunately, none of my clients caused drama for their PR agent today. How are you?"

"Good! I was calling because your brother mentioned he might bring the girls by this weekend. Would you like to drive up, too? You can bring Thor if you want, even though he terrified Jacob's girls last time. He could sleep in the mudroom."

My parents lived farther west in the Rocky Mountains, about a two-hour drive from Denver.

This could be good. Maybe Jacob would like to go hiking with me, too.

"I think I can do that," I answered. "I have a bunch of errands to run this week before I can fully commit, but go ahead and plan on me joining."

I always loved seeing my brother and his family, although I would admit that his four kids were undoubtedly overwhelming. Mom didn't mention if Lauren, Jacob's wife, would be joining. I wondered if maybe she was using the excuse to stay home with their littlest baby, my first nephew. He must be nine months old now, I guessed.

Jacob and his family lived about an hour from me, clear on the other side of Denver, and I really should try harder to see them more often. Their lives revolved around soccer games, gymnastic meets, and school pageants — a far cry from the quiet life Thor and I lead. Plus, his middle daughter, Caroline, was terrified of Thor. That always seemed to complicate any lengthy visits.

Thoughts of the weekend ahead were tabled as I pulled into the store's parking lot and turned off the engine. These stores always gave me a sick feeling. I'd gone in them several times for new ski equipment or something for Jacob and his kids, but I was in over my head. The moment anyone started explaining features and differences between products, I was lost. I was not outdoorsy, much to the chagrin of my very outdoorsy family. Smile and nod, right?

"Hey, man. Looking for anything specific today?" an employee asked as he walked towards me. His corporate polo-and-khakis-look was canceled out by the dirty, long hair he had tied at the top of his head and the bloodshot eyes.

"I need new hiking boots." I cut straight to the chase. "I'm going on a hiking trip in Europe and want to get them now to break them in."

"Backpacking Europe — gnarly," the young kid replied, doing a terrible job of convincing me he hadn't shown up to work high as a kite. Welcome to Colorado. "Where are you going?"

"Sweden," apparently making up my mind that I was going right then.

"That's dope. You skiing, too?"

"No, I'm going at the end of winter," I answered, ready to end this conversation. "Can you point me towards the boots section?"

"Sure, sure. Right this way. What part of Sweden are you going to be hiking? Snow? Rocky terrain?"

I thought about that for a moment. Had I ever actually looked at a map of where we were traveling? Sweden was pretty large, wasn't it? How did I not already know this?

Find a map of Sweden, I added to my mental to-do list.

"A little bit of everything," I stuck to vague answers.

"All right. Well, let's take a look over here." He motioned to a wall of boots. I grabbed a pair of thick wool socks off the nearby rack and began to try them on.

Without fully understanding what had happened, I'd suddenly dropped $500 in thirty minutes. Glancing down at my receipt made me realize quickly that this trip would cost me a lot more than that all-inclusive price.

I popped my trunk and put in my new backpack, boots, five pairs of cushioned hiking socks, and a water bottle with a fancy filtration system. I still needed a sleeping bag, more socks, other camping gear, and even clothes. The thought made me groan as I slammed my trunk.

This was too much.

Folding my receipt, I stuck it in my wallet, just in case I changed my mind about this whole endeavor, and drove home.

The rest of the week passed uneventfully before Thor and I drove up the mountains to my parents' house.

"Ready to go hiking?" I said aloud to Thor the following morning as I sat in the mudroom, lacing up my new boots.

"Sure, I didn't realize you were leaving right now. Let me get the kids ready," Jacob replied. Apparently, he thought I was talking to him, not my dog. Thor and I looked at each other; a knowing look in his eye acknowledged my crazy.

"Don't you say anything," I whispered to him through clenched teeth. He huffed and laid his head down on the floor, energized for this hike.

Thirty minutes later, Jacob and his two oldest girls were buckled in the back of his truck, ready to go. I loaded Thor into my Jeep and followed him up to the trailhead.

The girls took off at a run with Jacob close behind, shouting sensible parent things like, "Stay away from the cliffs" and "Not too far" as he chased his kids.

Thor looked up at me with an annoyed look, seeming to say, *"Why are we doing this?"*

"Come on; it'll be fun. You love walks. This is just a walk in the forest." I clipped on his leash, and we set off, following Jacob and his kids.

The weather was spectacular, sun leaking through the aspen trees. Birds chirped overhead, chipmunks scurried through the underbrush, and I even spotted a few mule deer off deeper in the woods, mostly fleeing at the sight and sound of Thor. While it had been hot when I left Denver, the altitude combined with the shade of the forest made the temperature practically perfect.

We walked up the path for a while towards a clearing up ahead. Sooner than I'd care to admit, I was winded and blamed it on the altitude.

I stopped, pretending it was Thor who needed a break, and fought the instinct to double over, hands on my knees. Instead, I took a sip from my expensive, fancy new water bottle. I poured some out for Thor, pausing for a moment more to let him drink before I turned to keep going.

Stepping in front of him, I walked forward until my

arm was about ripped out of my socket. My body was whipped around with the tension to see that Thor hadn't risen to follow me. He was now acting like he was suddenly made of concrete and refused to move.

"Let's go," I tugged on the leash again.

Nothing.

Not even an inch of give.

My 100-pound dog was ready for a standoff in the middle of the trail, and I had no hope of winning this one. Thor had one severe glare going as he stared off to my left into the trees, not even paying attention to me.

"I'll have Dad make you your very own steak tonight," I bribed, to no effect.

I followed his line of sight, but there was nothing there other than more trees. My niece had said the aspens looked like they had eyes carved into them with the knots, and I couldn't unsee the 'tree eyes' now.

They were watching me from everywhere.

The hair on my arms stood up as a strange feeling swept over me. Despite the heat of the late morning and sweat beading on my brow from exertion, I shivered.

I closed my eyes for a moment, taking a deep, calming breath before turning to my stubborn dog.

"Thor," I said, more forcefully to remind him who was the alpha in our pack. "Come. *Heel.*"

I swear to God, he laughed at me. Could dogs laugh? Whatever the sound was, it was more than a huff.

Frustrated, I plopped down on a log at the edge of the clearing, and Thor walked over to me, laying his head in my lap.

"Oh, *now* you'll move," I muttered, absentmindedly rubbing his head. "I shouldn't even be petting you. You're a bad dog."

His eyes seemed to glow before he sneezed so hard that dog slobber covered my favorite green cargo pants.

"Gross!" I cried, standing quickly. Globs of snot stuck to my hands as I turned, looking for somewhere to wipe them. Bending to run my hands through the grass below, I side-eyed Thor. His eyes were lit with mirth, mocking me.

I ran some water over my hands before wiping them again and finally sat back down.

My eyes drifted to the forest, and Thor settled at my side, staring with me. It was as if we were waiting for something, but I couldn't for the life of me imagine what it would be. A bear? I hoped not.

We waited on the trail for almost an hour until Jacob and his girls finally came in our direction. The sound of cute, excited voices talking to their dad reached me before a small brunette head popped out of the trees, followed by Jacob with a child on his shoulders.

My cheeks were flushed, and I was more than a little embarrassed to admit that two small children had hiked probably double what I did.

As soon as Thor saw that the kids were walking towards the car, he suddenly jumped to his feet. I followed him as he yanked me down the trail.

"I see," I sighed, doing my best not to faceplant. "Now that we're leaving, you're gung-ho for hiking."

❄

Later that night, I became the favorite aunt of the family (never mind, I was also the only one) when I suggested the girls and I camp outside in the backyard of my parents' house. My proposition was met with tiny squeals of excitement, making it almost impossible not to smile.

"This is so fun," my mom said as she pulled out blankets and pillows for us to take outside. The temperature in mid-July in the Rocky Mountains was lovely and sunny during the day, but it dropped significantly after sunset. I grabbed a few extra blankets just thinking about it. Fortunately, my nieces all loved to snuggle.

"I figured it'd be good practice," I replied before thinking through my comment. It took everything in me to continue acting normally and not slap myself in the forehead for letting it slip.

Her hands stilled for a moment. "Practice for what?" My nosy mother perked up, of course, picking up on the tidbit.

"I'm…," I hesitated, "I'm thinking about going on a trip to Sweden."

I intentionally skipped over many essential details, such as I'd already paid for it and was relatively sure I had decided to go. Probably. *Maybe.*

"Oh, I've heard Stockholm is lovely! Is André going to watch the girls while you're gone?" she added, assuming Sabrina would be joining me. I ignored the pang in my heart, wishing she was.

"I'm not sure Sabrina is going this time."

"So, who are you going with?" she asked, now focused

solely on me. "Have you met someone? Why didn't you say something?"

"No, Mom," I rolled my eyes. "I haven't met someone." It always returned to this. "I think I'm going to go alone."

"Alone?" Her eyebrows climbed her forehead, reaching for her hairline.

How could I be 31, and a single word uttered out of my mother's mouth had me reevaluating my entire life's choices? At that moment, I decided I was ready to stand my ground. "Yes, Mom. Alone."

"Well, I don't know what to think about that. What's the crime rate like in Stockholm? Is that where you're going?"

"I'm going to Stockholm first, and then a few other stops." I kept it intentionally vague.

"By train?"

"... Some. Yes."

"Are you driving while you're there?"

"No, I don't think so." *Add researching how to get around Sweden to the list,* I thought to myself.

"Well, how are you getting around then? Hitchhiking with strange European men?"

Without meaning to, I tucked my chin, staring down at my hands. "I'm going horseback riding and hiking," I mumbled as quickly as possible.

"I'm not your father — I can hear just fine," she said, now staring me down as only a mother can do. "You're horseback riding and hiking? Do you not remember the *years* of horseback riding lessons we paid for and how disastrously that ended?"

"Of course I do." I did not need to be reminded of my fall. Even though I had been ten, a broken leg and elbow had been enough to make me never want to touch a horse again. "But that was a long time ago; I was a kid. I can see now that it was as much my fault as the horse's."

"What about that Girl Scout camp we sent you to that you called us from in tears? You *begged* your dad to drive back to pick you up early."

Her eyes seemed almost sad, disappointed that I didn't have the same love of the outdoors like the rest of the family. Honestly, it was shocking that my family wasn't jumping all over this, considering they'd been begging me to join them on their adventures for years. I usually preferred to read about other people's adventures from the comfort of my couch.

"You're not exactly the most outdoorsy, honey. I don't think this is a good idea." She resumed folding the blankets in her hand. That was the end of the conversation.

I sighed, knowing this would be her reaction, but it was still hard to hear. "I'll think about it, Mom," I frowned down at the tent my dad had given me.

"I know you'll do the right thing, honey."

Those words always seemed to be the final stop on her guilt trip. She patted my arm as she walked out the door to her grandchildren.

I sighed. After giving myself a moment to regroup, I grabbed the tent and walked outside to the sound of three little girls squealing in delight.

Dad lit the fire pit on the patio, and the girls roasted marshmallows while Jacob and I set up the tent. The minute my mom laid the blankets inside, my nieces all piled in. Giggles filled the air, followed by a soft *thump*, then another. "PILLOW FIGHT!"

The stars were out in all their glory, lighting the night sky along with the almost full moon. I gazed up at it, contemplating what to do about this trip, my life… all of it.

"You coming inside, Aunt Shelbie?" Charlotte, the oldest, stuck her head out of the tent. Her wild curls were the same as mine, except a warm chestnut to my sandy blonde, and stuck up in every direction.

I smiled up at the stars, letting the unease from earlier go and choosing instead to be happy and in the moment with family. At that, I spun on the girls.

"You better make room because I call the middle!" I shouted, sending my nieces into a fit of giggles again.

After my nieces had drifted off, I lay in the tent, staring at the canvas ceiling. Fortunately, my dad's tent was well insulated, and the body heat of three little girls all crammed against me was enough that the dwindling heat of the day wasn't a huge problem.

My bladder, however, was.

The more that the tiny bodies piled on me moved across my abdomen, the harder it became to ignore how much I needed to pee. I would have to get up, and either walk into the woods nearby or make my way up to the house.

The decision was not a difficult one. There was not much I hated more than peeing in the woods. I had an irrational fear of poison oak on my butt, leftover from a tale my brother loved to tell me that had happened to our neighbor.

I knew now that it was a lie but had not when I had asked her if that was why she only ever wore dresses and never pants. Apparently, that was a weird thing to ask a grown adult. I could still hear my brother doubled over laughing when I thought about it.

Finally, I couldn't take it anymore. I began the slow and tedious process of moving sleeping children onto their sleeping bags. I peeled myself out of the pile of bodies and snuck out of the tent, aiming for the house. I was not going to pee in the woods today. That'd have to be one of those things I counted on muscle memory when the time came.

As I walked towards the patio, I glanced at the trees. The wind moved through the aspen leaves and rustled the grass. A chipmunk scurried across the yard, running to the grove, and I stopped.

Everything around me was still, and yet, it was all *alive*. An elk bugled loudly, resonating down the valley my parents' land was in. I glanced in the direction of the sound, squinting through the night to see if I could spot anything.

Suddenly, a thought hit me. Bears lived in these woods. So did mountain lions.

What on earth was I doing having small children sleep

outside with me? What would I even do if a predator happened upon us? What if the ashes of the fire pit earlier started a forest fire?

Terror gripped me, now focusing on everything that could go wrong. I stood there, paralyzed. The need to pee was forgotten, and I ran back to the tent, snatching up a child. Claire, the littlest, snuggled into my shoulder in sleep and was oblivious to the panic running through my veins.

As I stepped onto the patio, I heard a sound above me and glanced up the steps to the porch. Jacob sat there, watching me, with a smile and a wine glass in hand.

"I was wondering how long this would take," he laughed.

"Shut up." I handed Claire over and returned for the others.

"Watch out for poison oak, Sassy," he said, the only one I'd ever allow to call me that nickname.

"Screw you," I replied, barely audible over his chuckling. Claire asleep on one shoulder, he leaned down and scooped up Caroline as well. Charlotte snuggled into me, and we went inside.

The door seemed to slam behind me as I carefully laid down my niece and ran to the bathroom. I was ready for this night to be over.

4

I battled my way through Sunday traffic down I-70 with the rest of the Weekend Warriors, Thor asleep in the back seat. After unloading the car and walking inside, I noticed a missed text from Sabrina.

"I hired a babysitter tomorrow night, so clear your schedule. I'm coming over for a girls' night. I need a break, and I miss you," the text read. I smiled as I texted back, confirming her plan.

It would be great to have Sabrina over. She was the planner of the two of us. If I set her loose, she'd have my whole trip set out for me, and everything lined up within the night, all for the cost of delivery food and wine.

My own attempt at organizing glared at me from the fridge where I'd hung the torn-out page of my journal. I walked over to it, pulled it out from under the magnet, and glanced over my list.

Renewing my passport didn't sound daunting; I could handle that tomorrow on my lunch break. Look at me, so prepared and ready with over six months to spare. This might have been the most organized I'd ever been in my life. Sabrina would be so proud.

The next day, work passed quickly, and I left the passport office with a note saying I could expect it in the mail in a month. *Check.*

I sped home after work, walked Thor rapidly, much to his annoyance, and began to clean rapidly. The crumbs under couch cushions would have to wait another day — I didn't have time.

Clothes lay scattered all over my bathroom and bedroom floor and draped across a chair in the corner. I wasn't even sure which were clean and dirty, so I opened the door to my washer and threw it all in. I'd deal with it later.

I loaded all of my dishes into the dishwasher, slammed the door shut, and sprayed down my counter. As I finished wiping it down at record speed, the door opened.

Thor ran over to it, tail wagging as Sabrina came in. She looked perfect in her jean shorts and tank top, hair curling under on the ends. In the middle of the summer, her deep tan was the perfect shade, and I envied her. If I stayed in the sun too long, I burned. My freckles might merge, but that was as close to tan as I got.

"Hola gordito," she said, stooping to Thor's level as she let him lick her face and ears. His tail thumped loudly against the wall, pounding out a steady rhythm.

"You didn't have to clean for me," she said, looking up at me but still petting Thor. "I've known you long enough to know what to expect."

I laughed and shook my head. "If I hadn't cleaned up

first, you would have spent the entire night here cleaning for me rather than relaxing."

She didn't say anything to that because I was right.

"I have something else I could use your help with, though, while you're here. But let's order food first. Sushi?"

"Of course." She stood, dropped her bag on my counter, and pulled out a bottle of wine. Making herself at home, she walked into the kitchen and grabbed two wine glasses and the corkscrew.

"What can I help with?" she asked as she cut the foil on the bottle.

"I need to make a plan if I'm going to go on this trip, and nobody makes a plan better than you."

She placed her hand lovingly over her heart, embracing the comment as a compliment, which it was.

I pulled out my phone and ordered sushi before plopping down on the couch. She joined me a moment later, pulling her feet up under her as she sipped at her wine.

"It's so *quiet*," she said as she looked around. Thor chose that exact moment to locate the squeaker in his stuffed dragon toy, and it emitted a long, loud, high-pitched squeal. "Except you, Thor. I forgot what a quiet house sounds like."

I knew she meant the comment wistfully, but it stung a little. Her life revolved around Annie and Jasmine in a way I couldn't imagine, my only comparison being Thor. While, yes, I made many decisions based on him, I wasn't foolish enough to think it was the same as having a family.

The thought of kids had never really been in the forefront of my mind, probably because I'd never met anyone even a little bit worthy of fathering a child. I'd had several failed relationships early in my twenties that left me with an idea of everything I *didn't* want in a relationship, and then my options had grown slim.

I was an old soul. I'd been told that my whole life, and today's world of dating apps, talking stages, and casual hookups seemed like a waste of time.

My dog and a good book were usually enough, but lately, I'd had this strange feeling in the pit of my stomach. It was almost as if I'd forgotten something but couldn't remember what I'd forgotten. It was an annoying, nagging feeling, and I didn't know how to fix it.

Maybe it was just a keen awareness that another year had passed, and I still didn't have much of a purpose for my life outside of keeping Thor and me both alive. What a depressing thought.

I looked up at Sabrina, staring at me, and I realized I'd been quiet for too long.

"Sorry," I apologized, taking a sip of my wine. "What were you saying?"

Her hand reached out, touching my knee. "You okay? Something seems off lately."

I sighed. Something *was* off, but I had no idea how to explain it. "I don't know. Yes, I'm fine. Physically and mentally. I'm just in a slump right now, that's all."

Her eyes searched my face for another moment before she dropped the subject and grabbed my phone off the couch. She typed in my password, nosy as ever, and flipped through my emails. "Where's the info on your trip? I want to see what you'll be doing."

I leaned over, and together we scrolled until she found it.

"This looks pretty!" she forced a little too much enthusiasm in her voice. Her eyes searched the page as she scrolled down, reading every word as I knew she would. She paused, and her gaze shot to me before looking back at the screen.

I leaned over a little closer, seeing what caught her attention.

"So, uh," she mumbled, "when did you say your trip was?"

"During the Winter Nights Festival," I replied. "So that should be the end of winter. Why?"

"Shel," she looked up at me hesitantly, "You misread it. It's not at the *end* of winter. It's in September, at the *beginning* of winter. You have seven weeks now, and you're no longer 90 days out to cancel and get a refund."

I stared at her, my world suddenly shaky. I *what*? Frantically grabbing my phone from her hands, I scanned the screen in front of me.

Winter Nights Festival Two-Week Tour, it read in big block letters.

"This tour leaves from Sundsvall, Sweden, hiking along the Baltic Coast before traveling inland, as the country celebrates Winter Nights and the Northern Lights in the evening sky," I read aloud.

"Keep going," Sabrina said, staring hard at me as she awaited my reaction.

More details about the hiking paths, what I could expect to see, and the gear I'd be responsible for bringing came next. I scrolled a little further down and finally saw what she was referring to towards the bottom of the email.

September 29th.

Panic crept in as I read more, noticing what she mentioned with the 90-day cancellation refund availability. I swiped to open my calendar instead, glancing down to see that September 29th was, indeed, only seven weeks away.

49 days.

The next day was miserable as I held back yawns during client meetings due to the anxiety that kept me awake most of the night before.

I hardly remembered the rest of my time with Sabrina; the whole night was a blur of panicked haze. We'd eaten our sushi and watched a movie, but my mind had wandered.

48 days. That was all I had to prepare for this trip. And I couldn't even get my money back now. I had to go. I wasn't blind to the fact that I was in no way, shape, or form prepared for this trip.

Shit.

"Anything else to add, Shelbie?" my boss Jordan asked, and my head whipped up. He was eyeing me, eyebrow raised, knowing my thoughts were elsewhere.

"No, I think if we keep with this plan, we can keep you in good standing with the local neighbors throughout the construction process." At least I remembered the topic of discussion. Yay, me.

How I landed a heavy-highway construction client as my main focus was beyond me. I knew nothing about cars, roads… any of it. But I was great at mediating conversations with disgruntled neighbors in the area. Not the most riveting job on a day-to-day basis, but I didn't hate it either. It was not a passion, that's all.

After my meeting, I left for a lunch break, ready to clear my mind at the park across the street. A sigh escaped me as I plopped down on the bench and stared off into the garden.

It was pretty, with a small pond and a walkway around it. Trees lined the walkway, with benches set every few yards. Several young women — moms or nannies, I wasn't sure — pushed strollers, chased children on bikes, and ran through the grass.

A dog walker passed me with several leashes attached. The cluster of dogs was semi-orderly in a shocking way, even though the man holding their leashes was a big enough guy. I couldn't imagine asking anyone to walk Thor, especially not with other dogs. What a disaster that would be.

An older woman shuffled towards me, and my eye was drawn to her as she neared.

"Is this seat taken?" she asked, pointing to the end of my bench.

"No, go right ahead," I smiled at her.

My lunch consisted of salt and pepper pistachios and a tomato-mozzarella Caprese salad. Again, anything to avoid cooking. I cut into my tomatoes as I picked up my phone.

Sabrina had made a to-do list for me, as I'd asked, and saved it where I could easily access it.

Riding lessons would be my next priority. With my time crunch, I needed to find somewhere budget-friendly, too. I only had a few weeks left and needed as much help as possible.

My thumb slid across the screen as I scrolled, finally landing on an ad for a page that came highly recommended: Charlene's Riding Academy and Training Ranch.

Charming horses in the foothills of the Rocky Mountains were featured on the page, but I forced myself to look past the pretty picture and scrolled through reviews. Comments were split between discussing her talent at training difficult horses and teaching riding lessons, but all of them were positive. I decided to shoot off a message to inquire about lessons.

Pride swelled in my chest as I marked another item off my to-do list. That taken care of, I popped a few pistachios in my mouth and glanced at the quiet woman sitting next to me. She had stunning, long white hair braided, hanging down over her elbow.

"You made the right decision."

I turned, now facing her, but her gaze was still straight ahead.

"Pardon me?" my eyebrows raised, confused by her comment. Had she been looking over my shoulder at the riding lessons I'd just inquired about?

Her eyes were fogged over, however, staring out vacantly at nothing. I waited a moment more, seeing if she would expand on her odd comment, but got nothing.

I leaned forward, closer to her. She didn't even turn in my direction at my now blatant stare.

After a minute, I shrugged. She must be confused. I left the odd interaction behind me as I gathered my things to head back to the office. As the doors to my building swung open, I looked over my shoulder at the park, but the woman had moved on.

Later, my phone dinged on my passenger's seat next to me as I was driving home. I pulled into my parking spot and picked it up to read the message I'd received.

"Hey there, Shelbie. Charlene, here. This sounds good. Stop by my ranch tomorrow night at six, and I bet we can work something out between us girls. Wear jeans and boots."

The little checkmark next to 'riding lessons' gave me an ounce of satisfaction, one step closer to my trip.

5

My GPS guided me down a dirt road in the foothills outside Denver. Dust flew up on either side of the Jeep, dry from the heat of the summer. I slowed, rolling to a stop in front of a large gate blocking in a beautiful pasture. There were three mismatched barns, two tiny brick houses with metal roofs, and all the accouterments you'd expect for a horse ranch.

A woman leaned out of the closest barn, squinted, and pushed a remote to open the gate. I slowly rolled through the gate, turned off the engine, and opened the door as she walked towards me.

"When you messaged, I was afraid you'd be one of those uppity city girls," Charlene called in greeting, glancing at my now dirty Jeep with a look of approval.

It took me a moment to adjust to all that was *Charlene*. The woman before me was a cross between Dolly Parton and Shania Twain, ready for the stage. She was in great shape for a woman in her late fifties, if I'd guessed correctly, and over a head shorter than me. But I'd never seen such liberal use of rhinestones in everyday attire. Her leopard print shirt was very fitted with an enormous bedazzled cross stretching across her ample chest, matching the sparkly pockets on her jeans. A walking disco ball.

She had pretty caramel brown hair that complimented her bright hazel eyes. Her hair was heavily teased, styled in a half-up, half-down look, and she was clearly under the impression that if it touched the clouds, she could be forgiven for any previous misdeeds. The higher the hair, the closer to God, as the saying went.

This was a Western Woman.

"Well, come on already," I jumped to attention after realizing I had been stock-still. I followed her, nearly blinded as the evening sun caught on her shiny pockets when she walked to the closest barn.

"You mentioned you've ridden before, right?" she yanked me to attention, now realizing I'd been mute up until that point.

"Yes," I found my voice, "I rode as a kid, but it was an introduction to jumping. I didn't do any sort of distance riding. And also, that was a long time ago."

"It's never too late to get back in the saddle," she nodded. "Girls our age have to find hobbies outside of the menfolk. After my third husband bit the dust, I swore off men completely. He was the only one I even liked, and then he was rude enough to move to Heaven. What a jackass. Grab a brush and clean your horse while you tell me about this trip you mentioned in your message."

I was jarred at the abrupt dump of personal information and slightly terrified of this tiny, fierce woman. So I did as I was told.

"I'm going to Sweden," I said as I brushed a handsome black and white paint horse. The motion was soothing, both for the mare and me, as she let out a contented sigh. I leaned forward, stroking her big cheek while Charlene bent down, lifting the horse's hoof. "It's a two-week riding, hiking, camping trip through the Swedish countryside and foothills."

Charlene stopped cleaning the mud out of the horse's shoe, stood, and squinted at me, giving me a once-over. I stopped, slightly uncomfortable as an odd moment passed of us awkwardly staring at each other. Then she shrugged.

"Are you going alone?" she bent over and focused again on the hoof in front of her.

"I am." I did my best to muster strength behind the words.

"Good for you."

She surprised me with the support, not the first reaction I'd received from everyone else so far. "You think?"

My voice came out a little higher-pitched than usual, but I found I was suddenly desperate for someone's approval of this foolhardy plan.

"I think you're in way over your head; that's what I think," her answer as blunt as her hair was large. "But I think it's good for girls our age to be comfortable alone."

That was the second time she'd lumped her and me into the same age bracket, suddenly making me reevaluate my skincare routine.

How old does she think I am?

Does she know how old she *is?*

In companionable silence, we finished preparing two horses, hers a massive, almost white, palomino, and got ready for our ride.

"All right, let's not beat around the bush," she broke the lull in the conversation.

I thought over the blunt things she had said so far. Had we been doing that already? I'd hate to see this woman honest if this was her version of holding back.

"You've got six weeks, so we need to cover a lot of ground mighty quick. I'm not gonna help you much. You're gonna have to do this on your own out there unless you do the dirty with someone real quick into the trip and can whip some idiot into doing all of it for you."

Well, all right then.

After realizing my jaw had gone slack, I closed my mouth and grabbed the reins. I liked my independence, and once I got over the way she'd phrased it, that's what she meant. I nodded in agreement. "Let's do it."

"Good girl. Saddle up," she instructed, rounding the horse to watch me. I grabbed the saddle horn with my left hand and put my boot in the stirrup. As I shifted my weight to lift up, the horse took a note out of Thor's book, stubborn and unruly, and stepped forward. The motion almost knocked me on my ass, and I hopped to keep up.

Charlene smiled as she grabbed the halter, holding the horse in place this time. "Try again."

So I did. This time, I was able to push my weight down on the stirrup as I attempted to swing my leg over gracefully. However, nothing went according to plan.

I ended up halfway over, my face on the saddle's right side, but my body had not received the same memo. I was dangling in mid-air, staring at the ground, unable to move. A small hand shoved hard into my butt, forcing me up and over until I settled my weight in the saddle. My cheeks heated in embarrassment, realizing how out of shape I was.

"We'll work on that, I guess," Charlene muttered to herself, appearing so tiny now that I sat astride my horse.

She walked to her own larger horse and flew up and over. The motion was so graceful my mouth hung open yet again. I wanted to be able to do that, too. She kicked her horse, and off we went.

"We'll revisit the basics, rein positions, posture, and then do some trotting today. Let's see what you remember."

We walked our horses around the edge of the riding arena for the next half-hour, letting the horses warm up while I got reacquainted with riding.

"Fix your posture," she yelled across the arena. "This isn't English. Don't squish your lady balls. Ass down, zippers up."

"I need to see your tits! Keep those shoulders back!" I got next.

"Don't hold your saddle horn at the top. Would you grab your man that way? Hold the shaft, thumb over the top."

An undignified sound came out of me halfway between a sputter and a cackle, unable to contain it anymore. I was overwhelmed by the entirety of this woman. I wouldn't call myself a prude, but this was a trip.

"Okay, let's trot."

Thankfully, I'd remembered my industrial-strength sports bra as we picked up speed. I did my best to remember all of my instructions.

Ass down, zippers up. Tits out, grab the shaft.

A smile slowly crept over my face the more I repeated my new X-rated mantra, and I bounced across the arena while a breeze ruffled my curly ponytail.

I closed my eyes, hands loose on the reins and trusting that this horse wouldn't lead me astray. After all, Charlene taught mainly children if her ad I'd read had been accurate.

A deep breath had me inhaling the smell of mountain air, warm and calming, and centered me at this moment. I finished my lesson, remembering why I had always loved horses. Tension eased from my shoulders, and while my muscles ached, my heart felt lighter than it had in weeks.

I dismounted from the horse much more gracefully than I got on, although any dignity I'd had upon arrival was long gone.

"That was… something. You mentioned your trip is for two weeks?" she asked as I hefted the heavy saddle off the horse.

"Yes, with some hiking in between. Not all riding," I tried to make it sound less intense than I knew it was. My knee buckled as if the thought alone had my bones ready to drop out of my skeleton and run away.

Nothing got past Charlene as she glanced down at my knee and puckered her lips into a pout in concentration.

"You need a lot of practice. How much did you say you had to spend on riding lessons?"

"I can afford whatever $300 can get me."

She laughed at that. "That ain't near enough, girl. Tell you what. My ranch hand up and left, chasing after some bull rider like the buckle bunny she is, and I'm short-handed right now. Why don't you come by three days a week and help me? You muck some stalls and whatever else I need to be done, and I'll have you ready to ride in six weeks."

"Done," I agreed before I could think through this arrangement. I was ready to make any headway towards not embarrassing myself on this trip.

"One question, though," I asked as an afterthought. "Can I bring my dog?"

"What the hell," she replied.

I wasn't entirely positive that was a yes, but it wasn't a *no* either. This place would undoubtedly entertain Thor.

The next few weeks passed quicker than I cared to recall as my trip grew closer by the day. I finished my shopping list, shelling out cash for more outdoor gear than I'd ever use again in my life. This whole trip was a mistake, and I knew it.

Anxiety crept in on me daily as the days ticked down my calendar. But I was a firm believer in the silver lining. Sometimes, it was just harder to find. My silver lining for this trip was, oddly enough, Charlene.

I battled traffic diligently three days a week, sometimes more, as I worked off my riding lessons. My drive was spent listening to Swedish language lessons on my phone, Thor in the back seat panting and ready to explore her ranch.

As promised, she had me riding comfortably in a matter of weeks. My posture was 'acceptable,' and my balance was good. She was happy with my progress, and I was more than proud of myself for tackling this new skill set.

Evenings were filled with riding, manure, and laughter while I mucked Charlene's twenty stalls in her three mismatched barns. Despite the smelly task, the more time I spent with Charlene and her beloved horses, the more I loved it.

Charlene was unabashedly *Charlene* in a way I didn't know if I'd ever seen one person be before. Every day was filled with rhinestones and hairspray.

Some days we worked in companionable silence, and others, she told me wildly entertaining stories of her younger years. She was sassy and overly honest but always upbeat and ready to make me laugh, whether that was her intention or not.

It was the last Saturday before my trip, now only two days away, that I found myself driving out to her ranch, even though it wasn't one of my scheduled days.

I pulled in through the gate and parked the Jeep, Thor pacing the back seat, ready to unload. As I opened the door, Thor let out a strange, low growl — odd, since this ranch was his favorite place to be these days.

"What's the matter, big guy?" I stroked his head before moving to the side as I let him out of the car. He jumped and padded directly to Charlene's side, leaning heavily into her, a growl still in his throat and his hair standing on end. She bent down to calm him but was quiet.

The quiet wasn't necessarily what caught my attention, but something was most certainly off. Her hair was in a relatively flat ponytail today, and there wasn't a rhinestone in sight. She almost looked, dare I say, normal?

While everything she wore was still very fitted, the lack of pattern and sparkles seemed odd on the woman. I didn't even know she owned anything that wasn't bedazzled. This was certainly out of character.

"*Tjena, vad görs?*" I practiced my Swedish, walking towards her. Look at me, sounding so official. "Need a hand?"

"Sure," Charlene replied in a flat tone. This was the least energetic I'd ever seen her. Where was the sass? What could possibly bring this fiery woman down a notch?

"Everything okay today?" My eyes scanned her for some clue as to what could be upsetting Charlene so much that even Thor could feel it. We'd spent so much time together lately, and I was startled to realize I sincerely cared about her. So did Thor.

My anxiety over my trip that drove me out here this morning was suddenly forgotten as I eyed my... friend? Were we friends now? I guessed so.

"I'm fine," she waved me off.

Well, that definitely worried me. As a rule, if a woman muttered the words "I'm fine," chances were they were not. It was girl code.

"You've been blunt enough with me these past few weeks; it's time I return the favor," I decided on honesty

Charlene-style. "You're less sparkly today, figuratively," I waved my hand over her outfit. "And literally, for that matter. What's going on?"

A few moments of silence went by as we walked into the barn. "It's my sister," she finally replied with a huff. Charlene grabbed a halter and rope off the wall before sliding open her palomino's stall door. She did quick work of bringing him out and tying him off in the center of the barn.

Charlene had never mentioned her family other than her ex-husbands, plural, in passing, which I found odd. We'd talked a lot over the last few weeks, and I'd told her several stories about my family. How had I not noticed she purposefully excluded talking about hers?

"Is she okay?"

"Of course she's okay. Nothing bad ever happens to that tramp." She grabbed a comb and some spray from a bin she kept nearby and began to brush out her horse's white mane, not elaborating past that.

That was not the response I had anticipated but hadn't I learned that the unexpected was to be expected with Charlene? Thankfully, I held in my giggle at her words, and my jaw did not hit the floor. I waited silently, ready to hear the rest of the story.

"Marlene rolled into town last night on the arm of my ex-husband, Tony," she went on after a while. "Paraded all around town like a show pony ready for the fair and stopped at my bar for a drink. She knew I'd be there to dance on a Friday night. Then, of course, she and Tony needed a place to crash. So they came here, to her little house even though she moved out twenty years ago. I'd be fine if I never saw that woman again."

Suddenly the disdain in her voice every time she had mentioned her first husband made much more sense. I watched as her movements became jerky, working through some tangles.

"I'm so sorry to hear that your relationship with her isn't great," not entirely sure how else to respond at that moment.

"Well, it sure as shit ain't your fault." Her brushing turned a little aggressive at that. I leaned over to take the comb from her.

"Wanna talk about it?"

Charlene let out a long exhale and walked to pet one of the other horses leaning out of a stall.

The sorrel colt was already the biggest horse in the barn and the youngest of her horses she was currently training. I couldn't remember his name, but the horses seemed to blend together for me, except for Raven.

Raven was my favorite, a black and white overo paint horse with gorgeous coloring. She was the one Charlene had me ride the most often, and I was smitten.

"Not much to tell. Marlene is my twin. We grew up with Tony, and he was my high school sweetheart. We married right after high school and lived in a cute little trailer with a horse pasture. I'd open the windows, and the horses would stick their heads right inside. I loved that place. Right up until I came home early one day to find Marlene in my bedroom with Tony underneath her."

I was shocked into silence at her admission as waves of

cold fury built in me. How awful to be betrayed like that; how dare anyone hurt this sparkly, shiny beacon of light.

"He tried to say he got confused and thought it was me, but that's ridiculous. The woman looks *nothing* like me. She could never master teasing her hair just right — when is mine ever flat?" she went on. "And the eyeliner that woman wears? Put her on the corner and leave her to make her money.

"Anyway, I left Tony and slashed his tires on the way out. I soaked all of his tools in vinegar so they'd be as useless as him, took the horses, and never looked back," she continued as if those were all very reasonable things to do.

A long silence passed between us before I realized I was supposed to respond. I was equally shocked at the tale she'd spun and how casually she mentioned destroying property. Charlene was straight out of a country song.

"Good for you," I finally said. *Solidarity, sister.*

She nodded, and we worked in silence. Caring for her horses was therapy for her, and it was easy to see that. Her shoulders relaxed after several minutes of brushing, petting, and combing. This horse would be the most pampered steed in Colorado when she was done with it today.

"Want to ride?" At that, she turned to finally put away her brushes. "I need to take Bryan for a ride anyway. He's spent too much time in the pasture while I've been working the colts. It's his turn to run now."

Without even waiting for my response, she walked to another stall and hooked a halter around Raven, leading her out to join us. The sight of the pretty black and white mare brought a smile to my face, easing my anxiety. I was happy here with Charlene and these horses.

"Sure. This will probably be my last time for a while," I answered, glad she offered. I didn't know why I came out here today, but maybe a ride was what I needed. We both saddled our horses and led them out of the barn.

"Let's skip the arena today," she jumped into the saddle.

I did the same, grabbing the horn and pushing myself up. I may not have flown the way Charlene seemed to, but it was a drastic improvement from only a few weeks ago. I settled, reins in hand, and let Charlene lead the way. She needed this day to clear her head as much as I did.

We rode past the barns and the little house at the back of the property. I'd never honestly noticed it before. It had a bright coral pink door and tire tracks in the grass out front, which I assumed were from Tony and Marlene last night. Thor was sound asleep next to a rocking chair on the little porch, snoozing in the shade and right at home.

Charlene didn't even glance sideways at the house. She rode straight for a gate at the back of the pasture. We left and walked into the foothills on a narrow trail through the woods. Neither one of us spoke much as we walked through the trees.

I took the time to glance around at the stunning scenery around us. The smell of pine reminded me of home, fresh mountain air easier to breathe than the city's smog in the distance.

Why didn't I appreciate this more? It was lovely out here, under the shade of the trees. I'd lived in Colorado my whole life and somehow just... missed it.

"There's a clearing up ahead. Ready to run?" she called to me.

I grinned, eager to feel the wind in my face. We reached the clearing, and I nudged my horse into a lope, riding into the morning sun.

Charlene picked up speed ahead of me, riding as smoothly as if her mount was made of wind. She leaned down and let out a loud yip of delight.

This woman was something else. It was hard not to admire how she lived her life so completely. Her melancholy mood from that morning evaporated into thin air as she bounced back, riding full tilt on her beloved horse. I watched her ponytail whip in the wind behind her as she relaxed, at peace with the world.

It was enviable — she knew exactly what made her happy and then made it happen. Charlene was the definition of content even with three failed marriages and a crummy family situation, and I admired that.

I didn't know what I wanted from life, let alone how to make it happen.

We finished the ride, horses sweating in the mid-day sun and my knees sore from the stirrups, and headed to the ranch. Thor was waiting for me as we entered the gate and into the barns. I hopped off, stretching my legs to loosen the stiffness of the longer ride, and began to remove the tack from Raven's back.

Charlene worked silently beside me, but I could feel the earlier tension fading from her. She brushed her horse tenderly, removing the sweat and babying her children, as that's what these horses were to her. We finished a while later and returned the horses to their stalls.

Turning towards me, she looked down at her clothes before taking the reins from my hands to hang them up.

"I should burn this outfit," she muttered, startling me yet again with her random thoughts. "I'm fully confident that I look fabulous no matter what I'm wearing, but it's so *boring*."

She glanced over at me in my jeans and solid olive-green tee, not too far off from her own outfit currently, before shrugging. Unapologetic, as ever.

I chuckled as I shook my head.

Now that we were done, I sat down on the stack of hay bales in the back of the barn. Thor padded over to me and laid down on my feet. My eyes traveled the building, taking in the horses quietly munching and the neat row of saddles and tack hanging on the wall.

I was procrastinating. I should have headed to my Jeep to leave, but I didn't. Charlene noticed my hesitation, cocking her head to the side in an appraising look.

"Why are you doing this, hun?" Her tone was calm, soothing, and lacking judgment.

"Riding?" I asked, confused. "I leave in two days…"

"No, not riding. I'm not *that* dumb," she rolled her eyes. "Why are you pushing yourself so hard for this trip?"

I thought about it for a moment before answering. So many strange things had happened this summer that I couldn't explain, starting with purchasing this trip — uncharacteristic for me.

My dreams were more vivid, constantly filled with scenery I didn't recognize, places I'd never been.

Passing strangers had offered odd comments that had stuck with me for long after the fleeting moments of our conversations.

I'd even befriended the woman standing before me, as unlikely of a pair as we made.

If someone had told me at the beginning of the summer that this was what my life would look like now, I would have laughed. But, as much anxiety as I had over how much had changed in my relatively stagnant life since I booked this trip, I wanted to go.

"I feel…" I struggled to find the words. "Called? I don't think that's the right word, but I don't know how else to explain it."

Charlene waited in silence, giving me the time I needed to think through my answer.

"I don't know, Charlene," I sighed, leaning down to run my hands over Thor. "I think I need to do this for me. I need to prove to myself that I can do this. That I can live my life and make my own choices. Be my own main character."

She only nodded as she spun, walking out of the barn. I rose, took one more look around as I stretched my back, and followed.

"I almost forgot, I got you something. Hang on a minute." She ran over to her house and slipped inside before coming back to me with a box in hand. "These were mine, but I thought you needed them more than me."

Touched she had thought of me, I lifted the top and

pulled apart the paper. In it sat a pair of spurs. These weren't just any spurs, though — they had snowflakes etched into the metal with a small rhinestone in the center of each one. They were glistening in the sunlight and attached to small turquoise straps. My brown leather riding boots would be as fabulous as her while I rode in Sweden.

Eyes tearing up at the thoughtfulness of her gift, I smiled at her. She was giving me a little piece of her to take with me. I knew it'd give me the courage to borrow her strength, tenacity, and courage in whatever lay ahead. Seeing the tears in my eyes, she grabbed me in a crushing hug.

"You can do anything, girl," Charlene said as she released me, patting my arm. "Come see me when you get home. I need to hear all about it."

I nodded, hopped in my Jeep, and drove off before the tears could fall. If Charlene could move on from so much pain and heartache in her past and live a life as full as hers was, then maybe she was right. My life wasn't even half as terrible as the things she'd overcome to get to where she was today. I just needed to *start*.

My chest felt lighter as I drove down the dirt road and towards home. By the time I got home, I was so tired physically that my mind seemed to settle. I spent the following day packing, adding everything on the detailed list Sabrina had typed out on my phone of every possible thing that she thought I might need.

I was as ready as I'd ever been.

I jerked awake as a hand lightly tapped my shoulder. Pulling my noise-canceling earbuds out of my ears, I saw the flight attendant motioning for me to put my seat up. Everything was blurry from sleep, and my not-so-chic (but convenient) neck pillow was damp where I must have been drooling. Lovely.

An economy seat for ten hours from Denver to Munich was not the world's most comfortable ride, but the sleeping pill I had taken before takeoff had been one of my better ideas, if I did say so myself.

I stretched my arms above my head, glancing around as the entire plane came to life. The number of people they could get on these big planes was always slightly shocking to me, three rows across and too many to guess back.

No matter how far I leaned, I couldn't see out the windows from my seat between the two aisles. I'd have to stick to Google Earth for my view of Munich from above.

We landed smoothly and were herded off the plane and

through customs like a cattle drive. I admired my pretty, new stamp for Germany as I aimed for the next gate. Stockholm, the sign read in large letters. Just seeing the city's name printed in front of me was exhilarating.

My legs and back were sore from the long flight, and I felt every one of my 31 years as I waited for the next plane to arrive. Killing time, I bought myself a pretzel, sure that this was the German equivalent to the breakfast of champions.

We boarded shortly after, and I took my seat at the window, excited that I would get to admire the view this time. I skipped my earbuds — I was too anxious to pick up my audiobook where I left it, even though this fantasy novel was better than the last few I'd read.

My face was glued to the window as I watched the landscape change until the beautiful, blue Baltic Sea came into view. Suddenly, we'd started to descend. Colorful architecture poked through the clouds woven in between waterways.

Tiny, green, tree-covered islands were innumerable, dotting the seascape. As we approached the city, it was easier to see the fourteen islands Stockholm was known for. All of them were interconnected with so many bridges that I lost count after a while. I'd never seen a town so tightly settled along the water.

My eyes sparkled with the sun reflecting off the wings, mirroring my delight over the adventure awaiting me. Sweden was breathtaking, and I hadn't even stepped foot in it yet.

Home, something deep inside me seemed to say. It was a

strange voice, raspier than the inner monologue that ran inside my head constantly, but I brushed it off. Everything I had worked so hard for these last few weeks was now laid out before me, and I was excited.

As we descended to the airport, the coastal city turned to farmland painted with trees alight with fall colors. Even the buildings along the runway were painted the country's signature blue and yellow. Everything loudly announced, "*Välkommen!*"

I jumped out of my seat, impatient for the plane to unload and my journey to begin. With my first step inside the airport, I was already in awe of this country. A peaceful feeling of rightness seemed to settle deep in my bones.

My gaze shifted up. Everything was magnificent, even the modern light fixtures hanging in the terminal and geometric-patterned inlaid wood floors. As far as I could see, there was evidence of the clean lines that have made Swedish design famous.

Another passport stamp was added to my collection, and I boarded the train for Stockholm Central Station. All my previous doubts and reservations about this trip were squashed even further by each charming sight.

The train glided to a stop, and I grabbed my bags, aiming for the bustling platform. The intricate blend of old and new was already evident everywhere I looked.

I made my way towards Gamla Stan, ready to unload my luggage at my hotel and explore the city. I didn't know much about Swedish cuisine, but the smell of cooking meat had me dreaming of a traditional meatball. That was up next for lunch.

Outside of my hotel was a bike rental vendor. I stopped, handing over a few hundred kronor, what I thought was about sixty dollars, to rent an e-bike for the day. Every travel video I'd watched of Stockholm had suggested it. The only problem was that I had no idea where I was going.

My bike bounced across the cobblestone streets down narrow lanes as I wandered through the city. My head swiveled, watching where I was going while also taking in the stunning colorful architecture, modern decor, and medieval accents blended into this beauty on the water.

I stopped for lunch in King's Garden as my stomach growled loudly, ready for those meatballs. The savory pork and beef meatballs covered in gravy and served with mashed potatoes were precisely what I needed after my long day of traveling.

Reclining in my chair, I sipped my *saft*, a delicious berry drink the waiter had insisted I needed to try, and watched the town move around me.

This is truly wonderful, even alone, I thought to myself. The uneasy feeling I'd had for months seemed more settled, at peace, and I was content.

Grabbing my phone, I pulled up a map to plan the next leg of my ride through town, deciding on Stockholm City Hall to see the gilded *Queen of Lake Mälaren.* Then, I'd circle back towards Old Town to the Medieval Museum.

Pictures had not done the *Queen* justice; over 18-million

golden mosaic tiles depicted the history of this exquisite country. I was mesmerized by the enormous, glittering mosaic, even amongst the bustling crowds around me.

As the day went on, I was delighted I'd splurged on an e-bike, happy the motor could give my legs a break. Jetlag caught up to me, and I pulled over to a small cafe. I was all too happy to honor the traditional *fika* with a coffee and a princess cake. It was almost too pretty to eat, but the raspberry and whipped cream combination was as delicious as the day was magical.

Next, I rode to the Medieval Museum, stepping underground and back in time. Slightly creepy wax figures were dressed in period clothes depicting life in medieval Stockholm inside the city's original walls. However, I did my best to avoid them, focusing on the Viking ships and relics displayed.

Intricate wooden carvings were everywhere — runes, designs, and animals covering displays of saddles, swords, shields, boats… everything, really.

I was surprised that one exhibit was dedicated entirely to grooming. A wax figure stood behind it with a neat beard, trimmed and combed, which explained the accessories shown behind the glass. I scanned through the plaque next to it and was intrigued to read that Vikings were known for cleanliness, particularly unusual considering the period.

I strolled through the rest of the museum, learning about an ancient culture I'd never experienced until I saw a mannequin of a woman standing in front of a man and children behind her. The positioning seemed so intentional that I found myself drawn to it, reading the plaque in front of the figures.

"Women held a particular place of honor in Nordic culture, serving as the head of the household. This included far more than cooking and cleaning but also running the farms and defending their homestead while men were gone on voyages. Viking culture allowed for far more women's rights than other cultures of the same period. Adultery was a serious offense, and divorce allowed women to leave a marriage with half of their family's wealth."

Well, that was fascinating. I was delighted I'd decided to stop here, creepy mannequins aside. Those I could have done without.

I moved on, and the next display made me pause. Three women clothed in long, flowing blue capes with gold embroidery were hunched over wooden tiles strewn on a table, each carved with different runes.

"Although history remembers the power held by the men as raiders, stories have been passed down that it was the women who were believed to carry magic, the practitioners of seid,*"* I read on the plaque below.

"While not worshiped, the Norns were highly revered in Norse mythology, set to have spun the fates of mortals and gods alike. Viking culture held fast to the belief that their fates were predestined and death was inescapable. Seers were famous in their time and highly sought after to ease worries over the future.

"Often, these magic practitioners were also referred to as Norns, collectively. This was also the name for the original three, Urd, Verandi, and Skuld. The three sisters of Norse mythology were the sworn protectors of Yggdrasil, the sacred tree at the center of the world and passageway between the nine realms."

Chills broke out over me as I read the words. *Promised,* that same, raspy voice said inside me. Jetlag must have been getting the better of me because I didn't even understand my inner ramblings at this point.

Before leaving the museum, I shot off a picture of a particularly creepy mannequin shoeing a horse to Charlene. I walked back to my bike and decided to send a quick message to my mom and a picture of the charming fountains to Sabrina. Even though I was having a wonderful time alone, I missed my people.

By the time I reached my hotel bed later that afternoon, I crashed. As my head hit the pillow, I couldn't help but feel a rising sense of pride that I'd done this, all by myself, and had the most glorious day exploring. The next leg of the adventure was sure to follow in these magnificent footsteps.

7

My legs felt the fire of the bike riding in Stockholm the following day. Thank God I had chosen an e-bike, or I would have been done before the trip had even started.

I slipped out of bed and rose on my toes, stretching my hamstrings and calves to loosen up. Right then, I felt very *in* my 30s. Maybe that bike ride wasn't the best idea right off the plane. Too late for that, however.

Next stop, the Baltic Coast. I had one last day to explore the smaller town of Sundsvall before I met the rest of my tour later that night.

"This is going to be your year, Shelbie. I can feel it." Sabrina's words on my birthday echoed in my head. With that optimistic view, I boarded the train.

As I stepped into the quaint city, I pulled my jacket tighter around me, enjoying the crisp sea air in late September. A street market was set up for the day with local artists, farmers, and restaurants showcasing their wares in small tents. The tents themselves weren't that different from what I'd seen at home at local farmers' markets, but the draped fabrics in bright colors accenting the wares they showcased added a fun flair all of their own that felt very Nordic. I loved it.

The small inn I booked was the perfect bed and breakfast for my last night before ten days of sleeping in a tent. A pang shot up my back at the thought of what was to come. I was not excited about the whole sleeping on the ground thing.

The owners were a lovely older couple, Hans and Annika, and were as welcoming as all of Sweden had been so far. Fortunately — or maybe, unfortunately — they spoke English beautifully, so I hadn't had much chance to test out my basic Swedish skills yet other than ordering food.

My room was surprisingly large, with a small fireplace in the corner. I threw my backpack down at the foot of the bed, overstuffed with everything Sabrina had thought I might need for this trip, and sat on the edge of the bed. Sliding my shoes off, I rubbed my feet through the soft, white fur rug on the floor. I doubted it was real, but it fit the space perfectly. Everything was light birch wood, the bed and dresser matching and sleek in design, and a small bathroom was off to the side. It was simple but charming, the way so much of this country had been so far.

My stomach rumbled loudly, and I rubbed it, remembering the smell of cinnamon rolls from the street market. I had time to kill, so I went down the stairs and out to the street, ready to knock out some souvenirs.

Meandering through the stalls, I made my way through the coastal town. I admired the 18th-century architecture mixed in with modern amenities — a theme I'd already seen much of in Sweden. Everything about this country was welcoming, a homey feeling settling over me easily even though I'd only been here for two days.

First stop, cinnamon roll. It was decadent, not as covered in icing as I was used to from the States, but delicious all the same.

Next, I stopped at a local toymaker in a tent bursting with bright primary colors. There, I purchased cute little wooden carved animals for Annie and Jasmine. Bears, moose, elk, seals — everything I might see on my trip (but hopefully not *too* close) — all carved with exquisite detail. I was delighted with my purchase and hoped the girls loved them as much as I did.

"I've been waiting for you," someone voiced in a thick Swedish accent from next to me.

I finished paying before glancing over at the older woman in the next booth. She had beautiful, long brown hair greying at her temples, hanging loose down her back. But the most memorable part of her was her skin, so pale she seemed to glow.

Her booth was draped in deep violet fabrics, different from the bright reds and yellows of the toymaker, and windchimes hung on the corner. Smoky incense permeated the tiny space giving the whole booth an eerie vibe.

Even though her words were strange, I felt inexplicably

drawn to her. My feet moved without any conscious thought to approach her booth, and a sudden gust of wind came up behind me off the water, pushing me forward. Fabric fluttered in the breeze as the chimes sang a magical tune.

Finally, the wind settled down, and I glanced down at her wares, enchanting jewelry for sale. Different colors and styles of leather bands — some a simple strand, some intricately braided — were strung with beads and pendants, each engraved with unique markings. "Do you make these bracelets yourself?"

"I do," she extended her arm covered in bracelets tinkling softly as she waved a hand over her pieces. "But it's not the jewelry that's important. It's the runes."

I leaned in to look closer, touching one of the rune-inscribed bracelets.

"Look, do not touch," she scolded with more force than I would have expected before my hand could land on a bracelet.

"I'm sorry. I was admiring the detail you put in each bracelet."

"Of course I do. Magic is in the details. You never want to use magic without intention, or who knows what the results will be."

I smiled hesitantly, immediately dismissing the notion of magic. It might be my favorite thing to read about, but I was far from believing it existed.

"They're lovely." I smiled, ready to move on.

"They're calling to you," she drew my attention back,

wind chimes jingling again. "Can't you feel it? Choose one."

I grew uncomfortable at the idea of walking away. Sure, I didn't believe in magic, but she did. As much as I wanted to walk away, I also didn't want this woman to go home and hex me later. And maybe I did feel a slight pull, something drawing me forward for a closer look.

"These are runes?" I asked, noticing the strange letters hammered into the medal. She nodded. "What do they mean?"

"This is the language of the gods. They mean lots of things." She pointed out several bracelets. "Runes aren't like an alphabet as you would think of them. They can be combined to form words, but each symbol also holds a specific meaning and intention.

"Here." She reached across the table, grasping my hand and pulling it forward. Her touch startled me on contact, and I jumped. She dropped my grip but motioned for me to place my palm out, turned down. "Feel for which one is calling you."

I forced a smile, my hand now hovering above the table.

Why am I doing this? I really need to practice saying no.

I closed my eyes because that seemed like what I should do. My hand glided over the table of jewelry, moving left and right as I waited for… I didn't know exactly.

As much as I tried to focus, my mind wandered, remembering my brother's magic shows when we were younger. The thought made my smile genuine as I now half-expected a stuffed bunny to pop out of a hat.

Suddenly, an odd feeling spread over me, stealing my breath and blowing my hair off my neck. I felt my hand catch in the air, almost as if I held a magnet hovering over another one.

Promised, that same raspy voice said inside me again. I opened my eyes, shocked by the odd experience and looking for answers. My hand lowered, drawn down, as I brushed my fingers across a pendant on a red leather strap.

ᚴ

Her earlier words returned to me as I pulled my fingers away, but my eyes were glued to the rune. Nothing was extraordinary about this symbol, but it was as if a key had slid into a lock inside me. Warmth spread through me, overriding the chill in the air as I gazed down at the rune and the small dragons etched into the beads at its side.

"I'm sorry," I apologized, remembering her scolding as I looked at her. "Can I touch it?" I reached for the one that caught my attention. She nodded.

As I lifted it carefully, it felt warmer, heavier in my hand than expected. Another breeze that hadn't been there a moment ago lifted the curls around my face, sounding almost like the flapping of heavy wings. For a moment, I caught the scent of pine and fresh air mingled with something sharper; manly. It must have been from the incense.

"Yes, I thought so," she grinned, a complete shift from her earlier behavior. "This shall be quite the journey for you, both in body and spirit. Are you prepared?"

"I've been preparing for weeks," I replied, shaking off

an unsettling feeling. My mind recalled the semi-disastrous attempts I'd made these last few weeks before getting here — all of the hiking and camping practice hadn't panned out how I had hoped.

She chuckled — not a good sign, I felt — before leaning over and tying the bracelet to my wrist.

"My sisters will be anxious to see you." She patted my hand before letting go. A shiver ran through me as the bracelet settled onto my skin. I pulled my jacket tighter, the wind off of the coast chilling me.

"Today is my last day here, so I don't think I'll be back."

"Don't worry, they'll find you. It's fate. *Nornors dom vid näsen du får och ovis dåres öde. I vattnet du drunknar, om i vind du ror, för dödsdömd är allt fördärv.*"

I forced another grin, trying, and I'm sure failing, to hide my confusion at her Swedish. This was the first genuinely Swedish expression anyone had offered me. Most everyone spoke some English, and my audiobook lessons failed me miserably. Hopefully, whatever she had said didn't require a response because I had none.

She noticed my reaction, though, and chuckled. "*The Ballad of Fafnir*, an Eddic poem. It's my favorite one; the story of a man and a dragon. I bet you'd like it, too." She winked.

I nodded politely. Somehow, I didn't think Eddic prose would make it to my To Be Read list but noted. I did like dragons…

"How much do I owe you for the bracelet?"

She shook her head at that. "Nothing today. I'll come to you again."

My brows drew together in confusion, not following what this woman was saying. Was she giving it to me for free? I wouldn't be stopping in Sundsvall until my last day before leaving, and who knew if the market would be set up again that day. I felt guilty taking the bracelet, but when I tried to untie it to return it, her hand settled over mine, holding it in place.

"You will sacrifice plenty. Keep it as a gift from me to you. A Present." She chuckled at her joke, but it was lost on me.

I smiled, now slightly weirded out by this woman. The bracelet was pretty, though; a small ring of gold centered on a red leather strap. It would make a nice souvenir for me. If this woman weren't so odd, I'd consider picking one for Sabrina too, but I was ready to be done and move on.

"*Tack*," I said, hoping that I had pronounced it correctly but was now doubting every bit of Swedish I'd learned.

A chime on my watch dinged, not nearly as melodic as the ones swinging behind me. I glanced down at my watch and noticed it was time to meet my tour guide and crew.

Looking back out at the street, I walked away from the water and into town as the sound of wind chimes faded behind me, coming to a stop.

I walked towards the small cafe my tour information had listed as the meeting spot, perusing the booths lining the cobblestone streets along the way. There were fresh fish, fruits and berries of all sorts, knit sweaters and hats, exquisite carvings, and many bright and colorful things.

My eyes scanned the signs hanging above each small restaurant until, a few minutes down the road, I spied the cafe we were to meet.

A tall man with dark salt-and-pepper hair was standing with his back to me, leaning against a railing sipping a beer. He had a muscular frame with large shoulders under his form-fitting black long-sleeved shirt.

Good God, please let that man be Gustav, my tour guide.

I walked up behind him, fingers crossed that maybe this would be a perfect meet-cute, as he slowly turned and waved in my direction. I almost crashed into the table in front of me as I caught my first glimpse of the man.

Yes, he was muscular, but the attraction came to a complete halt there. His beard was splotchy and would have looked better clean-shaven. His nose was practically bulbous, a word I didn't find myself using often. But more noticeable than either of those features was his scowl, set so deeply in his face I couldn't tell whether he was upset or if this was his resting face.

"Shelbie?" he asked with a thick Swedish accent. I nodded as I let go of any lingering disappointment. "I'm Gustav. The rest of our group should be here soon."

I faked a smile as I leaned against the railing near him. An ominous feeling settled in my stomach as I watched the passersby, hoping for a glimpse of my companions.

Behind me, a loud group of young people speaking rapidly in Swedish approached the cafe. I turned as they all laughed, grinning at their jovial conversation. The closer they came, the more I wondered if this was the rest of my group. I watched as they walked up to Gustav, shaking his hand as he spoke to them. I was shocked to see the man *could* smile, hoping beyond hope that this was a good sign. The entire group turned to me as the group's apparent leader said, "*Vill du följa med eller?*"

I stood there for a moment, glued in place as my face reddened, before responding, "*Jag förstår inte.*"

I don't understand. At least I'd learned that much.

Gustav glanced in my direction, the scowl back, before turning to the rest of the crew and saying something else that I thought had the phrase "American" in it.

"Shelbie, meet the rest of our group. They speak a little English, but I will be translating for everyone, I guess," annoyance clear in his tone. "We leave tomorrow at 8 a.m. sharp. Meet at the bus station on the west side of town to depart together. *Fattar du?*"

"*Ja,*" my response mixed with the consent of the gang. I glanced over at them once more. All of them were in great shape and must have been in their early 20s.

Super.

I did not fit with this group *at all.*

I returned to my inn for the night, glad to have a soft bed for the evening, as dread slowly crept in on me.

"No," I scolded myself aloud as I slipped into a matching pajama set Sabrina had gifted me for my birthday last year. "I refuse to think anything but positive thoughts. I have done lots of hard things before. I can do this, too."

I didn't even have Thor to huff his annoyance at me

talking to myself. The thought sank me a little further into my depressed state.

As I closed my eyes, I imagined the swirling purple and green lights dancing over the trees and water, lighting up the sky. A smile spread over my face as I reminded myself why I was here.

I couldn't wait to see the Northern Lights.

8

A little after noon the next day, our group stopped for a picnic lunch overlooking the Baltic Coast. I sat a little off by myself, not intentionally distant but not feeling included either.

Gustav passed out lunches to our group. *Räkmacka*, the label read, but I had no idea what that meant as I unwrapped my food. I was pleasantly surprised to find a delicious sandwich with rye bread, shrimp, mayo, and other ingredients I couldn't place. It made sense to be eating seafood seaside, I supposed.

Loosening my boots, I was thankful I'd been wearing them every time I walked Thor over the last several weeks and had taken the time to break them in.

The thought of my big fur ball sent a pang through my heart. I hoped Sabrina and her girls were spoiling him. Looking up at the rest of my group, I was suddenly lonely. And wasn't lonely in a crowd the worst feeling?

My calves were already sore from the rocky hike, but

the views had been exquisite. This slice of land was a beautiful intersection of mountains, forests, and the sea, all in one. That morning, we'd set off through the Skuleskogen National Park, headed for *Slåttdalsskreva.* Hell's Gap, as Gustav begrudgingly translated for me.

After a hike through forests, grasslands, and fields of rocks like I'd never seen before, we ended up at this impressive sight, quite literally cleaving a mountain in two. The bluffs rose high above me on either side, blocking out the sunlight. It was easy to see how it got the nickname Hell's Gap; this could be a passage between dimensions in a fantasy world.

Sheared rock faces rose a hundred feet above me, blocking out the late morning sun. We walked through the crevice barely wider than a single car lane for about five minutes before reaching the other side. I thought I overheard someone in my group say something that sounded like *tvåhundra meter,* which I knew, from my very limited Swedish, was 200 meters. Too bad I didn't know the translation from meters to feet. Needless to say, it was huge.

A breeze rattled the leaves of the trees behind us gently, swaying quietly. The sound was broken only by gulls calling overhead and seals barking distantly on the beaches below. Birds swooped down, looking for any scraps of our picnic as I took a sip out of my filtered water bottle.

I closed my eyes, taking a deep breath of the salty forest air and attempting to squash my sudden dose of melancholy. When I opened them, Gustav shot me his signature scowl as he motioned for us to pack up. Shoving the last bite of my sandwich into my mouth, I bent to retie my boots.

I groaned as we stood, returning up the rocky hills. There were many days ahead of me, and I needed to dig deep.

By the end of the day, I was ready to collapse. We each set up our tents around a central fire pit. Trash was picked up and disposed of away from camp, and food was hung high in the trees because of bears. Wolverines. Wolves.

Yay.

I was so tired, sleep found me easier than I expected, particularly after my failed camping attempt at home.

Too soon, the sun was up and the sounds of the camp coming awake filtered through my tent. I stretched and unzipped my sleeping bag. Quickly changing clothes, I became desperate for a bathroom other than the woods.

Today would be our first day of riding. I didn't know whether the soreness from hiking or riding would be worse. As I bent to pack my bags, the soreness in my thighs reminded me that I would be delighted to sit for a little while.

I did my business in the woods as fast as humanly possible, narrowly avoiding imaginary poison oak. We hiked into the forest up paths with wood planks for easy passage. My group chatted happily, watching for moose, bears, and other exciting wildlife that might be inhabiting the woods.

Me? I was hoping I'd miss them altogether, but I kept that thought to myself. I did, however, admire the cascading waterfalls created by the last of the snowmelt, ready to freeze again in a few weeks.

Gustav raised a finger to his lips as he motioned for us to join him in a clearing ahead of us. We approached him on silent feet as I peeked over the shoulders of the others.

A moose stood in the middle of a forest stream. Sunlight filtered through the surrounding trees, hitting his antlers just right, seeming to set them aflame.

This was truly spectacular, and I was glad I was here.

We finished our hike through the woods, slowly making our way to meet up with a local transportation company, ready to give us a lift to the horse barns. I was delighted to sneak into the bathroom at the rest stop, eager for a toilet seat.

Taking this quick break to change, I pulled off my jeans and hiking boots, replacing them with thick riding leggings and brown leather boots. My new spurs from Charlene were right on the top of my bag, ready for me to grab once we got to the barns.

I loaded onto the bus with the rest of my group as we took off inland, away from the magnificent Baltic Coast. Without meaning to, I dozed in my seat, missing out on the conversations I was never included in anyways. The bus stopped, jerking me awake, at a quaint barn backing up to a forested area. Other than that, I had no idea where we were or how far we'd traveled from Skuleskogen.

My group unloaded, handing over gear to the assistants at the barn. Today would consist of a day ride, and we would be returning to camp here later.

I packed a small bag of some necessities plus my filtered

water bottle for the day's ride before handing over the rest of my supplies. Following the sounds of the rest of my group, I forced a smile on my face and entered the barn to see a dozen horses set out to be saddled.

My vision seemed to tunnel, blurring out the sounds and people around me as I instead focused on the horses. This was familiar and carried a sense of home. I'd spent so much of the last few months in a barn; it was easy to understand why I'd feel that way.

At the back of the group stood a beautiful dapple horse, painted with shades of brown and white like the leaves falling on new snow. Without even meaning to, I beelined for her, sure that this was *my* horse.

"That's Freya," someone said from behind me. I glanced at the attendant who was walking towards me before turning to the horse, reaching out my hand to pet her.

"Hi there, Freya." She leaned into my touch, and my melancholy feeling faded further down. My smile felt a little more genuine.

"Do you know much about the Norse gods?" the attendant interrupted this calming moment.

"Honestly, no," I admitted with a diffident tone. Another reminder that my research on everything Swedish had been lacking. That had been on Sabrina's to-do list, but I'd ignored it, not thinking I'd need to know about the spiritual history of the country.

"Freya was the goddess of love and beauty," he continued, so much kinder in his tone than Gustav had ever been as he filled me in. "But the Norse were a fickle people. She was also the god of war and magic."

Startled at the jarring combination of traits for one god, I turned and said as much to the attendant.

"The Norse loved a conundrum, sure," he smiled. "My Freya here, though; I named her that because she's magic. This girl loves to find her own paths, even ones we didn't know existed before, don't you, girl?"

I attempted to smile back, now a little nervous that I'd chosen the naughty, wandering horse. Hopefully, I didn't get myself lost. I rubbed her nose some more, thinking that maybe she'd go easy on me if I spoiled her.

"Want to help me get her tack ready?" he asked, drawing my attention back to him.

I nodded, giving Freya one last pat before turning to help. He handed me the pad, and I placed it on the horse as he leaned over to grab the saddle.

My heart dropped down to my toes as he turned in slow motion, and I saw the English saddle in his hands.

I didn't swear often, but no other word could replace it at that moment.

Fuck.

How had I missed that crucial detail? In all of my weeks of practice, not once had I ridden in an English saddle. My heart raced as my eyes scanned the barn, searching in desperation for some sign that this was a mistake.

I mean, it made sense. I was in Europe. Why would I have assumed we'd be riding Western? No amount of logic could ease my rising panic, in any case.

I racked my brain for everything I'd learned as a child: rein placement, how to keep my balance, all of it. The last time I rode in an English saddle, I had been ten years old. All these years later, I could still feel the phantom pains in my thighs from gripping for dear life with the absence of a saddle horn; the jolt in my back as I hit the ground hard enough to break an arm; the fear of riding after that fall, causing me to put a twenty-one-year hiatus on my riding lessons.

It was as if my eyes would fall out of my head as I turned to Freya, trying desperately to avoid eye contact with the rest of my group until I got my heart rate back in order. I was positive my pulse was pounding right out of my skin, evident on my neck and face at this point.

Breathe in. Breathe out, I reminded myself.

I took several deep breaths as my attendant side-eyed me. "I'll just help you get this buckled," he said, smartly choosing not to say anything about my evident panic attack.

Oh, God. This was about to be so, so, so bad.

9

Breathe in. Breathe out. I can do this. I've done lots of hard things before.

Breathe in. Breathe out. I can't do this. I'm going to fall and die.

Breathe in. Breathe out. I'm a lot older now. I can think this through logically and be okay. My body isn't nearly as able to bounce back as it did when I was ten.

Breathe in. Breathe out. Who will take care of Thor? I should have written my will before I left.

Breathe in. Breathe out. No. Don't go there. I can do this.

. . .

Breathe in. Breathe out.

With a will of steel, I somehow went through the motions of preparing Freya to ride. I leaned my head across Freya's large back, mustering any strength I had left.

I would *not* let the tears that were gathering fall. I just wouldn't.

Breathe in. Breathe out.

I moved my hand along her back, stroking her soft fur while purposefully avoiding the stirrups tied tight against the saddle. I couldn't even look at them without imagining them swinging down, wild and free, doing nothing to help me maintain my balance.

Breathe in. Breathe out.

My final mistake was running my fingers through her dark mane. My hand bumped against the saddle, and I glanced at where the horn should be.

Panic flooded as I slammed my eyes shut, squinting to block out everything around me. My ears were buzzing so loudly I couldn't focus, a combination of all of my anxiety over this trip that I had continually swept under the rug and remembered flashbacks of my fall as a child.

Breathe in. Breathe out.

Freya's large body nudged me, pushing me towards the barn doors. I opened my eyes and looked at the beautiful mare, reminding myself I was here. I could be present. She nudged me again and began to walk towards the doors. With her reins in hand, I followed her lead.

The attendant's eyes followed me as we walked out of the barn and into the forest.

"I'll go warm her up with a light walk," I mumbled, a little shocked I could even form words but making any excuse to get out of that barn.

He nodded, eyeing me still until we walked under the cover of the trees.

Breathe in. Breathe out.

"Lead the way, Freya," I said, now talking to horses as well as dogs. Why the heck not? I'd clearly snapped.

She sighed loudly, much more relaxed than I was at that moment. Her head bobbed as she pushed forward down a path. I followed, still holding her reins, but it was most certainly the horse in control, not me.

. . .

Breathe in. Breathe out.

I glanced into the trees, attempting to slow my breathing any way I could. Tears streamed down my cheeks as we silently walked. I forced myself to look up, noticing the vivid changing colors of fall mixed in with the many ever-greens. My pounding heart rate slowed.

Breathe in. Breathe out.

I leaned on Freya as we walked in companionable silence, now down a less defined path I hadn't noticed she'd pushed me towards.

"So this is why they call you the wanderer, huh?" Yep. Definitely talking to the horse now. She whinnied in response, making me glance sideways at her. "Since you're a magic horse, can you talk?"

She nudged me a little harder this time, and it made me laugh, bringing me a little more out of my head. I swiped at the tears on my face.

Breathe in. Breathe out.

. . .

Breathing became a little easier the farther we got into the forest and away from my group.

"I'm so lonely," I admitted to Freya, lips trembling as I attempted to hold back the flood of tears threatening me.

The more I thought about it, I didn't even mean right now. I was lonely even at home. I was lost with no sense of direction. When did my life get to this point? How did I let it slip by me for this long?

Freya said nothing to my admission, which shouldn't have been too shocking to me since she was a horse.

I held her reins loosely as we walked further along a rocky face leading down into a river valley. I glanced down at the water below, moving slowly across a shallow portion of the river. The gurgling sound of the water passing over the rocky bed was soothing, calming my speeding pulse more.

The path Freya led us down was wide enough to walk side by side, but just barely. Part of me registered that I should have commanded the horse to turn around, heading too far into the forest and away from our group, but that reasoning was drowned out by the circling thoughts filling my head.

"How do I find where I belong, Freya?" I asked my new horse therapist. "I don't fit anywhere anymore."

My thoughts strayed to home — Sabrina filling her life with love and tiny people, my parents settling into retirement, Jacob building his own family. No one pushed me out, but I was only a side character in everyone's story. I needed to write my own.

I turned to look at Freya, as if she might have the

answers, right as she shifted her weight and knocked me off-balance.

I quickly dropped the reins as I struggled to regain my balance perched on the lip of the rocky edge. Swirling my arms in my best impression of a windmill, my weight finally shifted.

In the wrong direction.

I landed hard on my ass, knees to chest, as I flipped over completely, free-rolling down the rocky cliff face. My vision was a blur of trees and rocks and clouds on repeat as I tumbled end over end, aiming straight for the water below.

After what felt an eternity, my body slammed to a stop as my head cracked on a large boulder, forcing my body half into the freezing river running below.

Everything went black.

10

I awoke with a groan. Attempting to open my eyes took entirely too much effort, and everything was too bright. I squeezed them closed again as I tried to remember what had happened.

The sound of running water was close by.

A river.

Why did I remember a river?

My legs and feet were freezing, I suddenly realized, but could not recall why that would be. I moved them sluggishly, and they met resistance. Were they in the river?

I laid still for a moment more, eyes shut, trying to muster any strength. I focused on my leg muscles and slowly pulled myself up, away from the water.

Birds chirped overhead in what must be trees nearby as the sound of leaves rustling was entirely too loud. Nowhere, though, did I hear other people.

I was alone; I was sure of that.

I cracked my eyes open and tried to turn my head.

Nope. Bad idea. I was going to hurl.

Lying as still as possible, I worked my memory in overdrive to piece together so many questions.

Where am I?

How did I get here?

What happened to my head?

I was sure I had a concussion the more I thought about it. I focused on the rest of my body, seeing if I noticed any other significant pain other than my throbbing head and swirling stomach.

A sharp pain radiated from my abdomen; maybe a broken or bruised rib, I thought. My legs were freezing from the water, but something felt wrong with my knee, too.

How did this happen?

Help is coming, the raspy voice inside my head said. Add hearing voices to my list of problems.

I closed my eyes tighter as if blocking out my vision could make this all go away. I must have drifted back off.

The sound of a voice near me finally drove me back to consciousness. I focused, trying to decipher what it was they were saying.

Do you see me?

Can you help me?

I projected my thoughts, trying my hardest to call them to me soundlessly, but nothing happened.

Suddenly, my vision went darker, as if something was

blocking the sun. I did my best to crack my eyes open, vision blurry but there.

A face peered at me from a horse, bending down to look closer.

Horses. That sounded right. *I'd been riding horses.*

Or had I?

Nothing was clear to me at that moment; my confusion was made worse by my cold and aching body. I worked harder to open my eyes, trying to focus on anything.

The rider dismounted and walked closer to me, squatting down. I couldn't entirely focus yet on his face, but I was sure it was a man from the masculine smell of pine and fresh air mingled with sweat.

"Are you okay?" a rich, timbre voice asked.

I laughed. Or, at least, attempted to. The sound that came out of me was the strangest one I'd ever made. Maybe something was wrong with my hearing, too.

"No," I managed to spit out, sounding as if I had cotton balls shoved into my cheeks. "I hit my head."

"Let's sit you up, and I'll take a look," I thought he replied. My ears were buzzing so loudly that it was hard to tell.

He grabbed my hand with a rough, calloused palm, and my body seemed to float into an upright position with a mind of its own. Unfortunately, my stomach was not happy with this new position as I turned quickly and heaved up the contents of my stomach.

Embarrassment should have flooded me, but instead, I was only relieved that I'd turned *away* from this man and avoided spraying him with spew. I didn't have to look far for that silver lining.

I pulled my legs towards me, now leaning my head between them, and moaned. This may have been the worst I'd ever felt.

Gentle fingers at odds with the roughness of his palm grazed my head, searching for injuries.

"You've given yourself quite the bump here," he finally acknowledged as he dropped his hands down to his sides.

I started to nod and then reconsidered the motion as my stomach lurched again. This was mortifying.

"Do you remember what happened?" he prodded, asking entirely too many questions.

Memories slowly returned to me, a vision of swirling trees and rocks and clouds. I'd fallen, rolled down a hill.

"I think I fell down that rocky hill." I pointed behind me as my voice became a little clearer, head still down.

Silence followed. My eyes were still screwed shut, but I didn't think I'd heard him leave. I couldn't bring myself to lift my head enough to check, but what a piece of shit this man was if he left me here like this.

"I think you must be more confused than you realize," he finally replied after the long pause. "There aren't any hills near here."

What?

Now I was racking my brain, struggling to determine what might have happened. The more I thought about it, the more I was sure that I'd slipped down a hill.

Yes. The horse!

What was her name?

Magic something.

"It was Freya!" I shouted, then winced at the sound of my own voice too loud.

Another long silence.

"What does the Goddess have anything to do with this?"

I chuckled. Now I remembered. Freya was named after a goddess.

"Not the Goddess; the horse."

"Did you have a horse?" His voice was tentative as if he was taking a moment to absorb my crazy.

"Yes, she's a brown and white dapple. They told me she likes to wander, but hopefully, she's around here somewhere," I said, remembering more details the more I talked.

The sound of crunching feet told me he must have risen, walking away to look for my horse.

I gasped as more memories flooded me. "She pushed me! She pushed me off the hilltop!"

He returned after a moment, a hand now resting gently on my back.

"As I said, I think you're more confused than you realize. I don't see any signs of a horse, and as I told you, there are no hills near here."

I knew I had plenty of crazy in me, but I was pretty sure those two things did happen. Maybe this was all a dream?

I gathered all my willpower and slowly lifted my head, cracking my eyes open to look at him.

Before me squatted a mountain of a man. He had warm brown hair with streaks of gold, longer on the top, and shaved closely on the side. It mingled with a beard equal parts massive and neatly kept, not a hair out of place. His chocolate brown eyes pierced me, searching my face and body for what I assumed were any other injuries.

He was dressed in furs, draped casually over one shoulder over a thin linen-looking shirt, tucked neatly into what appeared to be a pair of thick woven pants. I wasn't entirely sure of the material, suede maybe, but I did recall enough to know it would be weird if I reached out to touch his pants to determine the texture. His outfit was as rugged as it came, cinched tightly with a belt of rough leather and metal.

Yep. I was dreaming. Now I was sure of it.

No man had ever looked this good before in real life, even with his odd choice of outfits. He was the perfect combination of clean-cut and masculine strength.

"Can you stand?" he asked after a moment.

"Maybe?" I sounded so sure of myself.

"Let's get you up."

He took my hands, lifting me with ease, and my world spun. One hand landed on my shoulder and another on my waist, holding me in place as I fought to keep my balance. Something was wrong with my knee.

"Why are you out here?" he questioned after a moment, thankfully giving me a minute to compose myself.

I stuttered out a laugh. "Fuck if I know. Where is here?"

At his words, I glanced around me. I could have sworn I had been walking along a rocky path descending into the water, but he was right. I didn't see a hill anywhere near here. Tall pine trees densely lined both sides of the river, the boughs beginning well overhead. My vision tracked the trees up into the sky before my eyes came down to the man in front of me. He was squinting at me, questions running through his mind that I did not have the answers to.

"This is the *Indalsälven*," he said, finally, "but no clan owns this strip of the river. It's neutral ground. What clan are you from?"

Clan? What an odd choice of word. But maybe I'm dreaming, and dreams don't make sense.

Shit. Am I in a coma?

"I don't know," I replied after a minute, unsure how to answer but feeling like he expected me to.

More voices approached us from a distance, growing closer. Mountain Man, as that's what I was now calling him in my head, turned to look in their direction.

"Well, that's not the hunt I had expected you'd find," a deep voice came out loud with a laugh. Several other low chuckles accompanied his voice.

I turned towards their voices with as little movement as possible and saw six more men riding towards us, all dressed similarly in furs and leather.

My breathing hitched, the threat of so many men closing in on me when I was too injured to flee, sending my body into a pointless fight or flight response.

Attempting to calm myself, I focused on their horses instead. The more I studied them through squinted eyes, the more confused I became by their appearance.

These were big men, but those horses were strange. I counted twelve horses in total, and all of them were a variant of dun, ranging only from tan to gold, with what looked like skunk stripes down their manes. White hair with a black line down the center was cropped close on some of the horses and hung loose on the others.

While I'd never seen a horse with those markings and coloring before, that wasn't what was odd about them. Large, round bodies seemed mismatched with how short their legs were. Maybe it was the size of the men that rode them? These horses looked like tiny Clydesdales.

I laughed at my internal dialogue. Tiny Clydesdales. Now images of tiny beer carts were dancing through my confused head. Charlene would love these funky little ponies. Realizing I'd laughed out loud, I noticed all seven men now staring at me with questions on their faces.

Cool. Now I look as nutty as I feel.

Focus, Shelbie.

One rider dismounted and approached us. "Is she hurt?" the blond man asked, glancing at the hands still holding me in place. His beard was trimmed close to his face, unlike Mountain Man, and his hair was kept short along his scalp.

"She has a sizeable bump on her head, and I think maybe a twisted knee," they talked about me as if I wasn't there.

A sudden burst of independence came over me, and I shrugged out of his embrace.

"I'm fine," I said with more enthusiasm than I felt.

They both eyed me wearily.

"Where did you come from?" Blondie asked gently. *Here we go again.* "I'd like to help you get home safely."

"I've already told Mountain Man here that I don't know," now annoyed at the questioning.

They glanced at each other with a knowing look.

"We can't leave her here alone," Blondie said. "Arne says he heard wings overhead."

"Oh, I see," another voice called from farther back. "You're willing to leave *me*, your brother, for dragon bait, but not a woman." Several voices chuckled. "No offense."

"Those are tall tales, Magnus," Mountain Man cut in. "And besides, it's neutral ground. Even Raud's not stupid enough to capture anyone here."

Well, thanks, I guess. Good to know where we stand.

Blondie made a *tsk*ing sound deep in his throat at his comment. "He's getting more brazen by the day. I can't take the risk and leave her behind. They're saying he's trading in slaves now."

Okay, that sounded terrible. I definitely did not want to run into this Raud, whoever he was.

Mountain Man seemed visibly annoyed now — so much for my helpful hero. Before he could further argue to leave me behind, Blondie held up his hand to stop the oncoming words. He was obviously the one in charge here.

"If Signe heard that I left a woman alone and injured in the forest, she would leave me and take half of the clan with her," Blondie said. Whomever this Signe was, I liked the sound of her already.

"Are you even going to ask if I *want* to come with you?" I sighed, ready for the menfolk to stop acting as if I wasn't present.

Blondie chuckled, turning to me. "Oh, you and Signe

will get along fine," he smiled. "Would you like to ride with us until we can figure out how to get you home?"

"I don't even know your names," I replied as if that's the only reason I was hesitant to ride off with strange men in the mountains of God knew where.

Blondie extended his hand as if to shake mine. I raised my own, and he reached farther back than I'd expected, grasping my elbow. I did the same in return, only a little weirded out by the odd greeting. "Gunnar Eriksson. Of the Eriksson Clan. And this brute here is Domari, my cousin."

"Shelbie." I glanced between Blondie — I guess I should call him Gunnar now — and Domari, the darker-haired Mountain Man.

Domari did not extend his hand in greeting but solemnly nodded. "Will you be joining us, Shelbie?" Gunnar asked, finally finding his manners.

"What the hell," I replied. "This is a dream anyway, right?"

The men all gave me an odd glance before walking me towards the group of horses. My balance was precarious as my knee gave out under me and my world spun. I stopped to grip my head as Gunnar paused with me. He glanced over me in silent conversation with Domari before handing me off to him.

A scowl was set so deep in Domari's face that it reminded me of Gustav.

Wait, who is Gustav?

❄

"You're riding with me," Domari growled, not thrilled with this chain of events.

"Can't I go with the nice blond one instead?" I replied honestly, having lost my filter in the fall. "You're the Grinch of the group. I can tell."

"I don't know what a Grinch is, but you're right," a young rider laughed from next to us. This one was huge compared to the others, and the others weren't small either. He was shirtless with only a fur draped over one shoulder, doing nothing to hide the immense amount of muscle covering his body, most of it covered in dark black tattoos. "Maybe that should be your new nickname? What do you think, Grinch?"

Several of the men laughed while waiting for us to saddle up. I glanced at the horse Domari led me to. I was glad to see that it wasn't an English saddle, but not exactly sure what to call this one either. I leaned in close, running my hands over the leather and down the horse's sides. The stirrups were shaped like boats, a feature I found a little odd.

"Enough, Magnus," Gunnar said, stopping the prodding but with a smile on his face. "Shelbie, meet my men. The big one there is Magnus, my brother."

Magnus nodded at me politely, giving a large grin that extended almost to his eyes and took over his whole face. I'd bet he was around twenty or so, younger than most of the men in this party. His champagne hair was tied up in a knot at the back of his head, and he ran a strange-looking comb through his beard, grooming himself even now on horseback in the woods.

"You've met Domari."

"*Grinch*," Magnus mumbled under his breath, met with a scowl from my surly hero.

"This is Björn," Gunnar pointed towards a bear of a man, the oldest of the group, maybe in his late forties. His beard, sprinkled with grey, could only be described as epic, reaching halfway down his chest and tied in small ponytails by thin leather straps.

"Thorsten," he moved on, pointing at a thinner man at the back of the group with short ginger hair and a beard two shades darker.

"Kare and Arne," nodding at the last two men. I guessed they were father and son with matching short flaxen waves. Arne was doing his best to grow in the facial hair that the men sported, but he was sporting more of a patchy look in his early teens.

"I'm warning you," I smiled at all of them as I hung onto the horse in front of me, "even if I was at my peak, there is no way possible that I would remember all of your names."

Several men chuckled at that, the big one smiling broadly through his neat beard.

Gunnar nodded at my comment before continuing. "We're traveling upriver to our farmlands for Winter Nights. The seers will be there for the festival. If your memory doesn't return before then to point you towards home, we can ask the Gods for guidance."

Well, all right. This is one exciting dream. And what great names I'd invented! I smiled amicably at everyone as Domari nudged me towards his horse.

"Mjölnir will carry us both for a little while until you regain enough balance to ride alone," Domari said sternly, making sure I knew he wasn't happy about this arrangement.

I nodded, because what else was I supposed to do right now? Domari helped me up into the saddle and quickly swung up behind me. His arms looped around my waist as he gathered the reins in his left hand.

Arne took the first spot, leading the horses away from the riverbank and into the forest. Several other riders went before us while Domari held his horse, Mjölnir, back. I looked over at the other riders and then noticed the riderless horses were far from empty. Two of them wore harnesses attached to sled-like contraptions loaded down with furs, and I assumed meat. This must be a hunting party.

Is that a bearskin?

I did my best not to look shocked at their kills, glancing over massive moose antlers and several pelts. Where was my imagination even coming up with these things?

Domari finally commanded Mjölnir to walk, stepping in line before Björn took up the rear. As the horse began to sway, I focused on all of Charlene's lessons to keep my balance.

Ass down, zippers up, I repeated in my head. That memory had not escaped me. I chuckled a little, thinking about what she'd say when she heard I hadn't even gotten *on* the horse before I fell and knocked myself into a coma. Hopefully, I'd remember all of these dream men when I woke up so I could tell her about them.

"Lean back, *Hàski*," Domari muttered. His voice broke my train of thought as he pulled his hand around my waist and shifted me against him. Suddenly, my back was flush to his front, and I felt a blush rise in my face.

"You're tilting," he went on, the only reasoning he provided. "To the left. It'll hurt Mjölnir if we're not centered."

That, for the most part, made sense.

We rode in silence for several minutes down a well-worn path through the forest. This trail was used for others to tow similar sleds as the grooves on either side matched perfectly with their own.

"We're about a half-day ride to our boats," Gunnar turned to us. "Then we'll camp for the night before we split up." He must be talking to me since I was the only one who wouldn't have already known this plan. "Men, stay alert."

I nodded, then closed my eyes as my nausea returned with the swaying of the horse's gait. Before I knew it, my body had relaxed into Domari. His hand slid tighter over my waist as I dozed.

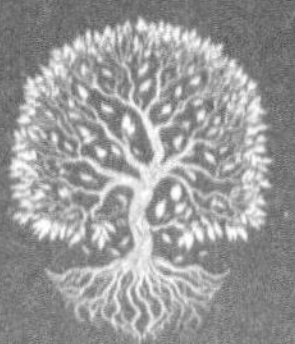

11

The horses stopped sometime later, and I was nudged awake. It took me a moment to gather my scattered thoughts.

Right. Hunters. Hit my head. Vivid dream. How odd I dreamt of sleeping.

I glanced around the clearing we had paused at, back along the river's edge.

"We're stopping to give the horses a break," a deep voice said behind me.

What was his name again?

"Help her off, Domari." I turned my head in the direction of the voice and saw a large blonde man. I thought his name was Gunnar, but I couldn't be sure. My head was still foggy at best.

Domari sighed loudly and swung his leg off his horse. His feet had just hit the ground when he reached up and grabbed my waist, pulling me down after him. The movement was jarring; my feet touched down, and my knee collapsed under me. I hit the dirt hard with an unattractive *oomph* noise as two men rushed to my aid.

"No wonder you can't find a wife handling women like this," the big one scolded. I looked up at the young man towering over me, completely blanking on his name. Even with the dirt on his face from what I would imagine were days spent outdoors hunting, he was handsome, rugged, and cocky; the twinkle in his eye matched the smile on his face. He was well aware of why my eyes lingered. Nevertheless, he was entirely too young for me, and I was positive I had no interest in anyone who meticulously combed his beard the way I'd already seen him do several times. I didn't mind the view, in any case…

"You all right there?" the one with the grey beard asked, finally breaking my blatant staring. This one was Björn; I was sure I remembered that one right. He looked like a Björn. He was a head shorter than the young one, but he had a large barrel chest, strong Nordic features, greying blonde hair, and kind eyes.

"I'm okay," I assured him after a moment, accepting his outstretched hand. "I think my knee hates me right now."

"Let's get you over here to a seat." He pulled me to my feet and guided me gently to a log, awfully attentive for such a burly man. I liked him already.

Björn nodded at me once I was settled and turned to walk away. I watched as the men loosened the horses' tack to give them a rest, taking the utmost care with their mounts. Charlene would like these men even if they weren't all stunning in their own way. That was just a bonus.

I had lost myself in my train of thought as someone walked towards me. My eyes came up right as Gunnar squatted down in front of me, arms resting on his bent knees. The fact that he was squatting, so my neck wasn't straining to look up at him, was greatly appreciated. He seemed thoughtful like that.

"How's your head?" Gunnar asked as if he could hear my comment on his thoughtfulness. I brushed my hand along the back of my head and winced as my fingers grazed over the sensitive, large lump leftover from my fall.

"It hurts," I replied honestly as he shifted to lean behind me. I turned my head as much as I could bear to let him see. "But my ears aren't ringing quite as much as before."

He raised his hand to touch it, then dropped it after a moment and stood. I raised my eyes to him as he circled the log I sat on and walked behind me, stooping down, appraising. "It's not bleeding anymore, so that's good, but it looks painful. That was quite a fall you took," he went on, tone devoid of judgment in a way I appreciated. "Any other memories coming back to you yet?"

I huffed, trying to stretch my mind in any direction. "No, just bits and pieces that don't make sense."

Domari exhaled noisily from his perch to our right, leaning against a tree. His arm muscles were flexed as he crossed them, glancing away from the group as if he had no time for this delay.

I rolled my eyes at him and then regretted the motion as my stomach lurched again.

"I'm not from here. I was traveling with a group, but I can't remember any names other than Gustav," I gave the only information I could come up with that I deemed worthwhile. I wasn't even sure I'd ever been told anyone else's names.

The men all exchanged concerned looks, silently looking for any recognition of the name.

"Where were you traveling to?"

I stared at him blankly. Honestly, I had no clue. I never did as much research on the geography of Sweden as I'd planned, trusting that that was why I hired a tour guide. Sabrina would be *appalled*.

"I don't know," I finally admitted, looking down. This was embarrassing. Not only had I let a horse knock me over, but I was wildly underprepared for this trip. Then, I'd gotten lost in the wilderness with men I didn't know. Tears threatened to spill, a combination of pain and fear of the unknown, but I screwed my eyes shut and refused to let them fall.

Gunnar squeezed my shoulder, assuming it was a memory loss problem again and not massive ignorance on my part.

"We'll figure it out," he said reassuringly. "It'll be okay."

And from the way this man carried himself, I knew he meant it. Why was this dream so *specific?*

The men watered the horses and let them graze for a moment longer before we loaded back up. I limped off into the woods to pee, praying this wasn't the moment my balance gave out, dumping me on my butt with my cheeks exposed. Grateful for answered prayers, that did not happen, and I made my way slowly to Domari.

"Make sure you help her up," Magnus called over. Now I remembered his name. "We don't want her to think all of the Eriksson clan is as awful as you, Grinch."

Domari frowned before quickly lifting me into the air and over the saddle. Waiting only a fraction of a second for me to settle my balance, he tugged on the reins and pulled his horse forward, ready to be done with this exchange.

"Aren't you going to ride?" I asked as the horse lurched forward, surprised he hadn't mounted behind me again.

"I'll walk," he growled. What happened to the man who'd found me by the river? Domari was as cold as the others were warm.

"It's not your fault," Magnus rode up next to us after a while, "he's always been this irritable." He smiled at me, opposite the dark and gloomy man walking alongside the horse.

"That's enough, *Knut*," Domari spat, annoyance in his tone. Magnus winked at me before kicking his horse to a faster pace, riding ahead of us.

I rode along in silence as the day dwindled. I grew up in the mountains and forests of the Rocky Mountains, but this view was still spectacular. We hadn't strayed too far from the water as I could still hear the river in the distance but could no longer see it through the trees. They surrounded us with tall, white, and grey bark. Some had already shed their leaves, but most were lit with copper, amber, and scarlet hues, making the grove look aflame. Light sparkled as it filtered through the branches overhead, casting a magical glow on the ground around us. There wasn't much wildlife around, but this was a large traveling party, and we were making plenty of noise between the horses and the sleds.

As the sun steadily sank beneath the treeline, it grew darker by the minute. The horses seemed to know the way as the men continued until I noticed a clearing up ahead. We stopped there, and by that time, I was shaking. Cold crept in from my clothes that had never thoroughly dried. The men dismounted and made quick work of unloading the pack horses.

Domari helped me off the horse, waiting for a little longer this time to let me go once my feet were on the ground. I nodded as I fought for my balance. As quickly as he could, he let go and walked to help the others, leaving me standing alone.

"He's not very nice, is he?" I said to the horse. Wasn't its name Mjölnir? The name sounded familiar, but I couldn't place it; maybe it was from my Swedish language lessons. No matter his name, this horse was a good one, responsive to Domari's commands and with an easy temperament. I ran my hands along his face, his nose, and through his funny black and white mane as he sighed contentedly.

In easy companionship, the others were chatting, laughing at comments I wasn't focused on. I watched their interaction and noticed others were undoing their horse's tack. That was something I did know how to do, thanks to Charlene's insistence that I do everything myself.

I glanced at the odd saddle, mesmerized by the beautiful, intricate patterns embossed in the leather — animals mixed with runes and geometric designs. My fingers ran over the soft material, distracting me until Domari came up behind me. He said nothing as he leaned over to undo the cinch, body flush against my back as he pulled the saddle down off his horse.

"You're cold," his brow furrowed, glancing down at me, shivering in front of him.

"Why, thank you, Captain Obvious. What gave it away?" My attitude had not been lost along with my memory.

He stared at me for a minute with an odd expression on his face; maybe that wasn't a saying in Sweden. Thankfully, these men all spoke English.

"You need to get out of your wet clothes." His tone was matter of fact, and it irked me.

"Gee. You could at least buy me dinner first."

What was it with this guy? My attitude was souring by the minute with the pain, cold, and all-around distress putting me on edge. Domari's demeanor did *not* help.

"Let's find you some dry clothes you can change into," Gunnar said much more tactfully than his cousin as he walked over to take Domari's place at my side. I glared at Domari's retreating back as he left to help the men. Gunnar chuckled next to me, shaking his head.

"Ready?" he asked politely, his hand slipping under my elbow to help support me as I limped across the clearing towards the sled full of supplies. His eyes roamed my body for a moment, but not in a leering way, before he turned back to the sled and motioned for Arne.

"Get her a pair of your extra pants," he ordered as

Arne jogged to our side. The teen nodded and returned to his horse and gear. While I was far from petite — big bones to match my tall frame — these men were all massive, muscles covering their bodies in peak condition. Even those who didn't stand much taller than me made me feel dainty in a way I had never felt before. I realized that the young teenager was the closest to my size.

"How wet is your top?" Gunnar asked over his shoulder as he sorted through the contents of the sled.

I glanced down, running my hands over the smooth fabric of my jacket. Only my legs had been in the river, so I told him as much.

"That's a strange cloak you have on," he said, eyeing me as he dug through his gear. "Are you sure you're warm enough? It looks so thin. You must be from a trading village to have clothes like that, as I've never seen anything like it."

At his words, I looked down at my jacket again, confused. It was a navy blue fabric with thin insulation and cute wooden toggles covering the zipper. Really, though, I'd loved the fur hood; it seemed Nordic, and I'd bought it especially for this trip. In all honesty, there was nothing too special about it. However, these men were wearing furs, so I could see his point in comparison.

Before I could answer, Arne returned to me with a pair of pants. Gunnar handed me thick woolen socks and a pair of lace-up boots. "If you pull the laces tight enough, I think you can make these work for now while yours dry."

I thanked them both and looked around for a place to change.

"We'll set up some poles for tents here in a minute. You can change inside," Gunnar said, reading my mind. I nodded in relief and sat down on the edge of the sled to wait.

The men chatted as they worked, joking back and forth in a friendly, familiar way. Domari didn't say much but did rise to the bait a few times to put Magnus in his place. He kept calling him '*Knut*' and said it in a tone that I knew was a put-down, but the meaning was lost on me.

After several small tents were set up, Björn, seemingly the group's father figure, came to lean on a tree near me.

"Are you feeling any better?" he asked. My smile was genuine, pleased he cared enough to check in on me again. I had hit the jackpot with these men finding me, even if they were strange European men I was hitchhiking with, as my mom foretold.

"A little," I shivered. "I think I'll be better once I change clothes."

He nodded, nothing else to say but lingering anyway to keep me company. I liked that.

Together, we watched the younger men set up the last tents and arrange a firepit in the center. After a few beats of silence, I turned to him and asked, "What does *Knut* mean?"

Björn chuckled to himself, a smile spreading across his face before answering.

"*Knut*. Knot. I guess, really, the youngest of the family, tying their family off at the end. Domari grew up with them after his parents passed, and Magnus was still a child when Domari left us a decade ago. He returned to find Magnus was even bigger than him, a shock to see for certain. However, neither he nor Domari is quite as big as Njal was, Domari's father. He was a giant of a man." His voice turned solemn, and I realized that Njal must have been a close friend of Björn's once upon a time. "It's good for Magnus. The boy has confidence in spades, and nobody puts him in his place quite like Domari," he ended with an approving nod.

That was much information to take in and somewhat changed how I watched their interactions. My gaze drifted over the men. They were all easy with each other, but now that I was looking for it, I could see the distance Domari put between himself and the others. I supposed that made sense if he'd been gone for ten years and only recently returned.

"Where did Domari go for ten years?"

"Now, that's not my story to tell," Björn answered, shaking his head. After a moment, he turned, thoughtful, before stepping away from the tree. "You should ask him sometime. Maybe you'll be good for him, another outsider. He could use that."

A guttural laugh left me at his words. "Oh, I highly doubt that. He has made it abundantly clear that he is not thrilled Gunnar made him bring me along."

Björn glanced over his shoulder at the man in question, pausing to watch him as Domari pulled out a whetstone and his blades from their holsters at his side, sharpening them with quick movements.

"Domari has lived his life in isolation, even before he

left us. He maintains his life by holding strict control. Finding a woman in a forest and bringing her home is not what I'd call *controlled* and, most certainly, unplanned."

None of that made much sense to me, but I turned to look at Domari again. His movements were calculated, exact, and focused.

"We should be at our village a little after midday tomorrow, and then my wife can take a look at you," Björn went on, and I slowly shifted my gaze back to him. "She's a healer. Yrsa loves to look after the lost ones, my Mama Bear." He smiled at the thought of her.

My heart warmed at the way these men talked of their women. It was clear that both Björn and Gunnar were highly devoted to their wives, and some of my stress over this situation seemed a little less heavy because of it.

Home, a voice deep inside me seemed to say.

"Can I ride with you instead tomorrow?" I decided to ask, hopefully sparing myself the awkwardness of every interaction with Domari. Björn laughed outright at that, which took me by surprise.

"I wouldn't mind. But if my wife caught wind that I'd let another woman ride my horse, with or without me on it, she'd have me strung up in the village square for adultery." His smile was entirely too large to be casually discussing a hanging. "The same can be said for all of our women. They're as ruthless as the worst of us." He patted my shoulder and walked back to the other men.

Gunnar motioned me towards a small tent, more of a lean-to actually, and I rose to limp towards him. Magnus came to my aid, but I waved him off as I continued forward, finding my balance again.

I thanked Gunnar as I went inside, more than ready to shed my wet clothes. I stripped out of my pants, socks, and boots and sighed as I pulled on the dry woolen items. My legs weren't warm yet, but it was a significant improvement already from my riding leggings and cold leather boots. I came back out of the tent and laid my clothes next to the fire Magnus was tending. Hopefully, they'd dry by morning, and I could wear them again.

Arne silently handed me a strip of dried meat and a piece of hard bread as I smiled in return. He blushed, and the men all laughed at his reaction. My smile dropped as I glared over at the men, silently accusing them of being rude to the kind boy. Several smiles greeted me — Magnus's eyebrows lifted in a jovial expression — but the men kept their mouths shut.

Domari shoved a large, rough mug into my hands made of a natural texture I couldn't make out in the dim firelight. What I did know, though, was that it was *warm*. Steam rose off the top, and I cupped my hands around it, inhaling the sugary scent as the heat seemed to settle in my chest. After a while, I took a tentative sip and tasted sweet, hot alcohol. A buzz shot straight to my head that was far from welcome after the fog I'd been working so hard to clear all day, so I settled for holding onto the warm cup instead.

"You can sleep in my tent tonight," Gunnar said later after we'd all eaten. "Alone. I'll take the first watch, and then we'll trade-off."

No one uttered a word, but I noticed the older Björn nod in approval at the command.

I thanked them and went to lay down on the furs in the tent. Exhaustion swept me under its spell before I had even taken the time to notice the sky darken further, stars shimmering above with the beginnings of green and purple wisps.

12

Shivers racked my body the following day as pain and soreness took a back burner to cold. My mind circled through everything I could remember, recalling more after a night's sleep.

My name is Shelbie Smith. I'm from Denver, and I'm 31. I was on a trip in Sweden, hiking and riding my way through the countryside.

My tour guide's name was Gustav, and he was rude. I'd never paid enough attention to where our destinations would be to know how to point someone in the right direction for me to catch up to them.

I never even got on Freya. I panicked at the thought of riding in an English saddle again. Then that stupid horse pushed me off a cliff. Now, here I am, injured, alone, and with no real idea how to get home.

My thoughts did nothing to warm me, and a sense of hopelessness settled deep in my bones. I was sick of this feeling, sick of the tears I was keeping at bay, sick of the cold, sick of the pain.

Enough was enough.

I threw off the furs I'd been covered in and rose with a new sense of determination. New plan: I'd ride with them to their village, spend a day there while I got my bearings, then figure out how to get to Stockholm. I no longer cared about how much money I'd wasted on this trip; I wanted to go home. I had nothing to prove to anyone by sticking this out, and I was done.

Lifting the flap of the tent, I stood. A gust came in off the water, sending a shiver down my spine as I zipped up my jacket and pulled up the fur hood. Voices spoke in hushed tones not too far off, and I paused to listen.

"We'll split up, and I'll go ahead with the men in the boats. I want you to bring the horses over the ravine and keep your eyes peeled for any signs that Raud is moving in our direction." That sounded like Gunnar, particularly the way he was issuing orders. "If he's going to make a move, it's going to be soon. He will want it to be before winter hits and raiding becomes too difficult."

"And you think, after all this time, he's still set on this?" Domari questioned.

I peered around the tents, craning my neck to see the men as I eavesdropped.

"I don't know," Gunnar sighed. "You know Father banished him upon threat of death should he return. Rumors are stirring that he's heard of Father's illness, and Raud is biding his time, waiting for the right opportunity. Hel," he huffed, "it wouldn't surprise me to see Raud show up at his funeral."

"He wouldn't dare disrespect the dead that way."

"Raud is far from the boy you once knew, Domari, if

rumors are to be believed," Gunnar replied. "It's not for me to say what he would or wouldn't do anymore."

Several beats of silence went by, and my mind spun on what I'd heard. That name had been mentioned several times now — Raud. Everything about the man sounded ruthless, yet Domari had once been close with the man.

"What about the girl?" Domari broke the silence, his tone returning to his cantankerous norm.

"She rides with you and Björn." Domari began to speak again, but Gunnar held up a hand to silence him. Part of me was shocked to see that worked, seeing as Domari was both larger and older. Clearly, he respected his younger cousin. "I think it's best to speak with Father about her before you arrive. Maybe he knows of other traders in the area she might have been separated from."

A soft chuckle followed. "You just don't want Signe seeing you come home with a woman."

"She's pregnant, Domari. You'll learn this someday when you finally settle down, but pregnant women should not be trifled with."

Another laugh. Domari was more at ease with Gunnar than the others, his mannerisms less constrained. "As if you'd ever trifle with her, to begin with. From what I've heard, you've been enamored since the day you met her."

"Should I be ashamed of that fact? You've met the woman. She's *terrifying*. I love it."

Listening to them speak of Gunnar's wife with such reverence warmed me to them. This Signe sounded like a badass. I was a little surprised to find I was excited to meet her.

Their conversation changed to more mundane things, and my need to pee finally forced me to step away from the tent. Domari raised a brow as I moved forward, both men glancing in my direction.

I waved. Why? I didn't know. I was awkward.

I pointed to the woods because I hadn't made it weird enough, and Gunnar nodded. Internally, I slapped my forehead at how stupid I looked as I hurried off into the trees. I flexed my arms and legs as I walked to relieve the stiffness from sleeping on the ground, trying anything to bring some warmth to my system.

When I judged I was far enough from camp, I leaned my back hard against a tree, trying to steady my knee as much as possible while I did my business.

I'm never camping again, I thought bitterly to myself. I'd now peed in the woods so many times I'd lost count, and it never got better.

How many fantasy novels had I read where the main characters went on a journey through the wilderness, and it painted such a glamorous picture? They talked about the trees, the animals, the sky, the enemies at their back, but yet, *not one* ever mentioned how miserable it is to crap in the woods.

The silver lining for today was that my knee didn't give out on me mid-squat — maybe a little stronger this morning — and I did not have to crap yet; both wins in my book.

Business done, I gripped the waistband of my borrowed pants and returned to the campsite. Domari crouched in front of the fire stoking the flames while cooking something that smelled delicious.

"Your clothes are dry," he said as I approached. This man always cut straight to the chase. No 'good morning,' no 'how are you feeling.' Nothing.

I nodded, acknowledging him but not in the mood to talk to the jerk yet.

"Your boots are different. I've traveled far, and I've never seen anything like it, even from the Far East." He reached out, handing me my thick riding leggings and leather boots. I looked down at them, confused.

The Far East? Who called it that anymore? I let the comment go, at a loss for what to say.

He handed me a bowl of something steaming, the scent rising into the morning air and mingling with the fog. My stomach rumbled at the aroma, and the heat sank into my bones. "We're about an hour's ride from our boats. Then, you'll be riding with me while the others go on."

If I hadn't been famished, I would have contemplated throwing my bowl at him for how nasty his tone was. "Don't sound so excited."

He stopped what he was doing, resting his hands across his knees. His gaze was penetrating, appraising, and cold. "I don't trust outsiders."

My head jerked back, surprised by his comment. "And I'm an outsider?"

"I don't know you. I don't know your clan. I don't know where you're from. So, yes. An outsider is exactly what you are, *hàski.*"

"Listen, *buddy.* I get it. You're the big, bad protector,

looking out for everyone here while you sharpen your knives and search the trees for enemies that aren't there," my hands flailed out at the trees around us to emphasize my point. "But I'm the one putting myself at risk here, riding off with strange men to a destination I don't even know. Sure, you say you'll help me, but God only knows if I'm about to be murdered and thrown in the river, never to be seen or heard from again."

He smiled at that. *Smiled?* Who smiled when someone mentioned they're afraid of being murdered? Psychopaths, that's who.

I chose to avoid how irresistible he looked as he grinned, eyes crinkling at the side as the humor spread across his entire face.

"I wouldn't throw you in the river."

My jaw dropped. "Is that supposed to be reassuring?"

Magnus approached and thumped me on the back, jolting me forward. "See, Domari? She doesn't think you're funny either."

Domari's grin turned to a smirk as he turned to the fire. The other men joined us, reviewing the plans for the day ahead as they ate.

I watched as I sipped a thick broth with meat boiled into it from my bowl. I didn't know what it was, and I decided not to ask. My stomach was empty from the amount that I was sick the day before, and whatever I was eating was fatty and delicious.

After everyone ate, the men quickly broke down the campsite and reloaded the horses and sleds. We were ready to ride again within the hour.

Domari helped me back onto Mjölnir, letting me ride alone for the morning. I listened as Kare quizzed his son on the different plants and paths we crossed, teaching him as they rode. This forest was made up of silver birch, which made sense. The bark was greyer than the aspens I was used to, but they were the same thin, tall style that made me think of Colorado.

Home, a voice filled with longing said inside me. I missed home, that was certain. Soon, though, I'd be headed back.

Björn, Gunnar, and the redhead whose name I couldn't remember for the life of me were deep in conversation over the coming winter and preparations to be completed when they arrived home. Domari said nothing to me, or any of the other men for that matter, walking alongside the horses in silence.

A half-hour into the ride, Magnus approached us, hand outstretched, leaning over to me.

"Give me your hand," he said, placing a handful of something reddish-orange in my palm. "Try these." He popped several berries in his mouth, chewing, before shooting me a wide, red-stained grin.

I smiled hesitantly before eating a few as well. The taste was crisp and tangy, slightly different from a raspberry, but along the same lines. "These are good!" I grinned.

He laughed, scrubbing at his teeth after seeing mine. "This is the only problem with cloudberries."

I'd never heard of a cloudberry before but continued to munch on them as he handed me more, running my fingers over my teeth every few minutes to wipe away the stains.

Magnus rode off at a quick trot, returning several times with more.

"Does he always do this?" I asked Domari, breaking the silent treatment he'd been offering me all morning.

"He's always loved sweets," he answered brusquely. "But yes, he has a nose for berries that could rival a bear."

Magnus rode near me for the rest of the morning, telling me of his new wife, Astrid. I gathered that he couldn't have been more than twenty, so he must have married young.

Soon, we descended towards the river, the dense birch trees growing further apart and letting in more sunlight. The sound of the rushing water reached me prior to glimpsing azure water sparkling in the sun. The river was wide, much more so than where I'd fallen, and on the shore were several large rowboats.

As we got closer, I blinked several times, ensuring that what I was seeing was correct. The boats anchored on the shore were longer than a rowboat and slightly wider. The bow and stern raised to a point with a circular carving at the tip. Small sails were laid flat in the boat's center, but several oars sat inside.

Flashbacks of my time in Stockholm came back to me, remembering the medieval museum, creepy wax figures, and ships. I swallowed, confused by my realization. These weren't rowboats.

They were Viking ships.

I understood that this country's history was thick with Viking culture but hadn't known it extended this far.

"Beautiful ships," I said after a minute. Domari glanced up at me, saying nothing, and nodded.

"Your clan likes to imitate Viking culture?"

His eyes met mine again, and the look he gave me was scathing. "*Imitate?* Just because we no longer raid doesn't make us any less Viking."

"I mean. Yes. Viking raids haven't happened in, like, a thousand years."

This time, Domari didn't just question me. He came to a complete halt, placing a hand on Mjölnir's neck to stop him as well.

"Where did you say you were from?"

"Well, I didn't, but Colorado. The United States."

Domari studied me for several more minutes before glancing off to the side towards the other men, then back to me. "And you fell down a hill. One that I couldn't find. With a horse that was nowhere to be seen."

"Well, when you say it like that..."

"Either you're lying, or there is more to this than we know."

Now it was my turn to be confused. What did that even mean? "Why would I lie about the few things I *do* remember?"

The more time I spent with this man, the more I regretted saying that I would travel with them. I should have looked harder for Gustav and my tour group. I should have found my bag and headed straight to the nearest airport, right back home.

Domari's eyes were lit with annoyance. "I have never

heard of any of those places before, and I've traveled farther than anyone in our clan. I spent ten years in Byzantine, aiding all of their *pointless* battles, conquering kingdoms far and wide. But, I am not an imitation of a Viking. I *am* Viking."

Wait. Did he say Byzantine?

I went over several odd interactions I'd had so far — questions on my clothes, their attire and traveling gear, even the scenery.

Something was off.

Now I was sure I was dreaming.

"This is going to sound stupid, I'm sure. But," I hesitated, "what year is it?"

"We don't track years the same here, but it was 1060 on the Julian Calendar when I left Constantinople."

I almost slid sideways off Mjölnir.

1060? Julian Calendar? *Constantinople?*

Domari peered at me, concern now mixed with questions in his expression. "Why do you ask?"

A panicked and unflattering chuckle escaped my throat. I was definitely in a coma — there was no question about it.

My mind reeled, attempting to catch any grasp on reality. This did not make sense.

I surveyed the men and immediately dismissed the notion that this could be some elaborate practical joke. First, they didn't know me, so that would be a lot of effort.

Second, this was too… much. The clothes. The hunting. The boats. All of it.

Either Freya pushed me off a hill, and I had somehow time traveled, or I, indeed, was dreaming a very elaborate dream.

I felt the saddle's leather under me, ran my hands through Mjölnir's mane, closed my eyes, and smelled the scent of pine heavy in the air. It all seemed so *real.* But how could that be?

My eyes snapped open suddenly, my head whipping in Domari's direction.

"What language do you speak?" If I hadn't sounded crazy before asking the year, I sure did now.

"We're speaking Norse," he answered hesitantly.

My eyes went wide, trying to make sense of it all. "Me too?" I asked to be sure I understood correctly.

"Yes?" The question in Domari's voice told me everything I needed to know. Yep, the crazy ship had left the harbor.

"Do you not normally speak Norse?"

I cackled. *Norse? No, I don't speak Norse. I don't even speak Swedish, as this trip had made so evident.*

"I speak English. You're sure you're not speaking English?"

"Ah. So you're from England. Were you captured?"

"No, I'm not from England. I've never even been there. I'm from the United States like I told you."

"Well, somewhere, you must have learned Norse, and now you're forgetting it. And yes," he spat, "I am sure we're not speaking English. The only time I ever spent in the country was in a war camp. I did not bother to learn the language."

As shocking as his answer was, that proclamation went right along with the little I knew about Viking culture. "Why were you in Constantinople?" I asked, halting my spinning thoughts.

"I was part of the Varangian Guard," he answered matter of factly. Too bad I had no idea what that was, so I smiled and nodded.

Silence filled the air as we stopped at the river's edge. Domari helped me off the horse and instructed me to stay close. Those instructions were laughable; I wouldn't dream of wandering off as I was far more lost now than before. Even if I hadn't time traveled, I had not the slightest clue where I was or how to get to the closest city. Plus, I had no money, no passport, no phone… I was utterly dependent on these men and their generosity, a thought that did *not* sit well with me.

The men quickly unloaded the pack horses, piling their meat and furs into the ship faster than I could comprehend. My mind wandered, trying to understand what was happening, and I must have zoned out. Before I knew it, the men were loading onto the boat, leaving Björn, Domari, and I on the shore with the horses.

"We'll see you in the morning," Gunnar said. "Safe travels through the hills, and watch for signs of Raud."

Domari nodded and turned to walk towards me as the men pulled their oars out and began to row upstream.

I don't know why it hadn't occurred to me until now, but the question popped out of my mouth before I could even think it through. "Why did you only row part of the way? Why not use horses *or* boats?"

Domari and Björn both turned in my direction at the question. Domari wore a puzzled expression as if he was still absorbing all that was my crazy, while Björn offered me a smile.

"The river is much deeper here," he answered in a kind tone. "It ebbs and flows as it approaches the sea, filling bogs and lakes along the way, but it has too many shallows to sail to our hunting grounds. We need the horses for the rockier terrain and to carry the meat to the boats. This next pass we're taking is harder for the horses to manage with their loaded packs. Over time, we came up with this plan."

"And you don't put the horses on the boats?"

"Sometimes we do, but here, no. They're too heavy, and our hunting party is too small."

Huh. Well, I guess that made sense.

We loaded the horses, and Domari climbed atop one of the other mounts, now freed up from its passenger. He clucked, and all the horses took off at a trot, following his lead.

Björn pulled up next to me, keeping me company.

"Why do you hunt so far from your village?" my next question popped out. Björn was friendly enough to answer me, so I decided not to hold back.

"Foxes," he said as if that summed it all up. Seeing the questions still in my eyes, he elaborated, "Our clan trades. It's the end of the trading season as winter is fast approaching, but we went on our last distance hunt for the season. Fox pelts are in high demand in Byzantine, even in Rome.

We are a wealthy village under Erik's wise rule, so we follow the foxes."

I nodded, intrigued by the idea of traders as the very little I knew about Vikings circled the idea of pillaging. "So, you don't go on raids?"

He laughed at my next question. "We used to, but no. We are no longer raiders. We leave that to our more savage brothers."

Interesting. I hadn't ever taken the time to learn enough about Vikings to realize they were so multi-faceted.

"Tell me about your village," I prodded again, distracting myself by asking questions I could get answers to rather than all the ones in my head left unanswered.

A warm smile lit Björn's face as he told me of the villagers I'd soon meet. We talked of a favorite goat he swore must be a descendant of Thor's own Tanngrisnir and Tanngnjóstr, pulling his chariot across the sky. He went on lovingly about his wife and all her many skills. Yrsa was a healer, I'd already learned, but she was also a fascinating woman in her husband's eyes and a fierce mother to their children, now grown.

Björn was a grandfather, which surprised me considering I didn't think he could be more than late-forties, but that was understandable if this was, indeed, Viking times.

I added quips occasionally, asking the names of his children and grandchildren, but for the most part, I let Björn talk.

Björn had always been close with Erik, their leader. Erik was Gunnar's and Magnus's father and an outstanding leader in Björn's perception. All had prospered under his reign.

I gathered from how the men allowed Gunnar to lead that he would be the next chieftain once his father passed. None of Björn's stories seemed to involve Domari, which I found odd. I knew he was Gunnar's cousin, and their village did not seem large.

Our horses navigated without much guidance as we traveled through a narrow pass, and Björn and I were closer to Domari. I took the opportunity to include him in the conversation.

"So, what's your story then, Domari?"

He glanced over at Björn, then huffed. No answer.

"No storytime for you?"

The only sound answering me was the clopping of the horses' hooves.

"Come on, let's hear it."

Domari sighed loudly. "Not much to tell," he finally said, realizing I probably wouldn't shut up. He was right. Just ask Sabrina.

"I grew up there. I was raised by Erik and his wife Frida, my aunt and uncle. I left ten years ago for Constantinople and returned home this summer."

Fighting against my need to fill the air with chatter, I nodded, accepting that that was all he wanted to share.

"We need to camp soon before we lose daylight. Winter is approaching fast," Domari announced. Björn bobbed his head, moving to the side to herd the horses tighter behind Domari.

"The last pass is the most dangerous on the river's edge.

We'll camp now and finish the ride in the morning," Domari explained, much more willing to discuss tasks and horses than his personal history.

I sat quietly, not having anything to add, and followed their lead.

13

The night passed uneventfully, other than my back screaming from multiple days of sleeping on the ground. As the sun was peeking through the trees, someone patted on my tent. I begrudgingly peeled the warm furs off me.

My breath fogged the air as I stepped outside, arching my back in a stretch. I'd slept in my clothes, trying to hold in any warmth, but I was still cold in the morning chill. Gratitude swept through me as Domari handed me a warm bowl and a piece of bread. The steam from the bowl warmed my face as I cradled it in both hands, savoring the heat. I sipped at it as I dipped the bread in the broth, letting it soak for a minute to soften.

Björn was already kicking dirt over the smoking fire and preparing to move on. The men loaded the horses, and I finished my broth, handing over my bowl with a nod of appreciation. Shortly after, I nudged Mjölnir to follow as Domari led the way.

Trees alight with fall colors were everywhere, both on this side of the river and across. Most of the leaves had fallen to the ground, but the peak of orange and red mixed with evergreens painted a beautiful landscape.

Shortly into our ride, the path began to transform. The trees grew sparser, and the dirt below Mjolniur's feet turned to rock as the trail steadily rose. However, these horses were made for this terrain. They navigated the rocky slopes effortlessly, although closer to the cliff's edge than I cared for, carrying us over a large ravine. The river rushed far below us as my heart beat wildly in my chest.

Mjölnir swayed as he walked, but his steps were sure. I did my best to focus on Domari's back in front of me, knowing Björn was also following close behind. I was as safe as I could be, considering the circumstances.

Soon, the path leveled out, riding along a plateau for a short way. Far in the distance, I could see white-tipped mountains rising regally into the clouds. Thick forests shot up denser than I'd ever seen. It was fall, and while the greens had faded to browns, it was easy to imagine how stunning this view would be in summer.

Home, that same voice said again in me, and I understood. It was easy to imagine why these people would make this their home. Ahead I spied the beginnings of farmland, clearings set in the trees that I assumed were pastures.

"Are we getting close?" I wondered aloud to Björn, who bobbed his head in response.

"My homestead is the first we'll pass," he said as the horses descended into the valley. "The women will be out working the fields by now. Maybe we'll meet Yrsa on our way into town." His eyes crinkled in delight as he said his wife's name.

It was interesting to hear these men talk about their women. The very little that I knew of Vikings had painted a portrait of a ruthless, greedy society full of pillagers and heathens. But between their passing conversations and what I remembered of the exhibits in the medieval museum in Stockholm, I was starting to see how very wrong I was. All cultures had extremes, and I was sure that there were plenty of ruthless, greedy Vikings out there too. But it wasn't these men before me. These men were the furthest I could imagine from that.

We rode on in silence while I continued to admire the stunning vista — the low point in the river made for the perfect farmland. The grass, touched with the beginnings of winter, stretched as far as the eye could see, right into the nearby forests surrounding them everywhere. Timber would be easy to come by for the many buildings that dotted the landscape.

Long, sleek wooden buildings grew closer, smoke curling into the sky from the centers. My jaw hung loose as we neared the village, and I took in the size of the buildings. These were long, narrow structures with poles along the perimeter, holding up a roof that resembled an upturned boat. As we rode down to Björn's home, I stared at the building.

Björn leaped off his horse as we drew closer, excitement evident in his movements. He brought his hands to his mouth and let out a loud whistle. The front door, partially ajar, flew open as three children ran out. Two women followed, one younger and one older, in long, woolen dresses cinched with wide belts at the waist. A wide grin overtook Björn's face as he walked to the older woman, engulfing her in a bear hug that sent the children into giggles. He knelt, scooping up the small children in one move, and had all three draped across his arms and shoulders as they squealed in delight. It was impossible not to feel the warmth spread through my chest at the sight of a loving family, delighted to have their patriarch home.

Domari dismounted and untied two horses, leading Björn's mount and the other two into a nearby pasture. He removed their tack with quick efficiency, tossing it over a thick wooden fence.

Yrsa, the older of the two women, had captivating auburn hair threaded with strands of grey. Soft wrinkles around her eyes and mouth matched the warm smile she aimed in my direction. "You must be Shelbie," she patted my leg gently.

I nodded politely with a grin. "Pleased to meet you."

"Gunnar stopped yesterday and told me of your many injuries," she continued. I nodded, remembering the men had mentioned she was the town healer. "Why don't you come inside, and I'll take a look at you before you ride into the village?"

I thanked her, dismounted on shaky legs, and stretched my muscles before following her into the house.

My eyes were immediately drawn up, the high ceilings astonishing to me. A hearth sat straight ahead, alight. Something was cooking over the fire, but I could tell from its placement in the exact center of the home that this was for both warming and cooking. Heat radiated from the hearth as we walked by it, but the herbal, clean smell intrigued me most.

"Come," Yrsa said as I paused near the fire. She led me to the side and back to a platform built into the walls covered with furs and woolen blankets. "Why don't you have a seat and tell me what happened?" she asked in a kind tone.

I turned to sit and was surprised by how soft it was under me. By no means would I call it a mattress, but it was lovely compared to a saddle or the hard ground.

Yrsa's soft but strong hands came up to me, pulling my legs to the side as she helped me spin. She was gentle in everything she did and warmth radiated from her just as it had from the hearth.

"I'm sure Gunnar already told you, but I hit my head and blacked out," I started. "I'm not entirely positive of the details around my fall; my memory is a little spotty."

Yrsa nodded, listening intently as I did my best to skip the part where I thought I might have time-traveled or imagined this entire thing. No need to sound even crazier than I already was. She asked simple questions, which I appreciated as we chatted. This woman was a mother to the fullest extent. I couldn't help but like her already as she looked after me as if I was her own.

"My knee is the sorest here, inside, and I think something's not quite right with my ribs."

"Let's take a look," she said clinically. "Can I ask you to lift your shirt? The men are outside and won't dare intrude."

I glanced towards the door, further down the building than I'd realized, and nodded as she helped me remove my jacket. Yrsa ran her hands over the smooth fabric, brow furrowed as she felt along the zipper underneath the toggles, but asked nothing. Next, she helped me lift my shirt to reveal an atrocious black and blue bruise covering my right side. Yrsa bent low to inspect it, poking lightly but never with the intent to hurt. I gasped at one point, and she glanced up at me.

"You've broken a rib," she straightened. "I can't believe you've been able to ride for days like this. We need to bind it to give you more support and ease the pressure. Why don't I get you something to change into, and you take off your clothes?" She paused as if deciding what to say next. "Interesting choices, your clothes. You're not from here."

My head came up at her words. It wasn't a question, and I tilted my chin, staring into her eyes before I answered.

"No, I'm not."

Yrsa patted my leg affectionately again. She rose, no further questions asked, as she padded to the other side of the home.

I came to my feet and glanced around, aware that this home was one large room. Privacy was hard to come by. Seeing no one else, I stripped out of my pants and shirt, dirty from our ride, and folded them neatly next to me.

Yrsa returned shortly, a thick brown woolen dress similar to hers in one hand and a wide woven cloth in another. She took in my sports bra with a questioning eye but, again, said nothing as she placed the fabric on the bed.

"Let's wash you first," she said. I reached for the dress and watched her back as she turned, walking away again towards the rear of the house. A large basin sat there, and she reached in, dipping a bucket and a cloth into it before returning to my side.

I smiled gratefully at her. With quick efficiency, I washed my torso with the wet cloth. When I was done, she took it from me and motioned to stand. Yrsa wound the binding tightly around me, tying it off at the end once it was wrapped securely. The pressure plaguing me for days reduced almost instantly with the added support, and I breathed a sigh of relief.

"Keep this tightly wrapped, and I'll recheck it in a few days," she said. "Now, lift your arms, and I'll help you get the dress on." I did as I was told, letting the fabric settle over me. "We'll skip the belt for now to ease your pain. Let me see your knee now."

I sat back down and hiked up the dress, allowing her to prod around my knee with the same quick efficiency she'd used on my ribs. It was swollen and puffy but not as bruised as my torso.

"You've twisted it, but it will heal. How is your pain? I have some tonics I can make to ease the swelling if you'd like."

I'd kill for some Advil right now but nodded in appreciation at the offer. Whatever she had, I'd take it.

"And last, your head. May I take down your hair?"

My curls were as wild as they'd ever been. Blood mixed with dirt, matting parts down while the rest frizzed to its maximum potential. I pulled on the ponytail holder, letting it hang loose, and turned on the bench. She stood behind me, parting my hair to inspect my wound.

"I'll clean it up some," she said, reaching behind her to grab something that looked like soap. "Lie back with your head hanging off the edge, and I'll get you fixed up."

I did as I was told and relaxed onto the soft furs and blankets, letting this woman take charge. My hair hung down, but not enough to touch the dirt-packed floor. I closed my eyes as she began to massage my head, searching for wounds as she cleaned. She hummed a tune, soft and tranquil, relaxing me even more. I heard her rise from behind me, but before I could turn my head to see, her hand brushed gently on my shoulder.

Warm water rinsed over my head, and she massaged some more, humming resumed. This was the most content I'd been in a week. I must have dozed off as she gently shook my shoulder sometime later, my hair now washed and combed, free of debris and dirt.

"I'm so sorry," I said, appalled that I'd slept through my exam. She smiled politely and patted my shoulder again, ever affectionate.

"You needed it. I'm glad I could help. Leave your hair free while your head heals a little more. I patched you up, but it wouldn't hurt to take the pressure off of your healing scalp."

I thanked her again as she helped me from the pallet, hugging the small woman earnestly. I hadn't even made it to the village, and I already loved these people.

❄

Yrsa walked me outside to find the men. Domari must have gone out to the fields to help on the farm as he was nowhere near the home.

She bent to speak to one of the children playing nearby and whispered of promised treats if he ran to fetch Domari and Björn. The boy ran off at full speed, racing through the pasture with a delighted grin.

"I imagine Domari will take you to Gunnar's home next," she said, turning to me. "You'll stay there with them."

I pouted internally, sad that she wasn't offering to let me stay with them, but sensed some underlying politics I didn't understand. I didn't want to leave Yrsa and Björn's loving home. His wife had won me over as quickly as he had on our ride.

The two men approached us a few minutes later, and Domari walked straight for the horses, ready to move on. Björn eyed Domari but said nothing before approaching me.

"What did I tell you about my woman?" he said with a broad grin as he pulled his petite wife into his side. She smiled as she patted his chest, looking lovingly into his face. "Did she get you fixed up?"

"Your wife is magnificent," I replied genuinely. "I feel better already." And I was startled to find it was the truth.

"I'll make that tonic for you and have one of the boys run it over to you later," she said, helping me to Mjölnir's side. "Take it easy until then with that knee."

"Yes, ma'am," I said with an affectionate tone. "I promise."

Yrsa shot Domari a look that was as stern as every look she'd given me was kind, and he sighed as he approached me. His hands came around my waist as I placed my good leg into the stirrup, and he lifted me up and over the horse's back. Waiting the shortest amount of time possible to assure I wouldn't tumble back out of the saddle, he turned to his horse, threw his leg over, and nudged the band of horses into a walk.

"Thank you again," I said over my shoulder as Mjölnir followed the horses in front of him. "Both of you."

The couple waved at me as Yrsa leaned up closer to Björn's face, and he leaned down to let her whisper into his ear. Whatever she said shocked him as I watched his head rear back, glancing down at his wife, then at me. His brow furrowed for a moment before Yrsa pulled on his arm, and he turned to follow her to the farm.

Yrsa was a wise woman; I was confident she knew that something was off about me, but there wasn't much I could do about it now.

Domari said not two words to me as we rode towards the center of the village. We made one more stop, and Domari unloaded two more horses at another house; Thorsten's, I realized, seeing his flaming red hair in the field.

Ahead stood two large longhouses, closer together than the others had been, in what appeared to be the center of the village. A clearing was in front of them, and in the distance was a raised platform. Domari passed through the clearing and rode straight for the house on the right while the remaining horses and I followed. He stopped, dismounting and untying his horse plus three more, before walking them into a nearby pasture between the two houses.

He hadn't said anything to me, so I sat astride Mjölnir, still pony-tied to two more pack horses, and waited for him to return. While I waited, I turned in the saddle, looking around. The building to the left was newer, the wood brighter and taking on less of the aged grey tone most of the structures had. The one on the right, though, was massive. Three times as wide as Björn's, I was willing to bet that this was the main structure of the town.

Following my line of sight, Domari pointed. "That's Erik's," to the right, "and Gunnar's," to the left.

"You grew up here with Erik?" I said, remembering the few details he'd mentioned before. He nodded and helped me down off Mjölnir's back.

"I did, yes, but I no longer live there," he replied as my feet hit the ground. I nodded to show I was good before he let go of my waist. "I have been staying in Gunnar's house since I returned."

Domari gathered Mjölnir's reins and the two remaining horses before walking towards Gunnar's home, aiming for the pastures I could barely see along the side of the building. Standing awkwardly behind, I assumed I was supposed to follow.

I paused as I peered inside the house for a moment, right as a heavily pregnant woman chased two small children out the door. They squealed as they ran outside. She stopped, hand resting on her back as her gaze drifted from her children to me.

"Come in," she waved me forward. Domari had paused at the corner of the house, and my eyes drifted to his familiar face, even if he was rude. He nodded, and someone must have taken the horses from him. They exchanged a few words before Domari turned, walking back towards me.

He bowed slightly to the woman before stepping into the building. I followed close behind.

"This is Signe, Gunnar's wife," Domari said after a moment. "This is her home."

I nodded, looking around the newer space. This building was immaculate, or as much as it could be considering the dirt-packed floors.

"You'll be staying with us." It was not a question but a command. Power oozed off of this woman in waves, and she made me want to hop in line to do as she said. Even though I was nearly a head taller than her, this woman was intimidating.

I looked down at her face, beautiful alabaster skin sprinkled generously with freckles, giving her a youthful appearance. Her deep green eyes seemed unreal, the color of the forest growing everywhere around their lands. They contrasted beautifully with her pale strawberry blonde hair braided back from her face.

This was a woman who *glowed* when pregnant. I'd never understood that phrase until right then, noticing the light that shone from the inside. It wasn't physical, but more a feeling.

She was in charge. And she knew it.

"Thank you for your hospitality," I said, realizing I'd been staring for a beat too long.

"Of course. What else could be expected of the chieftain's family than welcoming strangers into our home?"

I didn't sense sarcasm but was confused at the statement as I glanced down at my hands.

"Since Domari took our last bed, you'll have to share with him or fight it out between you," she said, and my eyes snapped up at this new information.

"Your kindness does not go unnoticed," Domari said, shooting a glare at me before I could say anything.

Signe chuckled, and it settled into a smile, the first she'd shown us, with a mischievous look on her face.

"He can show you the way," she went on, "then come find me, and I'll show you around. You can help me prepare dinner. Domari, Gunnar is already working on the outbuilding. Return the remaining horses to Kare's and then go help him."

Domari nodded, allowing this younger, heavily pregnant woman to boss him around more quickly than Gunnar. I eyed the two, glancing back and forth, before following Domari.

He walked down the left side of the building towards the rear, a little away from the fire but still close enough to keep warm at night.

"I think I missed something back there," I whispered after we were out of earshot from the imposing hostess. "She expects us to sleep *together*?"

He looked over his shoulder at me and shrugged, saying nothing.

"You're kidding me, right? I have so many issues with this."

"And I'm sure you'll tell me all of them." His tone was full of annoyance, probably for his cousin's wife and me.

I'd had it with this man.

"Listen, jerk. I'm all in on a one-bed trope, sure. Hand me a dark-haired, morally grey man and a small inn any day of the week. Only one remaining room the two main characters have to share? I'll eat that shit up. I don't care that its cliche; I love it. But this, in real life," I gestured back and forth between him and me, "is *not* happening."

At my words, he walked towards me. Our height difference was suddenly evident as I looked up into his face.

"I don't know where you're from, but I guess they don't teach manners the same in *Colorado* as they do here," he growled.

Oh, he was mad now. His dark brown eyes shone bright with anger. Why did I think this was suddenly kind of hot?

"To refuse Signe, to ask to stay elsewhere when you've been offered lodging in the *future chieftain's* own house is a grave misstep you don't want to make. Feuds have been started over less."

I said nothing, my eyes searching his furious gaze, trying to understand the culture I'd fallen into.

"Store your things here, and we'll discuss later," he said and turned to his platform. Conversation over.

I stared at his back for a moment more, flexed with tension and twice as wide as mine. He was unloading his gear, removing more knives than I knew he'd been carrying, and placing them gently on the bed in a row.

My eyes strayed to the bed, plush with soft-looking furs and mats, topped with woven blankets. I hadn't slept on a bed in days.

Nope.

No.

I wouldn't even let myself think it.

I dropped the small bag I'd been carrying with me since my fall, as well as my jacket and pants I'd replaced with the dress from Yrsa, on the bed.

"I'll just sleep on the floor," I said resolutely — my least favorite trope.

He glanced over his shoulder at me for a moment before turning around. "Suit yourself."

Before saying anything else, I stopped myself and turned on my heel. I winced at the pain in my knee and returned to Signe at the hearth.

Her eyes were focused on me, a sly grin on her face as she watched me approach. I steeled my expression, remembering the manners Domari had mentioned. This woman was one to be respected. I had no hope of ever getting home without them if this was real, assuming I didn't wake up soon having imagined the entire thing.

I failed to mention to anyone how awful I was at cooking, but now hardly seemed the time. I quietly followed Signe's instructions, focusing intently on my tasks as we prepared smoked beef and vegetables for dinner. She loaded it onto trays and turned to take it outside.

I reached across and took the heavy tray from her. "Let me," I said, my line of sight drifting down to her swollen belly. "You're carrying enough around already."

"Thank you," she said, kindness in her tone. "After the twins, I lost a baby. The men around here took it harder than I did, which is saying something."

I turned to her with a sad smile, unsure what to say. "I'm sorry for your loss."

"It happens often, but that doesn't make it easier. Gunnar was elated when we found out about this one. He's sure it's a boy. Between you and me, though, I wouldn't mind another girl." She smirked at her admission, a signature expression for her, I was coming to realize. "We got lucky with the twins — one of each. Much to his dismay, though, his little Revna is the fiercest of the two, not Ulf. He's terrified of his sister."

We both chuckled at the thought of the little girl dominating her brother. Honestly, that wasn't shocking to me after spending the day watching their mother.

Everything Signe did was fierce; I didn't know another way to describe it. Even the bread she kneaded wouldn't dare disobey her and her forceful hands. Gunnar's words from days before rang true. She was terrifying, and I loved it.

Dinner passed easily, the men draining horns of ale as quickly as they could pour them. I smiled, listening to the conversation and chipping in where I could. Revna climbed into Domari's lap, leaning on his chest as the sunlight dwindled, and he tucked her under his chin.

I guessed the twins were about four and endlessly entertaining. Revna yawned sleepily as the moon peeked out from behind the clouds. Domari rose easily, carrying her to the door. Signe swatted at Ulf, who argued with his mother for only a moment before he silently followed them.

I watched their retreating backs, confused at the shocking swing of this man's personality. The moon lit his profile as he leaned down and kissed Revna on the head, waiting for Ulf to enter the house.

"He loves those children," Signe said, drawing my attention. "He'll be a good father someday."

And there was that smirk. Good lord, this woman might be worse than Sabrina, setting me up like this.

"Leave them be," Gunnar chipped in, patting his wife's arm. "How is my baby today?"

"We'd be a lot better if this one would stop kicking me in the ribs," she said, annoyed at her unborn child as she rubbed her swollen belly. I smiled genuinely as the conversation shifted. The two continued to talk as Gunnar's hands rested lovingly on his wife, touching her any way he could. A thumb across her hand, a hand resting on her leg, a kiss on her shoulder. He adored her.

I turned my head to give them a moment of privacy and, instead, shifted my gaze to the moon overhead. Domari returned several minutes later, and Signe rose.

"It's time to put this baby to bed now, too," she said, eyeing Gunnar. "Care to join me?"

He rose quickly, eager to follow his wife inside, leaving Domari and me sitting in silence. Domari was chuckling as he watched them retreat before turning to me.

"I wouldn't go in there right now if I were you," he said after a beat.

My eyes grew large at his insinuation, suddenly realizing the lack of walls in these homes. Well, that was awkward.

"Be glad you're not staying at Erik's," he went on. So chatty, all of a sudden. "I stayed there for two nights before I had to leave. Magnus and his wife, Astrid, are insatiable. My ears can never unhear that."

I laughed at that, cringing internally at the thought of having to listen to others do the nasty every night.

"You live here now?" I tried to change the subject as the sound of soft moans drifted into the air from the house behind us. My cheeks heated as I did my best not to listen, but it was distracting.

Domari looked towards the house briefly before shaking his head and taking a sip of his ale. "Yes, for now. With Signe pregnant and after losing her last baby, any help they can get is better than nothing."

That was kind of him. I saw how he was with those children, so I took it to mean more than helping around the farm.

"Gunnar will be chieftain soon," he cleared up something for me that everyone had been beating around the bush. "Erik is not well, and much responsibility has already fallen to Gunnar. I'm happy to be an extra hand."

I was starting to see that Domari's relationship with Gunnar was more than cousins, closer to brothers. They'd grown up together from the little I'd gathered, so I supposed that wasn't surprising.

Domari reclined on his arms, gazing up at the night sky. Some time had passed in silence, no longer awkward or loaded, and the sounds of the activities in the house faded.

I yawned, attempting to cover it but failing, and he turned at the sound.

"You ready for bed?" he said with a smirk as he raised his brow. I rolled my eyes at the insinuation, especially after hearing what just went on inside.

He chuckled as he rose to his feet and aimed for the door. I stared up at the stars for a few moments more, searching for answers to so many questions. The glittering orbs held nothing for me, though. I sighed and followed him inside.

I tiptoed past two platforms built into the walls, one containing a now sleeping Signe with Gunnar's arm thrown over her protectively, the other holding the two small children sprawled across the bed.

In front of me, Domari was laying soft furs and blankets on the floor next to the bed. I smiled, glad to see he was being gentlemanly at last.

He lifted his arms, removing his shirt to reveal sculpted muscles I couldn't help but drool over. This man was breathtaking. In addition to the ten dark bands along his forearms and the knot tattooed on the side of his neck, a large, black shield was painted across his right hip, disappearing behind him. Before I could turn my head, he caught me staring and smiled.

His eyes were locked on mine as he walked towards the pallet on the floor. Then, he paused before taking one giant stride and stepped right over it, throwing himself down on the bed instead.

I stood there, mouth agape, glancing back and forth

between him on the bed and the pallet on the floor. *So much for manners,* I thought to myself.

I huffed, removing my boots and settling down onto the pallet on the floor to the sound of Domari's quiet laughter.

No matter how I tossed and turned, nothing eased my aching back, sick of sleeping on hard ground. Trying my best to hide the turn of my head, I glanced over to see Domari relaxed, ankles crossed with an arm thrown behind his head. His eyes were closed, but I had a feeling he was not yet asleep.

Several more minutes ticked by, my body screaming at this decision before I finally stood.

"Move over," I said gruffly, shoving a finger into his side. My hand practically bounced off his warm skin, hard muscle covering all of him.

His eyes were still closed, but he smiled. Brown eyes shone up at me in the low light of the hearth as he took in the sight of me standing at the side of his bed, waiting. I crossed my arms impatiently, and he chuckled as he moved towards the wall.

"As you wish."

14

I nuzzled under the blankets, warm and soft. The weight settled heavily over me, a feeling I could get used to. It was lovely, the pressure across my middle holding me down and keeping the heat in. I wiggled a little, stretching my legs after the best night's sleep I'd had all week, and bumped my leg into something hard.

"Quit moving," a deep voice said close to my ear, and my eyes flew open at the sound. I turned my head slowly, catching a glimpse of dark, mussed hair.

I slept with Domari.

And it wasn't a weighted blanket on me; it was his arm thrown over me.

My eyes expanded, all the words I was attempting to keep on lockdown in my head causing them to bulge, surely. I laid as still as my body would allow, forcing every muscle to obey me in my quest not to touch Domari.

"A little too late to pull away from me now." I glanced towards him to find a sleepy smile on his face, but his eyes were still closed. "You were on top of me most of the night. And you talk, even in your sleep."

I thought my eyes couldn't bulge anymore, but I was wrong.

Oh, God. What had I said?

I was too old to be embarrassed to sleep next to a man, especially since nothing had even happened. We'd *slept.* That was it.

Pull it together, Shelbie. He's hot, sure, but he's a real asshole.

Silently lecturing myself, I slowly gathered the strength to throw my legs over the side of the bed and place my socked feet down on the packed dirt floor below me.

"There's an outhouse over that way," Domari pointed straight across, eyes still closed, reading my thoughts.

I rubbed my hands over my face, trying to clear all my racing thoughts, and stood. Unable to help it, I glanced back behind me.

Domari had thrown the blankets off himself in the night, our shared body heat providing plenty of warmth. His chest was laid out in front of me in the dim glow of the hearth, and every glorious inch was carved muscle. Scars laced over his chest, the largest of which covered his left shoulder completely, mixed in with his dark tattoos. *A sign of a true warrior,* I thought. Dark lashes perched on his perfect face. But, if I was being honest with myself, what *wasn't* perfect about this man?

His personality, maybe.

"Are you done staring yet?" he asked, his voice still rough from sleep.

I jumped to attention, spinning too fast on my sore

knee, and headed in the direction Domari had pointed for the outhouse.

By the time the sun had risen, the entire house was awake and moving. Signe had honey-glazed bread prepared on the table next to the hearth along with cheese and sausage, easy to grab on the way out the door. Domari and Gunnar left shortly after, ready to work on the farm.

I washed my face and body quickly in the water bucket Signe had pointed out to me, missing my shower desperately. My ribs were still tender; it was easier to wear the loose-fitting dress Yrsa had given me than my outfit with a waistband hitting at the wrong place on my torso. Thankful that Yrsa had washed my hair for me the day before, I tucked my wild curls behind my ears and approached Signe at the hearth.

She smiled as I walked closer, hardly looking up from her task. I watched her silently, in awe of the number of things this woman could do at once. She stirred something in a large cauldron over the fire, kneaded several loaves of bread, and wrangled children with ease.

Revna and Ulf played noisily on the floor near her with small, carved wooden animals, not too different than the ones I had bought in Sundsvall for Sabrina's girls. The thought of them had me rubbing my chest. I desperately missed my own family, be it blood or chosen, as I watched this home filled with love.

"How did you sleep?" Signe asked, stirring the pot both literally and figuratively.

"Fine, thanks," I replied, avoiding the subject.

She smirked but said nothing, continuing her tasks. "In a moment, I'll put these loaves to rise, and we'll head out to the farm. We have a lot to do before tomorrow."

At my confused expression, she rolled her eyes. "Did the men tell you nothing?"

"Honestly, no. Not really. Other than Björn, he was wonderful to me."

"That's not surprising. That man is a papa if I ever did meet one. We are so grateful to have him and Yrsa in our village. Oh! That reminds me," she stopped to wipe her hands on her apron, "Yrsa's grandson stopped by early this morning with a tonic for you." She leaned over and handed me a small sack of dried herbs. "Let me get you some water, and we'll heat it. Yrsa has the best tonics. I wouldn't have made it through these pregnancies without her."

My heart swelled in gratitude, thankful for these women taking such good care of me.

Signe shuffled off and returned a few moments later, placing a smaller pot over the fire. She held her hand in a grabbing motion, and I handed her the herbs. Dumping them in, she stirred it several times as the smell of something sweet and tangy wafted into the air. Signe leaned down over the pot and inhaled deeply with her eyes closed as a smile spread across her face.

"I swear the woman has magic even if she won't admit it," she said after a moment.

Is magic real here? I honestly didn't know enough about

Viking history to know if they believed in magic, but the exhibit of the three women hunched over runes at the medieval museum surfaced in my mind, mixed with her words now. *Maybe.*

"So, what is happening tomorrow?" I asked, circling back to our original subject.

She pointed her spoon at me in a gesture I took as appreciation for the reminder before stirring it again. "Winter Nights starts tomorrow. Our whole village will gather at Erik's for a feast in the evening, and the day after, there will be games aplenty. The men haven't talked of much else for months, boasting and betting on who will win each event this year. It's a glorified pissing contest."

I chuckled at her commentary, loving the way this woman called it like it was. She and Charlene would love each other. She handed me the tonic in a wooden cup a few moments later, and I sipped at it, pleasantly surprised at the taste. The warmth spread through my body, easing muscle aches and soreness as it went.

We worked on the farm in easy companionship, Signe careful not to ask too many questions. She must have been warned that my memory was foggy, and I appreciated it. Even now, the things I thought I knew didn't make sense.

My mind still reeled at the thought of me speaking Norse fluently when that shouldn't be possible. My brain collapsed on itself at the concept of working on a Viking farm. Time travel wasn't real, but the implications of that were also daunting.

Was I in a coma?

Was I dying?

Did my family know where I was?

I had far too many questions and not nearly enough answers. Signe sat back on her heels, stretching her back, hand on her belly. We had spent the morning weeding her garden, pulling onions and other vegetables. She squinted out over the field where she'd sent her twins off to feed the chickens and where the men were working.

"Gunnar will run these men into the ground to get that outbuilding built before the first snow," she muttered. She shook her head before scanning over the fields. I followed her gaze, seeing Domari off by himself tending to the horses.

"The man who returned to us is not the same one who left," Signe sighed. "He needs to find his way back to us again."

"What do you mean?" I asked, staring at the gruff man I'd met a few days ago. "He wasn't always this grumpy?"

At that, she laughed, turning her smile on me. "Oh, he's always been earnest," she smirked, "but his heart was the largest of our clan. You can see it in how he takes care of that mount. He loves deeply; he's just forgotten how to aim that at people."

I couldn't decide whether to pry or let it go. The moment passed as Signe instructed me where she wanted me to take the large basket of produce we'd picked.

The afternoon was spent in front of the hearth, assisting Signe in whatever she asked of me. Villagers came and went, the open door an invitation to anyone passing the town that they were welcome. I was surprised at the easy way Signe carried herself in conversation, directing both men and women with confidence fit for a leader's wife — or maybe a leader in general.

Everyone was friendly to me, albeit distant, for the most part. Kare stopped by with his daughter, Bodil, carrying a large portion of smoked meat. Signe pointed him to Erik's longhouse next door, and Kare nodded at me as he left. I smiled, happy to see so many warm faces in this town.

As the sun began to set, the men returned inside. Domari carried Revna on his shoulders as she pulled on his ears, turning him left and right. He smiled up at her as he pulled her down, letting both her and Ulf climb him like a tree. Gunnar walked straight to Signe, pulling her from her task and into a passionate kiss. I averted my eyes, offering the two a semblance of privacy as Signe broke the kiss and swatted Gunnar with a spoon.

"How was today?" Gunnar aimed the question at both Signe and me.

"Good," Signe said. "Everyone is ready for tomorrow."

He nodded, turning to me. "And you're settling in all right?"

"Yes, thank you for asking."

"Wonderful," he grinned. "We'll find you some answers and help you home in no time. I am happy to have you in my village and home until then."

My heart warmed at the sincerity in his tone. This was a good man.

"Two guests in the same season," he sighed happily. "It must be a good omen from the Gods that we should be so blessed to have my brother home at last and a new friend as well."

I glanced up at Domari at his words. His face was shut down from emotion, but he nodded at the words. *Brother*, not cousin. Gunnar's love ran deep for Domari, but could he see it?

Everyone filed out as Signe shooed us from the house and towards the fire pit again. I carried a tray of smoked fish and herb-seasoned bread that smelled delicious. We passed around the platters, each taking a small serving.

Even after seeing it yesterday, I couldn't help but think the ale horns the men drank out of seemed so very stereotypical. History books had gotten this part of Viking life correct. The rest, I wasn't so sure. I hadn't seen a horned helmet yet, and these people seemed far from the ruthless barbarians of Viking legend.

I sat back, observing. Adoration showed for Signe in Gunnar's every move, from how he served her food to the easy hand resting on her leg. Domari sat farthest from me, off by himself, until the twins decided to take over his lap. Ulf was busy chattering about something I couldn't hear. He flexed his muscles, and Domari copied the motion, comparing. My eyes lingered, watching him far more at ease with these children than the other adults I'd seen him around. My sudden laugh drew everyone's attention as I noticed Revna attempting to add tiny braids into Domari's beard.

"It's a good look," I nodded at him, Revna taking on her mother's smirk. "I think you should leave it." At that, Domari smiled, and my heart made an odd pitter-patter sound I was unaccustomed to.

After the fire died down, Gunnar carried his twins

inside, followed by his wife, once again leaving Domari and me alone. I reclined on my hands, staring at the night sky, the silence stretching longer tonight than yesterday.

The sound of Domari kicking dirt over the dying fire drew my attention as he silently walked past me and into the house. I rose to follow and, this time, did not hesitate when he lifted the blankets for me to join him on the bed.

15

The next morning, I awoke with a jolt. Clanging sounds were already rising from the hearth. Domari had shifted against me again in the night, or maybe vice versa, I couldn't tell. Either way, we consistently seemed to find each other by morning, locked in an embrace that made us seem far more friendly than we were.

Domari and I both rose from the bed, and Signe shouted to join her when I was ready. I hurried through a quick morning routine, washing my face and straightening my borrowed dress, now crumpled from sleep. As I reached the hearth, Signe thrust several large trays into my hands, yelled for her children, and the four of us filed out the door to Erik's.

The doors were wide open, and fragrant, delicious smells wafted from within as we approached. Signe called out a greeting to Frida, standing at the hearth. She was an older woman, perhaps in her early fifties, with beautiful, braided greying hair and the warmest smile I'd ever seen.

The children sprinted into her embrace, and she dropped her responsibilities to stoop, chatting with them.

Signe patted her mother-in-law on the shoulder lovingly and went to one of the many tables along the room's perimeter. It made sense to me now why Erik's longhouse was so much larger, as this building was meant to accommodate the entire village. Long, wooden tables were set along the room's perimeter, pushed towards the platforms set into the walls for seating.

We went to work setting out wooden platters and bowls that were too lovely to be dinnerware, each with intricate carvings. After preparing the room for guests to join tonight, Signe steered me towards the doors.

"Let's go check the chickens and spy on the men," she said conspiratorially.

We walked towards her longhouse and around the side. A wooden fence was around a large pasture; horses, cows, goats, and sheep mingled together. Before we approached them, we could hear men at work to the tune of hammers pounding, wood sawing, and rowdy conversation.

I glanced over at the barn; a single story built as a smaller version of the house behind us. There, on the roof, was Domari. He was shirtless despite the cold air, hammering in the last of the wood panels.

"He's so handsome," Signe smirked at me again as she traced my line of sight. "If I weren't a married woman and feeling twenty moons pregnant, I'd be more than happy to share his bed."

Glancing in her direction, I rolled my eyes. She busted into laughter at that, shoving me in the shoulder. I swore the sound of her laughter could change a life. It was a high, magical sound so full of joy that I couldn't help but chuckle with her. After the last two days together, I had a girl crush on this woman. She was magnificent!

I wasn't the only one mesmerized by the sound of her laughter — it caught Gunnar's attention immediately. He turned in our direction with a smile I could only describe as goofy. No matter how long they had been married, this man was infatuated with his woman. And who could blame him?

Gunnar approached us, first kissing Signe, then leaning to kiss her swollen belly, before turning to me. "How are you feeling today?"

I thought about it for a moment, a little shocked at how much better my knee was feeling and thinking back on the tonic I'd drank several times yesterday. Maybe Yrsa *was* magic.

"Better," I said genuinely. "Your village is taking wonderful care of me, and I am so grateful."

He nodded at that, seemingly pleased to hear it, before turning and talking details of the evening with his wife.

I watched the men work for a few more minutes, taking sly glances at Domari. He glistened with sweat in the sunlight. He caught me looking, and I swore he flexed.

"Did you meet Astrid yet?" Magnus said, approaching with a wave.

Confusion set in, trying to think through all the villagers I'd met already.

"Trust me, you'd know if you'd met her," he went on. "She's more beautiful than the moon."

"And you're dumber than a goat," someone yelled. All

the men laughed, and the conversation shifted to trading insults. Even Domari had a smile on his face; I noticed the next time I snuck a glance at him. He stood a moment later, inspecting his work.

Astrid may be more beautiful than the moon, but this man was more beautiful than a *god*.

He squatted and then jumped to the ground, grabbing his shirt and walking towards me. Wiping at the sweat on his face with his discarded shirt, he stopped next to me and turned to inspect the barn.

We stood there in silence, the two of us, almost touching shoulders. I finally turned towards him, expecting him to say something.

"It's a nice-looking building, sure," he paused, "but not worthy of the drool escaping your mouth, just there." He pointed at my face, and I swatted his hand away. He chuckled, a deep rumbling sound, still watching the rest of the men work.

"You're so full of yourself," I replied after I regrouped, shocked by the shift in his personality. Sure, the joke may have been at my expense, but maybe he was starting to warm up to me. I couldn't keep the smile off my face, in any case.

"There's a lot of me to be full of," he said, glancing my way with a smirk before he turned to leave.

Did he just make a dick joke?

I stood there, virtually frozen at the imagery now running through my head, until Signe came up next to me. She took a look at my expression, then glanced in the direction of Domari's retreating back, and her grin turned sly.

"Come, girl," she said, pulling on my arm. "Let's get ready for tonight."

Signe led me into the longhouse and straight towards her bed, dragging me behind her.

"How's your head today?" she said, bending over a large trunk of clothes. She was looking for something specific as she sorted through them, discarding one after another. Finally, she held up a deep emerald gown with white threaded embroidery along the sleeves. She turned to me, holding it up, squinting as she took in my size.

"It will be too short on you, and your chest is bigger than mine. But the last time I wore it, I was newly pregnant, and my chest was heavy, so maybe..." she said, primarily to herself.

I stood there, waiting, as I didn't know what to say. I was almost a head taller than the woman, and while she wasn't petite, I was most certainly larger than her.

"Let's try it," she decided, pulling my arm closer to her again. "Here, give me that plain shift," her hand made a grabbing motion. "We can't send you to your first Winter Nights in our village in *brown.*"

She helped me out of my dress and pulled the emerald one over my head, gathering my long curls and dragging them out of the neckline. I was surprised at how low cut this gown was, as all of the other dresses I'd seen on women so far were a conservative and practical high-neck cut.

However, this dress wasn't made for practicality. It was made to be elegant.

"Gunnar brought me this from his last trading expedition," she explained. "He said he thought it would match my eyes."

He was right — it did. She had the most stunning eyes I'd ever seen.

"The green will look beautiful with your lovely curls, though," she said, happy to share her treasured item as her hand settled on my hair. "Do you think I could style your hair, or is your head still sensitive?"

I thought about it before I answered, telling her I felt much better.

"Excellent." She clapped her hands in excitement, and it was easy to share in her joy. I thought I had it as bad as Gunnar at this point; I'd do anything to make this woman smile like that.

She shoved me down forcefully onto her bed, motioning for me to turn around. Sectioning off pieces, she began to braid sections tightly along the side of my head in three rows, bringing them together in the back. Fluffing my curls along the top, she finger-combed her way through them with gentle hands and twisted them on the ends. The braids laid like a halo across my hair, holding it off my face and keeping my curls in check.

Signe's eyes twinkled with eagerness as she pulled me up towards her, spinning me so she could see her final product. My brown leather riding boots peeked out underneath; the dress was too short. She glanced down with puckered lips, clearly unhappy with the inability to change those, too, before shrugging.

"You look fit for the gates of Asgard, ready to sit among the goddesses," she said in a sigh, arms crossed as she hugged herself in delight.

I looked down, trying to see what she saw. This color of emerald was lovely, and the combination of my sports bra squishing my boobs plus the dress's tight bodice did give me ample cleavage, more so than I was typically accustomed to.

I glanced up, and Signe was still staring at me fondly. "Now it's my turn. Can I help you?"

She waved me off, grabbing a dress off the bed and quickly changing. "Not much can be done when I'm this pregnant," she said, pulling on a dress with ties along the side. I reached over, helping her tighten them to give her a more fitted style.

"You glow," I replied, not willing to let this exquisite woman dismiss her own beauty. "Besides, Gunnar looks at you as if you hung the moon."

At that, she laughed, a twinkle in her eyes. "Didn't you know, girl? I did."

16

Signe and I finished dressing as voices drifted in through the open doors. We emerged from the house to see dozens of people milling around, chatting, laughing, hugging. The air was celebratory, and it was contagious.

After watching so many men sweating outside earlier, I was surprised to see how *clean* they all looked. Hair was combed and trimmed, beards were well-groomed, and everyone smelled pleasant, which was a refreshing surprise.

Signe grabbed my arm as if for support, but it was a ploy to drag me towards Gunnar and Domari. Gunnar was deep in conversation with several men I had yet to meet, including an older man, a greying version of Gunnar himself. This must be Erik.

He was a handsome man with long, grey hair that was well-kept and trimmed to just below his collarbone. His blue eyes held a fog, and his skin had a yellow pallor that made me recall the conversations I'd overheard about Gunnar becoming chieftain soon.

Ignoring the circle of men, Signe walked us right into the center of the conversation, dropping my arm only as she reached for her husband. He stopped mid-sentence, shooting his wife a doting smile, before returning his attention to the other man.

Domari stood among the men, both included and apart, as he was situated a little way back. His eyes found me and roamed my body, taking in Signe's styling. I could feel her watching the silent exchange, that signature smirk plastered on her face.

His gaze slid from mine as Erik turned towards him, whispering something into his nephew's ear. Domari nodded silently, then retreated. He allowed Erik to pass and quietly escorted him into the house.

Several others followed in their footsteps, and Signe pulled me along. The two men approached the largest, most central table, and Erik stood at the center. Domari whistled loudly, and the boisterous room fell silent.

"Thank you for gathering here, my people," Erik said in a deep voice as more villagers entered the building to listen to his words. "We have had a long and prosperous summer, blessed by Thor himself." A round of cheering followed his words until Erik raised his hand.

"I am grateful to have so many of you gathered here tonight to celebrate with me. Let the Gods hear our thanks in Asgard." There was another round of cheers as drinking horns were raised. Chanting began, and horns of ale were passed to those who didn't already have one.

Signe pushed one into my hand with a whisper. "It's rude to refuse."

I didn't even need to turn to know her smirk was plastered on her face. This woman loved to meddle.

Erik glanced around the room, placing his hand on his chest. Even through their fog, his eyes were alight with pride, and he raised his own horn. The room erupted in cheers as everyone drank, and I followed suit.

The ale was a thick, dark substance, much stronger than the beer I was used to. I looked down into the horn, studying the drink. It wasn't exactly *bad;* I'd had way worse in college, but it would take some getting used to.

"Don't let the men see you are inspecting their ale," Signe whispered at my shoulder. "They take great pride in it. Just watch. Soon they'll all have a silent drinking competition, seeing who can act the least drunk. It never ends well." She laughed at her comment, reminiscing. I took another sip at her urging, and the warmth from the alcohol seeped into my bloodstream.

She pushed me towards the table where Gunnar was already perched to his father's right. Signe sat down, leaning heavily on her husband, as he bantered happily with the other men. I hesitated for a moment. This was the head table, and the leaders were sitting here. I didn't belong.

Before I could turn to leave, Signe's arm came up and pulled me down next to her. I sat hard, my ale sloshing in my horn as the soft furs underneath me caressed my skin.

Bread, cheeses, meat, fruits, and vegetables filled the tables to bursting now, interspersed with pitchers upon pitchers of ale. The hearth lit the house at the center of the room, as well as torches along the walls mounted in sconces. There were small, odd-looking lamps in bowls on the tables with two wicks stretched out with oil; both ends were aflame. I was glad the doors were open as, even in the evening chill, it was warm and smoky in the room.

A few other neighbors stopped to introduce themselves to me, and all here were friendly. Several rounds of toasts went around the room, calling everyone to drink repeatedly, and I did as I was told.

My insides sloshed as I watched the scene in front of me. Everyone was loud; ebullient laughter boomed from Magnus's direction as his petite wife rested under his arm, leaning into his broad chest.

Björn stood with a small boy hanging from his leg, conversing with several men I didn't recognize.

Domari leaned against a post not far from Erik's side and had a string of people waiting to talk to him. He smiled politely and responded to each one but was never the one to initiate the conversation. It didn't escape my attention that many were young, attractive females. I eyed one particularly curvaceous blonde as she leaned heavily into his side, speaking close to his ear. He smiled at whatever she said, and a hot streak shot through my body. Rather than admit I might be jealous, I took a large swig of ale and glanced away.

Gunnar and Erik were deep in a discussion that appeared more serious than the general atmosphere. Although they were only a few seats away from me, it was too difficult to understand what they were saying. I watched as they exchanged words, Gunnar much more heated than his father, but Erik brushed him off.

"What are they arguing over?" I whispered into Signe's ear next to me. She licked her fingers, sticky with dripping fat from the meat in front of her, and leaned in closer.

"Raud," she answered. "I don't know the man well, but he used to be a part of this clan." She popped some fruit in her mouth before continuing, "He's returned home from raiding season and has turned his sights on the local villages instead of farming his land to prepare for winter. They're saying he and his men murdered most of the last village and raped the women before burning it all to the ground." She paused to greet someone who had stopped at the table and then leaned back to me, "Gunnar is worried that we may be next. There have been rumors circulating that he is still angry with us, even after all these years, but mourning will do strange things to a person."

Her words rocked the fragile peace I felt in this strange world, reminding me of how ruthless the Vikings of history were. Before I could ask more, Domari settled next to me. He sipped at his ale while Signe elbowed me under the table and raised her brows with a smirk. At my expression, she burst into laughter.

Domari's eyes surveyed the room, keeping an eye on everyone, in equal parts on guard and with amusement. I peered over at him, watching, and stayed silent for once.

"I think I can hear your thoughts, damming themselves in your mind, waiting to burst free," he said, eyes still on the room.

I looked away and rolled my eyes — a typical response to him these days.

After a while, he turned towards me, but I did my best to avoid the obnoxious man. "You look lovely," he said, shocking me with the kind words. "Green suits you."

I was silent for a beat, glancing at him now, searching his face. "Thank you."

We listened to several men in rowdy conversation, trading insults as currency, each laughing harder as they escalated. Domari's eyes betrayed the joy he was feeling from this evening even though his face remained stoic, sipping his ale, watching the exchange unfold.

"Drink up," he said, glancing at me out of the corner of his eye. "Don't let anyone see you are resisting. It'll be considered an open challenge as to who can get you the drunkest."

I took a swig, realizing this was the second time I'd been warned of this. I could already feel the alcohol coursing through my veins, potent and heady.

"So far, you and Signe share that honor," I said as a belch, long and low, bubbled out of my chest. I slapped my hand over my mouth in shock, and Domari chuckled.

Sometime later, the singing began. Björn posed at the center of the room, singing a ballad of two mates, fated to be together but torn apart by a never-ending battle. He was a big man, and his voice matched, deep and full, resonating through the hall. The room was silent as they all listened raptly.

Tears sprung to my eyes, emotional in my intoxicated state, as I listened to him pour his heart into the song.

Without realizing it, I'd reached down, gripping Domari's arm for support. He glanced at my hand perched on his large tattooed forearm but didn't remove it before taking another sip of his ale.

How was he not trashed by now? I thought to myself. I'd been keeping count at one point but had lost track. Whatever the number was, I was sure he'd drunk double what I had, and I was well past tipsy.

Several men and women rose after Björn, reciting poetry and playing music. The room's mood was content and celebratory after a long and prosperous season.

Signe patted my arm, drawing my attention, and I realized I was still holding onto Domari. I let go and turned to look at her while the room spun. I forced my eyes wider, hoping they'd focus easier, as I took in her smug expression.

"Care for some fresh air?" she said, rubbing her belly. "I could use a walk."

I nodded and turned to help her up, swaying slightly on my feet. We left the hall, arm in arm, and stumbled out under the stars as she took a deep breath and stretched her back.

"Between the food and sitting in the same position, I needed to get up," she explained. I waved away her excuses, happy to keep her company. We stood there against the side of the longhouse, listening to the sounds of the party happening inside as we watched the stars glistening overhead.

"I'm sorry that I'm pushy," she said, and I laughed at her apology.

"Are you?"

She chuckled in return at my boldness brought on by too much ale. "No. Not really." There was that smirk again.

"It's fine," I nudged her with my shoulder. "I'm kind of in love with you anyway. Not in like, I want to be with you way. Well, I mean, maybe, if you're into that sort of thing, I might be down." She smirked at my drunken rambling. "But more like, I want to *be* you. You're so badass. I want to be a badass, too. We could just kick ass together, don't you think?"

"Thank you," she said, a broad smile filling her face. "And yes, men everywhere would flee at the sight of us, thinking the Valkyries had come for them."

"Yeah," I slurred, sounding as drunk as I felt. A few beats of easy silence spread between us as someone took up singing inside again.

"Gunnar was thrilled to see Domari when he came home," she turned the conversation. "He was gone for ten years, and it nearly broke Gunnar that he couldn't go after him."

I absorbed that for a moment, unsure what to say at the new information. "Why did he leave?" I finally asked.

"It's a long and complicated story," she said with a shrug. "Aren't they always?"

Our talk was interrupted then. Several men came through the doors, arms slung over each other's shoulders. I spied Magnus in the center, tears in his eyes, mooning over how much he loved his wife. The young, gorgeous girl walked a few steps behind them, smiling as she held her hand over her belly.

"I hunger for the heat of your hearth," Magnus said,

shrugging off the men holding him up as he spun towards his wife. "I thirst for the thickness of your thighs around me," he went on in a bad attempt at poetry.

Signe laughed next to me, watching it unfold.

"Aye, we get it. You like to bang her. We all would," one of the men said to him, forcing laughter out of the others, but Magnus's gaze turned furious. Stormclouds took over his face as he seemed to impossibly grow several inches, towering over the men in front of him.

However, his petite wife was not afraid as she stepped into him. She placed her hands on his chest, now bared under his untied shirt, and ran her fingers up his skin in a seductive move towards his jaw. It was enough to draw his attention down to her. The steam of only a moment before seemed to evaporate as he gazed upon her sweet face before him.

"Only you," she whispered. "Only you, *elskan min.*"

Tears again welled in the big man's eyes as he took his wife's hand and led her towards a tree in the distance, pulling her into his lap as he slid to the ground.

"Looks like he lost the drinking competition," Signe's eyes were alight with amusement.

"I'd say so," I agreed as a warm feeling settled inside me at the sight of the giant man crying over his woman. My blood was singing from the alcohol, everything funnier and happier and just... *more.* "Does he know she's pregnant yet?"

"Good gods, no," she snickered. "See how bad he is already? No one needs to listen to this for the next dozen moons."

I shook with laughter as I reclined against the wall, letting my head rest to still the spinning world around me.

Signe ran her hand over her heavy belly, silent a few moments more. "Have you remembered anything new about where you were heading?"

I paused before answering, thinking through how to answer her.

"Truthfully, no," I chewed on my lip. "But it's not because I don't remember. It's because I never knew to begin with."

She turned, staring at me appraisingly as her expression became grave. "Were you a slave?"

I sputtered at the question, which seemed terrible, as there was absolutely *nothing* funny about slavery. But I'd done this to myself, booked this trip without thinking through the details, made these decisions without any coercion, of sound mind, and landed myself in serious shit. "No, nothing like that. I just... didn't ask enough questions."

She stared at me a moment more, waiting for me to elaborate.

My mind wavered on what would come next.

Should I tell her? Maybe I should tell someone. I suppose it's possible they could know more than me about whatever is happening.

"I'm not from here," my drunk mouth decided to say before my brain was entirely on board with this new plan. "I don't mean *here* here," I gestured around with my hands at the scenery, now appearing as drunk as I was. This explanation sounded much better in my head.

Signe was quiet, waiting. I sighed loudly and closed my

eyes, trying to regroup. "I need another drink for this story."

Signe pushed off the wall next to me and walked inside without hesitation. My eyes followed her movements before she returned a few minutes later with not one but two drinking horns. She shoved one into my hands and made a hand motion for me to continue.

Here goes nothing.

"I don't know what to say, as I don't have the answers," I started. She nodded as if that made perfect sense, which I was positive, it didn't.

"I left my home to go on a tour of the Swedish countryside, which is what I was doing when I fell, and Domari found me."

She squinted, trying to follow my words. I realized right then that they probably didn't even call their own country Sweden yet.

I took a large gulp of ale, hoping for some liquid encouragement to keep going.

"*Anyway…*" I spurred myself on, "that's where it gets confusing. We'd been hiking for a day along the coast, then left to go horseback riding, and I slept through the drive there, so I don't have any idea how far we'd gone from our original starting point. The next thing I knew, I had a panic attack, walking that stupid horse Freya along the stupid water's edge, and she knocked me down the stupid hill. Then BAM," I raised my hand in the air, ale sloshing out of the side of the drinking horn. "Now I'm here."

I glanced over at her, still confused by my words, and slurped my ale. "That doesn't make any sense, does it?"

"Nope," she said. "Not even a little bit."

Yeah," I sighed, "it doesn't really to me either." I paused, sipping more ale, which was the last thing I needed at this point, deciding whether to go on.

"See, here's the thing," I turned towards her and decided to go for it, all in on the crazy. "I'm from the year 2021. So for me to be *here*," drunkenly gesturing at the scenery again, "I either time traveled or imagined the entire thing. I am probably dying in a coma in some foreign hospital with my family none the wiser wondering what the hell has happened to me, and I'll never go home again."

"Ah," she paused as a perplexed expression settled over her.

"Does that make any more sense?"

"Not really," she admitted with a chuckle. "But sometimes, that's life."

We both nodded, silent for a moment, thinking over her sudden wisdom. Many things in life didn't make sense, and you had to move on and adapt. I didn't know how that applied to this situation, however.

"Were you happy there? In, what did you say? 2021?"

I thought about it for a minute before answering. "I don't know, honestly," settling on the truth. "I love my family, and I have a wonderful best friend and the world's best dog. His name is Thor, coincidentally, but not named after *the* Thor." I paused, a smile on my face. "You would love him. He's huge and black and has an amazing personality. By amazing, I mean he hates everyone, except sometimes me, and gets me into trouble more often than not."

My mind trailed off at the thought of Thor. I missed him terribly. "What was the question?"

She laughed, staring at the stars. "I think you answered it enough."

I shrugged, finishing off the ale in my horn as she handed me another.

"I think I'll puke if I drink anymore," I said, burping loudly again as my eyes bulged. She let out a guffaw, genuine laughter filling the air, and tears spilled from my eyes as I joined her.

We stood there for a moment more, smiling, gazing at the stars.

"Are you happy *here*?" she said, quieter than before.

"Yes," I answered quickly and surprised myself with honesty as I bumped her shoulder, reaching down to squeeze her hand. "I am."

At that moment, the doors slammed almost off their hinges. More men paraded drunkenly out of the building, Gunnar and Domari at the rear. Threats were being tossed left and right over tomorrow's games, and I wondered how these men would even be able to participate as hungover as everyone was bound to be.

Gunnar walked towards us, a drunken leer aimed at his wife. "It's time I take you home," he said, his head bending to her neck, kissing it. She laughed, swatting his arm, before turning to me.

"Will you be okay?" she said, genuine concern in her voice.

I waved her off with an odd *psh* sound. "I'm fiiiiiine. Go make babies. Or, wait, that doesn't work right now."

"Doesn't hurt to keep practicing for the next one," Gunnar said against his wife's neck, hands drifting to lift her dress. She slapped at his hand and walked off. He followed a step behind.

I closed my eyes and leaned against the side of Erik's house as I listened to the sounds of the people around me. I could feel the peace of the night, the heat of the alcohol in my system, and the easy calm spreading through my body. My problems couldn't be fixed this evening, and I made a mental decision to let them be for today.

Someone settled in next to me against the wall, and I cracked my eyes open to see who. Domari's tall frame cast a shadow over me with his brown hair mussed from the evening's revelry. Inhibitions lost several drinks ago, I studied him, taking in all that was *Domari.*

He was handsome in a way that almost burned. His loose white shirt untied at the neck betrayed more about his drunkenness than anything else. Aside from watching him sleep, which I hated to admit to myself how much I'd loved, Domari was always tense — always controlled.

Right now, his shirt was rumpled, untucked from one side, and his dark chest hair spilled out of the large gap his shirt left exposed. I could stare at his chest for days.

He propped one foot up against the side of the house as his head tipped against the wall. His eyes never glanced in my direction, but his closeness was too intentional to mean nothing. This was a big house — he could have gone anywhere else. Instead, he chose to be by my side.

"This was fun," I said in an attempt to break the silence.

He nodded, taking a sip out of his drinking horn but remaining silent.

"Oh, okay, so you're going back to the dark and broody thing. Right. No more talking for you."

"You talk enough for three people."

At that, I spun. This man knew how to push my buttons.

The only problem was I was three sheets to the wind. My spin turned into more of a crumple, and the ground rose quickly to meet me. How Domari's reflexes were still so good after even more ale than me, I didn't know. The next thing I knew, he had scooped me up, holding me by the arms, and pinned me against his chest.

We stood like that, staring at each other as my hand rested against his chiseled chest, skin to skin.

One beat. Two. Time seemed to slow, the sound of the revelry all around us fading into the distance — just the two of us, locked in time.

"Kiss her already," someone yelled loudly, "or maybe I will."

"Your wife would string you up by the balls right here in front of Erik's house if she heard you say that," another yelled to raucous laughter.

Neither one of us moved, alcohol doing weird things to my judgment.

"Should I?" he said on a low breath.

My mind was so muddled; I couldn't follow the conversation.

"Should you, what?" I asked, chest heaving.

His eyes trailed down my body, watching as my breasts

threatened to spill out of the low-cut dress while I struggled to catch my breath.

"Kiss you. Right here, in front of my entire village for all to see. Should I kiss you?"

My mouth hung open, unflatteringly, until I snapped it shut. I stared up at him, searching his eyes for the answer.

YES, I wanted to scream. *Dear lord, YES!*

But I didn't say that or anything. I closed my eyes, head still tilted up towards him as he shifted his weight closer to me.

A moment passed by, longer than I thought it would take for him to kiss me already.

His beard tickled my cheek, now close enough to share breath, and I gasped, waiting. This was torture. His nose grazed my jaw until he bent to murmur, "I think I'll wait until I'm positive you'll remember it, *hàski*."

With that, he shifted, swinging me around until I was back leaning against the house, alone. My eyes snapped open, mouth hanging agape, as he walked away slowly into the night.

17

I opened my eyes to only a squint and then quickly screwed them back shut. The room was spinning. My stomach lurched, swirling as fast as my vision. My mouth was full of cotton, and I needed water *immediately*. I felt awful. Groaning, I rolled over on soft furs, attempting to work my way towards the edge of the bed.

My feet reached the lip and dropped over the side as I struggled to sit up. Several moments passed, my head hung low as I sat, trying to calm the storm raging in my insides.

"Ugh," I whimpered. I worked myself into a standing position and rose slowly, trudging towards the outhouse. Luckily, I remembered where it was. As I came out, hand on my stomach, I heard a low rumble of laughter I recognized immediately.

"Don't you dare say anything," I groaned in Domari's direction.

He laughed again but obeyed my instructions, silent.

I shuffled to the bed, sitting on the edge. If I laid down,

I was sure I'd die right there, never to move again. Hang-overs in your thirties were so much worse than in your twenties; no part of my body was spared.

The moment lingered, and I could hear the rest of the house coming alive. Still, I sat there, palming my head and attempting to ease the violent cry for help my stomach was calling out.

A drinking horn was shoved into my hand, and I gagged at its sight.

"It's a tonic from Yrsa," Domari said. "And I brought you some bread. Eat this, and then come find me outside." He turned on his heel and walked towards the door.

I sat there, staring down at the concoction and bread, remembering the miracles her last tonic had worked on my knee.

"Bottom's up," I said to myself. This time, I grimaced at the taste but finished it. Shoving the bread into my mouth, I rose on shaky feet, shuffling towards the door.

The sun was too bright, the sounds too loud — every-thing was *too much*.

I grabbed at the wood on the doorframe, pausing before walking out into the sunlight. Domari approached the front of the house, Mjölnir in tow and already saddled.

"Come on," Domari motioned to me, "let's go for a ride."

I moaned at the thought of bumping along on horseback.

"It's not too far, and I promise it's worth it," he said at my look of trepidation.

I nodded, walking towards his horse, and used all the

assistance he would give me to climb on. He rested his hand on my leg, letting me settle for a moment once I was in the saddle, before hopping up behind me.

"We'll go slow," he said in a quiet voice near my ear, beard tickling my skin.

I attempted to smile, but I didn't think it worked the way I wanted. Good thing he was behind me and couldn't see my odd countenance.

I closed my eyes, trying to prevent the horse's swaying from sending the contents of my stomach flying as Domari's hand settled around my waist. The heavy feel of his arm draped across was comforting in a way I wasn't prepared for, holding me in place and keeping me safe. I leaned into him, resting my head on his chest, feeling settled.

We rode like that for a while, and I caught glimpses of the scenery around us when I bothered to crack my eyes open. Mjölnir carried us through pastures covered in morning dew and into the edge of the forest leading towards the mountains in the distance. Eventually, the horse came to a stop as Domari patted my side.

"We're here," he said, still speaking quietly. I appreciated it, as although the tonic was working, my senses were still overloaded.

He helped me off, and I turned, looking around. Fog filled the forest, obscuring much of the view, but I thought I could make out a clearing up ahead. As we approached, a large pool of water appeared, steam rising off the surface, spiraling in the cool air. Large rocks framed it like a natural hot tub out in the woods. I stared at it longingly, reminded of a steamy shower at home.

He took my hand and helped me over the rocky path up to the shoreline without saying anything.

"It's the perfect depth for bathing," he said. I looked up at him, something close to awe in my eyes.

"Thank you," I said, ready to shuck my clothes and head straight in. He nodded, settling me on a rock at the shoreline, and turned to leave. I watched his retreating back, mixed emotions running through my system.

"Are you staying?" I shouted too loudly, cringing at the sound of my voice.

He turned at that, watching me with appraising eyes, before stopping where he stood. "Get in; then I'll return."

A shy grin crossed my face, appreciating the privacy he offered me. Maybe he did have some manners after all. I turned my back to him, sliding out of the borrowed green dress I still wore, and undid my boots. Indecision racked me as I debated whether or not to drop my bra and underwear as well. I was dying to be rid of them, so I stripped down in the cold air, shivering. I quickly slipped into the water, wearing only my red leather rune bracelet.

Sinking to my shoulders, I turned, eyes closed, letting the steam and the warm water settle everything, from my aching head to my soul. Without meaning to, I moaned. Everything felt lovely. I tipped my head back in the water and stood like that, enjoying the heat for several more moments before opening my eyes.

Domari returned as promised, now perched on the rock I left my clothes on. He stared at me unabashedly. The intensity of our eye contact should have had me blushing, turning away, seeing as I was naked beneath the water's surface. Maybe it was the last of the alcohol running through my system supplying my sudden confidence, I didn't know, but I met his stare head-on.

Flashes of our almost kiss from the night before filled my mind, a promise for another day. The way his beard had scratched across my skin, his nose skimming my jawline. I shivered despite the heat of the water.

"Feeling better?" he said after a moment, realizing we'd been quiet for too long.

"Much," sincerity filling my tone. "This is perfect, thank you."

He nodded, turning his gaze to stare off into the distance.

"Do you bathe here normally?" I asked, unable to be quiet for too long.

"Yes. We take great pride in cleanliness. Our bodies stay with us even into Hel. We honor them."

I nodded in understanding, having noticed how the entire village was fit and clean.

"Speaking of," he rose to his feet, and my eyes followed him, curious. Domari returned a moment later and tossed a bar of rough-cut soap to me. It had an herbal scent mixed with a more astringent smell that cleared the sinuses.

"Tell me about the competitions today," I said as I dipped the soap in the water, skimming it over my arms and neck.

A beat of silence went by, Domari saying nothing, and I glanced over at him. His eyes were locked on me, drifting between my eyes, my lips, and the swell of the top of my breasts rising just above the water. While he watched, I dipped the bar of soap down lower over my abdomen and smirked as his eyes caught on the steaming water around me, watching my every movement.

Clearing his throat, he finally answered. "We compete over everything. Rowing, fighting, agility. All of it," he said, eyes never leaving me.

I watched him, unsure of what would happen next, as I spun away from him. I flipped my hair over one shoulder and raised my arm to rub the soap over my shoulders and neck, wet hair sticking to my skin. "Will you compete?"

"It's expected of me, yes." A moment of silence as I dipped my head in the water, running my fingers through my curls. "Gunnar will want me to. I've been gone a long time, and he's bringing me back as his right hand, even though these men have not seen me in a decade. He will want me to showcase why I am worthy of the honor."

"And what will that look like?" I said, waiting for him to elaborate. I glanced over my shoulder at him and saw the heat in his gaze.

"Combat."

That word probably should have been a warning to me, but instead of backing off, heat spread through me that had nothing to do with the temperature of the hot spring.

"You'll fight each other?" I bent in the water, running the soap over my legs.

"Not to injure, no," he answered in a voice slightly deeper than usual, "although injuries do happen. It will be hand-to-hand combat, swords, horsemanship, spears, swimming. All of it."

I half-turned and paused in my cleaning. "Are you expected to win it all?"

He smirked at that, eyes on mine as they sparkled in the early morning sun. "No… But I could."

I rolled my eyes at the cocky response, and he chuckled.

"Because you were in this Varangian Guard? That's why you're so much better?" I turned, soaping my other leg and enjoying the steam.

"Yes," he said, not taking the bait. "I was an elite trained soldier for a decade, paid to be the best of the best."

"Why did you choose that?" I glanced at him again as I began to wash my hair. My raised arms made it so my breasts were barely below the water's surface, and his eyes were locked there. I channeled Signe with my smirk, shocking myself with my body confidence at the moment, but it was easy to feel with the way he was watching me.

Eventually, he looked away, gazing out at the trees. A loud sigh escaped him before he answered.

"Because I couldn't protect my clan," he whispered, the most honest I'd ever heard him. "I needed to be better. Stronger. *More*. I wasn't sure I'd ever return — that I'd ever be good enough."

The vulnerability of the comment caught me off-guard, and I dropped my hands to the water. Indecision racked me, unsure whether I should prod, urge him to go on, or let it drop.

I twisted slightly towards him and waited in silence for several moments more, pausing to see where he decided to take the conversation. Surprise filled me as he stood, pulled his shirt over his head, and undid his pants. As he began to tug them off his hips, I spun away from him, eyes wide as my body went rigid under the water, waiting to see how this would unfold.

A gentle splash sounded behind me as he walked into the water, not close enough to touch me, but quite close considering we were now both naked. His gaze lingered on mine only for a moment as he passed me and walked deeper into the spring.

Once he reached the middle, he turned, facing me, and threw his head back, letting his body float in the water.

I wish I could say that I didn't stare, but I did. So much muscle covered his body, now shining in the water. Water beaded in his dark chest hair, and I'd be lying if I said I didn't stare at where I knew his hips were floating below the surface. If my face hadn't already been red from the heat of the steam, it was now. My pulse was pounding, heat pooling low in my belly as I rubbed my legs together under the water.

Steam rose all around him like a god laid to rest in the center of this spring. He laid there for several minutes, floating in silence, before dropping his feet and running his hands through his long, brown hair, brushing it out of his face.

I sank further into the water, my mouth now submerged so he couldn't see my jaw unhinge and drool escape as he walked through the water towards me. Water dripped from his beard and onto his chest, glistening off his many muscles. This picture in front of me would feature in *many* of my fantasies from here on out.

His focus was lost, though, not settling on me this time. Something different had settled in his eyes, resolute.

"Erik and Frida raised me; you already know that." I nodded at his words, trying to recall what we'd been talking about, waiting for him to go on. "I'm older than Gunnar by three years, but my parents both died long ago, so almost all of my childhood memories are with them. Gunnar is like a brother to me." He paused for a moment, gathering the words for the rest of his story.

"Gunnar had a sister, Tove," he went on. *Had.*

I had never tried so hard to keep my mouth shut, but at that moment, I knew he needed to speak these words, so I zipped it tight.

"Tove was a year older than Gunnar. The three of us were inseparable. We did everything together," he said. "Signe reminds me a lot of Tove. Both were meant to be warriors." He was now lost in his memories, eyes glazed.

"Erik stopped our clan's raiding days after a battle that took too many of our men, including my father, his brother. He pulled away from the *jarl* we had followed for decades and left with those of us who sought a more peaceful life. We were children, and so many had been orphaned in the raid like me."

He sighed deeply, skimming over the story of long ago. "We grew up here, the sons and daughters of traders, but stories were still told of the glory and riches of days past. The wisdom that has come with Gunnar's age was not his at the time. He and Tove disagreed with the more settled lifestyle Erik was now demanding of us. He was determined to prove himself, especially considering how fierce his older sister was.

"Gunnar caught word of a clan nearby fighting stallions — a pointless waste of life for sport — and got it in his head that we could steal them before the fight. I disagreed, unwilling to disobey Erik outright, but Gunnar kept on. He convinced Raud and Tove that it was a great idea."

Raud. I'd heard his name several times before. Before I could ask, he went on, "I was the only one with any sense of the four of us, so I decided to go with them. We split up; Gunnar the lookout, Raud heading for one stallion, and Tove and I went for the other. The plan was shaky at best, but we were young and stupid."

He turned, eyes back on me, as he finished his story. "The details don't matter, but nothing went as planned. The stallions were far more guarded than Gunnar had realized, and Tove was caught in the crossfire."

I moved towards him in the water, now only an armswidth apart, but his gaze never met mine, head hung low.

"Accidents happen, Domari," I said, trying to ease the guilt I could see racking him. "It's not your fault. She chose to be there."

He turned his head, unable to look at me, swallowing hard.

I reached out, placing my hand on his arm, offering any comfort I could in this vulnerable moment.

"Anyway," he said, clearing his throat, "I joined a band of men set for Constantinople days later and was in the service of the Emperor for ten years."

"What brought you back?" I questioned, running my thumb over his bicep, feeling the strength beneath.

Before answering, he looked down at my hand on his skin, lingering there.

"A seer came to town," he said. "It was a chance encounter, or as much as anything can be when fate is involved. She told me I was needed here and fast. I resigned that day; sure something had happened to my clan."

I thought about that, taking in how serious he took the visions of a seer.

"I came home to find Erik dying, whether anyone wants to admit it or not. Gunnar is a grown man, responsible and calm, fit to lead."

"But he needs you," I said, only stating the obvious. "They all do."

He glanced off at the forest but covered my hand on his arm with his.

"This land, these people, are your home," I went on, my tone holding a little envy at the thought. "Even I can see that they're so glad to have you back in the few days we've been here."

His thumb rubbed over my hand absently as he closed his eyes.

"And do you think I haven't noticed how they watch you with stars in their eyes? The men want to *be* you, and the women want to be *on* you." At that, he finally cracked a smile, breaking his somber facade.

"Thank you," he said after a moment, fingers slipping between mine to hold onto me. My pulse galloped at the simple touch.

"For what?"

"This. All of it."

"Consider it returning the favor for saving my life."

His eyes found mine at that, trailing down to my lips, to the water blurring the image of my body below the surface.

Then, something shifted in his gaze, and his fingers intertwined with mine became a heavy grip, pulling me through the water towards him. His other arm laced behind me, pulling me flush against his chest as his mouth descended on mine. My heart pounded in my chest as he kissed my lips gently, his whiskers tickling my skin.

"I don't regret it," he said, my mind whirling to remember what we had been talking about as his lips scraped across my skin, fire pulsing in my veins. "If saving you brought me here, then I am glad fate stepped in, guiding me to you, helpless on the rocks," his words sent shivers down my spine to match the feeling of his fingers trailing low over my back.

"Even though I talk too much?" I smirked through heavy-lidded lashes. I leaned into his touch as if I could get closer than I already was, breasts smashed into his muscled chest.

"I will consider it my job to silence you," his gaze now full of hunger.

Our mouths crashed back together in a rush as he pushed us backward in the water. Both hands drifted down to my ass, gripping as he pulled me even closer. My back arched as it met a cold rock wall behind me, and I threw my hands up, locking them behind his head, unwilling to let even an inch of space remain between us.

His lips left mine for a moment as he kissed his way down my cheek, my jaw, my neck, my collarbone. I was made of molten lava as his tongue licked low across my chest, just above my breasts still covered by the water. My head tilted back against the rock as I was lost to sensation, everything this man made me feel, made me want. His mouth found mine again after a moment, and his tongue pushed gently against my lips to deepen the kiss, forcing a moan out of me as our breath mingled. If steam hadn't already been swirling all around us in the hot spring, it would have been now.

Every part of my body was aware that if I wrapped my legs around him, if he lowered me just an inch, just a fraction, his body would be there, pressing against my core. But that wasn't what this moment was about, no matter how much I fought with my own desires.

Chests heaving, he broke our kiss with a nibble on my bottom lip. "That," he said in a husky voice, "I think you will remember."

I chuckled at that, my heartbeat still racing in my chest, not ready for this moment to end. Between the buoyancy of the water and his arms around me, I was glad I couldn't fall because I was weak in the knees. No other kiss I'd ever shared had come close to this.

His arms loosened around me, but not enough for me to slip out of his embrace. Resting his forehead on mine, a beat went by, neither of us sure what came next.

As my mind cleared, I blushed, which seemed stupid after I'd just had every inch of my body plastered to this man. He smiled down at me before brushing one last kiss across the top of my head and letting go.

"What now?" I said, never one for silence.

"Now, I go humiliate the rest of my village," he replied, turning to leave the hot spring, flexing his back muscles as he rose unnecessarily slowly out of the spring. Water streamed down his carved backside just as firm and muscled as the rest of him. He turned, glancing over his scarred shoulder with a smug expression as he caught me blatantly staring at him.

"Are you coming?" he said, waiting for me.

I laughed to myself at the double-entendre, remembering every second of the kiss from moments ago. *Come back in the water, and I sure as hell will.*

I didn't say my thoughts aloud, though, as I sank further into the water, deciding whether I could pull off a sexy Sports Illustrated exiting the water move as he had done.

Probably not.

Dunking myself one last time while I waited for my heart rate to slow, I waded into the shallows. Domari stood on the shore with his pants hung loosely over his hips, untied, as he watched. He dried himself off with a large cloth he'd packed, a look of hunger in his eyes. At the last moment, before too much of my skin would be revealed, he took one long glance and turned his back, holding the cloth out to the side for me.

18

Domari's hand across my waist felt almost salacious as we rode back to the village. I was now hyper-aware of every place our bodies touched. I could feel his heartbeat, calm and sure, as his thumb trailed small circles over the surface of my dress. Every part of me was still reeling from that kiss. It was steamy in every sense of the word.

Silence had never been my strong suit, particularly not when I was uneasy — nonsensical words brimmed in my chest, ready to spill out. My hands trembled as I fought to contain them, focusing on enjoying the easy peace between us and taking in the scenery.

The fiery copper tones of fall were fading, but the enchanting green of the pines standing tall was left behind. Two large ravens perched high on a branch above us, watching as we rode by. I bit my lip, trying to relax, when I felt a rumble against my back.

"It is impossibly hard for you to be quiet, isn't it?"

A whooshing sound left me quickly, expelling air far too fast and in an unflattering way. I let the breath I'd been holding go.

"Yes."

My back vibrated again with his laugh before he leaned in, resting his chin on my head.

"Go on."

Thousands of questions rolled through my mind, some so pointless I could never admit them aloud. I settled on an easy, non-invasive topic. At least, I hoped.

"What will come first today in the competitions?"

He sighed against my back and adjusted his arm on my waist before answering.

"Did they not have competitions in Colorado?"

I thought about that before answering. I wasn't sure I was ready to break this truce between us by admitting my theory that I had time-traveled. Or was in a coma, imagining him. I didn't know which one sounded worse.

"Yes, sometimes we compete in sports or baking, or, I don't know… Anything."

He nodded, accepting my answer. "It is the same here. Our village hosts, but other clans are welcome to join us. You'll see more people here today than those you met last night."

I could understand that — the more competitors, the better the show.

"There are lots of physical contests; fighting, mostly. Those come first. The water events are always my favorite," he went on, seemingly lost in his telling. "As the night goes on, the finer arts will come out. Poetry, singing, the sort."

"You have singing competitions?" I suddenly imagined Vikings perched in red, spinning chairs.

"Yes," he nodded, "Björn always enters and usually wins."

Understandably, after I heard him sing last night, I could still hear the notes of his ballad, deep and genuine, reverberating through my bones.

"Is it only men?"

He chuckled before answering. "No. Well, some villages don't allow women to enter, I suppose. But you've you met our women. Not much can hold them back from anything they set their minds to. That's how Gunnar met Signe. She beat him at an agility course. That year they had the contestants jumping between moving ships to cross the river. The way Gunnar tells it, Signe didn't jump. She *flew*," he said in a reverent tone. "The men say Gunnar was too busy watching her to notice he'd completely missed the next boat, now past him, and landed hard in the water below."

I laughed with him at the story, seeing exactly how that could have happened.

"I heard they're running that course again this year," he continued. "It should be a fun one to watch."

I nodded but had nothing to say to that. He went on to tell me of other events I'd see — mock battles, swimming, anything they could think of to pit themselves against one another. My body relaxed, at ease in Domari's presence as I listened.

"Signe was born during a Winter Nights competition," his tone betrayed the smile I knew was spreading across his face. "Gunnar thinks that must be why she's so strong."

I jerked upright at his words. I might not be ready to compete in any of their events, but no one did a birthday party better than me. "Wait... It's Signe's birthday?"

"I suppose, yes, it could be," he pondered.

"Do you do anything special for birthdays?" I asked, my excitement level rising immediately.

"We celebrate a child's first birthday," a solemn tone took over his voice. Suddenly, I realized the hardships that must happen here with a new baby. This was not an easy life to live. "After that, no."

Well, that wouldn't do. We rode the rest of the way to the village in silence as my mind raced to think through how I could make this celebration happen.

I leaped off of Mjölnir when we arrived in the village. Domari shot me a strange look as I set off for Erik's as quickly as my knee would allow.

"Everything okay?" he asked my retreating back.

"Yep!"

I was a woman on a mission, and I knew who could help me — someone who happened to love sweets and had a nose like a bear. I approached the doors of Erik's long-house, looking around the property first before entering. Magnus stood inside, helping his mother carry heavy platters to tables that had been moved outside for the day's events.

"Magnus!" I shouted, slapping my hand over my mouth at the volume my excitement had driven me to. Frida's head shot up with an assessing look as I approached. "Sorry. I didn't mean to barge in."

Frida smiled, waving me off. "My home is always open to you."

My heart warmed at the words, genuine and welcoming, as this entire village had been. My mind returned to the topic at hand.

"Could I… borrow you?" I asked Magnus, staring up at the big man. He was twice as wide as me, my head reaching chin-level on him. His shoulder-length blonde hair was pulled into a knot on the top of his head, and flour dusted his shirt. The easy smile dropped at my words, the corners dipping, as he took me in.

"Are you all right?"

Magnus's young, handsome face transformed so entirely that I had to fight my instincts not to take a step away from him. His side was suddenly hulking, casting a large shadow at the thought of a possible threat to me. I'd seen the same look cross his face last night when the men had made a joke about Astrid and had been glad I wasn't the target of that gaze. Thank goodness he seemed to like me.

"Yes, I'm fine," I laughed uncomfortably, clearing my throat. "But I need your help."

"Anything." His face relaxed, returning the jovial smile I had grown accustomed to on our trip into the village. I was amazed at how quickly he could shift from one to another.

"I need to bake," I said. "A pie, or a cake, or… I don't know. Something sweet." I debated what Domari had told me about the lack of birthday celebrations, determining how to phrase my request. "To… thank Signe for hosting me. She's done so much; I want to spoil her in return."

His eyebrows scrunched together in thought, pouring over options.

"There should be lingonberries left," his mother chimed in. "You can show her the way."

Magnus's azure eyes came alive, the childish glint in them not too long gone in his early twenties. He spun, grabbed a wineskin, and then my hand.

We quickly jogged through the field and towards the forest, Magnus pulling me behind him. I laughed at his contagious exuberance and was glad my knee had healed.

"I used to sneak out here alone a lot," he said, slowing as we entered the forest. He took a swig out of the skin before handing it to me.

My sip was tentative, leary of my not-long-gone hangover. I was pleasantly surprised to find it wasn't ale this morning but something sweet and fruity.

"It's mead," Magnus said as I looked down at the skin. "I stole it from the supply for tonight." Part of me felt guilty for that, but his mother was standing there, so I decided not to dwell on it.

"Mother would send me to gather in the forest when I was too small to head off with the older ones," he continued after I passed the skin back to him.

A hint of resentment snuck into his tone at the comment, but it didn't overshadow his easy nature. I silently did the math, thinking through what Domari said about his, Gunnar's, and Tove's ages. No one had said years exactly, but I would assume Domari to be about my age, placing Gunnar and Tove in their mid-to-late twenties, making Magnus several years younger than them. Suddenly, the passing *Knut* nickname made much more sense. He was the baby of the family. And what a *big* baby he was.

Magnus ducked under a low-hanging pine bough, aiming deeper into the forest. I followed in his footsteps, boots crunching across the fallen leaves, letting him lead until he stopped at the edge of a large bush in a clearing. He knelt, still far too high off the ground, and leaned down, massaging the leaves.

"The bears beat me to them," he said in exasperation, glancing around.

I stood a little straighter, turning to look over my shoulder, sure I was about to have a run-in with a bear. Stepping a little closer to Magnus, I waited for his next move.

"Come. I know of another patch," he stood, not sharing the unease I was having over the idea of bears nearby. He chuckled, taking one look at my large, fearful eyes, even though I was trying to hide them.

"Here," he shoved the skin in my hands again and winked, "liquid courage. But know, I could take a bear any day." His eyes sparkled at the thought, so full of himself at his young age. I couldn't help but shake my head at his cocky nature, smiling as we walked farther east at a quick pace.

"Why are we in such a hurry?" I asked. "Racing the bears?"

He laughed. "No. I have to be back soon to enter the hand-to-hand combat battle. I told Astrid I would win it in her honor." His grin ate his entire face, spreading ear to ear.

He turned, stepping between two pines and into another clearing. He ducked down and pulled red berries off the bushes with a loud whoop. I followed his lead, stooping to the next bush.

Magnus leaned over, pausing my hand. "Pinch here, don't rip them."

I did as he showed me, his watchful eyes taking me in as he sat back on his heels, sipping at the mead. He watched for a few beats before he nodded in approval and returned to his task. He didn't bother with asking me why I didn't already know these things, and I liked that about him. His friendship was readily offered and just plain simple.

I looked down at the mound of berries in my hand, now overflowing, before he pursed his lips in thought.

"Here," he pulled his shirt over his head.

If Domari was muscled, I needed to develop a new word to describe Magnus. Power oozed off of him in easy waves. But while Domari's muscles seemed battle-hardened, laced with scars that told stories of his many adventures, Magnus's skin was pristine. Dozens of Nordic tattoos painted his chest and neck and covered his hands.

I was staring, I realized far too late. He grinned at me before flexing, moving his pecs in a wave. I rolled my eyes so hard that I could hear my mother warning me they'd get stuck there. His laugh was booming, forcing one out of me as well.

"It's easy to see why Astrid chose me, right?" I could see every single tooth in his mouth with his wide grin.

"Absolutely," I said. "If you were ten years older, I might feel jealous of her."

He laughed, returning to his task. "Put the berries in my shirt so that we can carry more that way. Astrid loves lingonberries right now, so I'll pick more for her."

"Makes sense that she's having cravings."

He stopped, hands stilling, and turned to me.

At the solemn look on his face, my mind reeled, thinking if I'd said something wrong. I knew I'd seen Astrid leave the feast the night before with her hand on her belly, and Signe had told me she was pregnant, right?

Then, my mind caught up. Signe said that no one had told Magnus yet to keep him from being even more of a blubbering mess. My face dropped, my eyes large, as we stared at each other.

"What did you say?" he asked me, all of his happy nature now gone.

"Um...," I stalled, trying to think quickly on my feet, "because, you know, all girls have cravings during their time of the month." There. Mention periods and I was sure to scare him into changing the subject. I snagged the skin, taking a large swig, and hiccuped. I *hiccuped*... That's how old and out of shape I was with drinking like this.

"She's not bleeding," he didn't even flinch. "Trust me, I would know."

Right. Domari said they went at it like rabbits.

I spun back to the lingonberries, shoving one in my mouth to try to delay myself further. I chewed, tasting the bitter, harsh taste, and screwed my face in disgust. Spitting savagely, I turned, tongue out, and reached for the skin of mead. He handed it to me, eyes never leaving my face in a terrifying way.

I took a large swig, difficult to swallow after last night but much better than the disgusting taste of the berry. Dropping the skin down to my side, I sighed.

"What do you know?" he demanded, hand outstretched, taking the skin from me.

"I think she might be pregnant," I winced. I was furious at myself for ruining this moment for him. For *them.*

He sank, hitting the ground hard, staring off into the forest.

"I don't think I was supposed to tell you," I stammered, trying to figure out how to backpedal through this conversation. "I'm so sorry to be the one to share the news. That's not my place at all."

He took a long swig of the mead. In fact, I'd call it more of a guzzle.

"Say something," I said after several moments had gone by. I'd screwed up so bad.

"Why wouldn't she tell me?" vulnerability filled his tone. "Am I not good enough?"

I could cry, knowing I'd done this. "No, no, no. I don't think that's it at all," I said, my hand reaching out to his shoulder but unsure if I should touch him. He guzzled again. Briefly, I wondered about the capacity of that skin. However much it held wouldn't be enough at this point.

"Then, *why?*" he turned to me, tears gathering in his eyes.

How this big man could be so sensitive blew my mind, and I loved it about him. He was also drinking the mead out of the skin so fast; I was getting a little concerned about how we would make it home.

"Give me some of that," I said, stealing the skin from him. I took a gulp and winced, dreading a repeat of this morning's hangover. But, I needed to reduce the amount he could drink in such a short time. He was still staring at me when I put the skin down. I sighed loudly, unsure what to say.

"In the short time that I've known you, you have been nothing but kind," I decided on flattery. He had a big ego, so maybe I needed to feed it to fix this. "Any woman, Astrid included, should consider themselves *lucky* to be by your side, let alone carry your child." He turned, now looking out into the forest, contemplative. "And think how handsome they'll be," I went on, attempting to lighten the mood.

"Of course, they will be," he scoffed. "She's the most beautiful woman to walk the land." He turned, staring at me. "Sorry."

I waved the backhanded comment off.

"And if they look anything like me," he turned, a grin returning to his face, "they're sure to be confused for a god." He snagged the skin, draining it, before jumping to his feet.

He staggered a little, grabbing a nearby tree. I didn't understand how such a big man could be such a lightweight. First, last night, and now this.

Standing, I scooped up the lingonberries in his discarded shirt and slipped my elbow into his.

"Come on," I pulled him in the direction I thought we had come from. "Let's go find your baby mama."

Magnus burped loudly, pounding his chest, before turning to me. "Baby mama," he said, hearts in his eyes. "I love the sound of that."

I nodded, hoping I'd at least kind of mended fences here, choosing to worry later about how Signe and Astrid would feel at my betrayal of this secret.

We walked arm in arm through the forest, Magnus singing me raunchy songs of battles fought, women won, and glory seized.

It took us much longer to find our way back than it had to get to the lingonberries, wandering without Magnus's full attention. As we exited the forest, competitions in play could be heard across the field.

Something shifted in Magnus as he instantly sobered, chest rising, eyes tightening. I looked up at him, worry lacing through me.

"Everything okay?" I dropped his arm.

"Sweets will have to wait, Shelbie. It's time for me to prove that I can defend not just my woman," he answered, "but my child, too."

With that, he left me, stomping off towards the growing crowd. He approached a brawl happening in what I was assuming was an organized fashion for the sake of the competition. Magnus let out a blood-curdling roar as he drew near, charging into battle, fists blazing.

I stood in shock, wondering how the drunken, love-sick man of an hour ago could now be raging into battle. Blood splattered, fists connecting left and right across the field, as the men began to drop out one by one. I wasn't sure of the rules, but it looked as if they hit the ground, then the contender was disqualified.

This was brutal… and also a little exhilarating. Domari was standing off to the side, a spectator only. His eyes caught mine, and he stared at the shirt I still clutched in my hands with an odd expression. He uncrossed his arms and stood a little straighter as he glanced between me and where Magnus had charged into battle, questions in his eyes.

I smiled, shrugging, before turning back to the fight.

Men were dropping out quickly now, the fight down to seven men. Two came at Magnus at once, another roar leaving his throat as he seized one by the shirt and threw him violently into the other, sending them both crashing to the ground. Two down, five to go.

I was now riveted, unable to look away, rooting for Magnus with every fiber of my being. He fought with every inch of his body, twisting and turning in ways I didn't know if I'd ever seen a human move; everything was intentional. Each footfall was methodical, adjusting to ensure his balance was never challenged.

This was so violent, and I *loved* it. My pulse raced with him, watching his every move in slow motion. It was hard to believe this wasn't a real battle, with nothing at stake but pride. Men were slowly ganging up on Magnus, hoping to change the tide of the fight. He stopped, looking into the crowd, eyes scanning past me, searching.

Without thinking, I darted my eyes around, knowing whom he was looking for. Astrid was on the other side of the battle, and Magnus would be caught off-guard while searching for his wife.

"TO YOUR LEFT!" I yelled, heart racing as fear for him swept over me, so invested in this fight. His head whipped to the left as Astrid pushed towards the front of the crowd. I could see tears welling in Magnus's eyes as his gaze locked on his young wife.

"For you," he landed a punch at an oncoming attacker without even looking, "For our *family.*" A high kick, two more men down.

Astrid's sleek, long blonde hair flowed behind her, giving her an ethereal glow that only added to her perfect visage. The crowd parted around the goddess of a girl, now standing right at the edge of the chaos of the fight. She put a hand over her heart, then another over her belly, before nodding at her young husband with a smile.

He turned at that sign from her, leveling the remaining fighters so fast I could hardly keep track.

The roar he let out, pounding his chest in victory, was nothing short of exultant. I screamed, jumping up and down as I clapped, a smile of Magnus's caliber taking over my face.

I glanced over to see Domari watching me. He smirked, eyes twinkling in the sun as he turned and pulled off his shirt.

He was up next.

19

After the fight, the men cleared out, faces swollen and blood-smeared but jubilant. I stood at the edge of the crowd, purveying the scene, seeing many people I'd already met — Thorsten, Gunnar, and Kare off to the side — talking to several men I hadn't. The sound of hands clapping backs, laughter, and merriment filled the air. Women were scattered through the crowds, both onlookers and participants, preparing for the next match.

I looked anywhere but at Domari, every muscle on display as he ran through warm-up exercises with a heavy wooden sword. Signe approached me, grabbing my arm and pulling me into the crowd without a word. Gunnar stopped mid-conversation, feeling the proximity of his wife now several yards away, turning eyes filled with admiration on her and her heavily swollen belly.

"Where are the kids?" I whispered as we pushed forward in the crowd arm in arm.

"They're with Frida and Erik, overseeing the event," she pointed towards the platform. "But I wouldn't miss these fights for the world."

I glanced over at her, hearing something change in her voice, to see her grin shift to almost feral delight. She loved these games, and her pregnant belly prevented her from qualifying.

"Will Gunnar compete? Or is that not allowed since he'll be chieftain next?"

"Oh, he's up next," she said, a grin eating her face. "Against Domari." Mirth twinkled in her expression, delighted at the idea of the two men facing off. Heat flooded my body as I turned back to the two men, both shirtless. I was unwilling to miss a single second of what was to come.

Even if I hadn't wanted it to be, my attention was glued to Domari, observing his every move. He was a giant of a man, standing taller than all but Magnus in the crowd. Gunnar swung a wooden sword, muscles flexed, showing his tattoos along his arm and neck. Signe let out a small moan next to me as she gripped my arm. A laugh rumbled out of me, and I couldn't help but agree with her. It hadn't even started yet, and my pulse was hammering in my body.

The sounds of whooshing blades swinging through the air filled my ears, and I was curious to see if this battle would take on the same style as the last. A loud whistle cut through the air, drawing the attention of everyone in the area. We all glanced to where Erik and Frida sat perched on the platform, the children at their feet playing with wooden soldiers.

"The next battle will be one of the blades," Erik announced, his voice shaking as he spoke. I'd missed this announcement earlier as Magnus and I had arrived late.

"No foul play will be allowed. This is to be a fair fight… Begin."

Men and women stormed the field, fewer contestants than the fistfight had been, but no less rowdy. Arne fought alongside the teenage girl I'd seen with their father two days prior. They both had their red-blonde hair braided down their backs, Arne's shaved on the sides, whereas the girl's was pulled tightly to mimic his style. They had matching black ink smeared across their eyes — a pair in all they did.

"His twin, Bodil," Signe shouted to me over the noise, following my line of sight. "Like my own Revna, she is made of fire. They will do well today if they stick together."

The air was full of sound, wood clashing on wood, war cries, and grunts — so much grunting. I scanned the crowd, looking for a dark head standing out against the sea of red and blonde.

There, towards the rear of the crowd, Domari and Gunnar fought back to back. A circle of men surrounded them, each taking their shot at the future chieftain and the renowned Varangian Guard.

No one stood a chance, however. The two were synchronous in movement; it was apparent they had been doing this for years. The ten-year gap in their bond hadn't changed a thing.

I glanced over at Signe. She was alight with excitement, feet dancing on the ground as if she itched to join in the battle.

Sweat splashed through the air, many of the men shirtless and women down to thin layers, as the battle moved on. Time slowed as I watched, comprehending how the world came to remember these ruthless Vikings a century later. This was a *peaceful* clan, and they fought as if they'd been handed a sword in the cradle.

I couldn't peel my eyes away from Gunnar and Domari as the crowd thinned, now down to a handful of competitors. I was surprised at the number of women who had lasted so long, but they moved in a whirlwind compared to the heavier men. I was positive that if Signe hadn't been resting her hand on her belly, she would still be standing out there, undefeated even now.

Muscles rippled under Domari's skin with each swing, his gaze in equal parts locked on his opponent and scanning for the next. My eyes darted around the battle, watching one after the next go down, stepping out as a sword stopped just short of their body, neck, face. These Vikings fought with precision and control; even a blow could be halted so swiftly it was hard to tell that their opponent had been spared. Only the sight of contestants leaving the circle relatively uninjured told the tale of the mock brutality at play.

Signe was screaming next to me now, unable to control herself any longer. Sights and sounds seemed to fade as I watched Domari with intensity. My pulse raced as I fiddled with my bracelet — anything to occupy my hands as I watched the show unfold.

This was hot.

Like, *really* hot.

I needed that skin of ale back from Magnus.

Two women came at Domari and Gunnar, rotating places at the last minute to throw them off, but the men moved so swiftly that the surprise move didn't succeed.

The last man rushed Gunnar, shoulders dropped low in a charge, ready to plow through him.

Domari moved so fluidly that I could hardly comprehend the strike. He swung his sword high over his head and down across the man's back, dropping him. Domari crouched low, and before he could rise to his feet, he swung his leg out to the side, spinning. His eyes came up as he stopped his blade at Gunnar's throat.

The grin on Gunnar's face rivaled his younger brother, every tooth on display, as his chest heaved from exertion. He raised his hands to the sides, spinning for the crowd to see, before dropping his sword and bending the knee at Domari's feet.

Domari stood, staring down at his younger cousin and brother kneeling before him, head bowed as he panted.

The crowd was silent as the importance of this moment sunk in. This was the future leader of their clan, bowing down before another.

"Rise," Domari leaned down to grip Gunnar's arm, pulling him to his feet.

Gunnar pulled him into a fierce hug, thumping Domari on the back. The two whispered something to each other that had Domari's eyes crinkling in amusement. At that, Gunnar spun, raising Domari's hand into the air.

The crowd roared. Cries of delight rang through the air as the two men spun in the center of the field.

Warmth filled my chest as I watched a slow smile spread over Domari's face at the acceptance he felt at last.

After a moment, his eyes found mine locked with intensity, and his grin expanded. He dropped his sword, walking towards me with purpose, as my heart beat faster in my chest. Every step closer to me felt like a push of fate, the pen hitting the paper to write my story at last.

As he approached, he leaned down and locked his arms around me, lifting me into the air. I threw my arms around his neck, laughing at the sudden movement. He slid me down his chest, locking his mouth on mine.

Whistles and shouting broke out among the crowd, reminding me that the entire field had now witnessed this kiss. This was far from the private moment we'd had in the hot spring.

This was a statement, a declaration for all to see.

He slowly lowered me to my feet, sliding down his body in a way that lit every single one of my nerves on fire.

"Please don't say you won that battle for me," I said, ringing a chuckle out of the big man in front of me.

"No," he shook his head slightly and glanced over the crowd. "I won that battle for *me.*"

The afternoon passed similarly with more mock battles using weapons I didn't even have names for. Then came the cooking; women and men brought out covered dishes, laying them on the table in front of Erik's house. People formed a line near it, and Signe grabbed my arm, pulling me to do the same.

"Don't tell anyone," she whispered, "but this is my favorite part. I want to try every dish that someone might think is worthy of competition."

I glanced at the table, noticing Yrsa standing behind one of the entries, and grinned. Taste-testing I could get behind.

We walked through the line, sampling each entry from savory to sweet. I was surprised by the variety and seasonings, not knowing what to expect for a Viking meal. Signe whispered commentary to me over each dish and the cooks who'd baked them. There were entrées made of chicken, pork, venison, fish, and mutton. Loaves of bread were decorated beautifully with herbs and fruit baked in. It all smelled heavenly.

My heart warmed at the easy conversation, at how readily Signe pulled me into the heart of this village. The more I thought about it, the same could be said of everyone I'd met so far. I scanned the crowd, full of villagers from near and far, all enjoying themselves. Horns of ale and mead were passed out, sloshing as they were rattled together in cheers.

After making our way down the table, Signe led me over to a tree, pulling me down to sit on the ground next to her.

"My feet are screaming," she reclined against the tree. I did the same, happy to sit with her in easy silence. A group of men stood nearby, laughing loudly, recounting the day's battles. Gunnar's back was to us, Domari at his side. He shifted, as if he could feel my eyes on him, and winked, raising his ale to me. I beamed back at him.

A surge of euphoria spread through my chest as I watched him incorporate himself into the circle of men, no longer standing on the sidelines. He was still the quietest of the bunch, but he smiled easily and laughed with the men. What a change from the man I'd spent the morning with, guilt-ridden and aloof.

A huge body dropped down beside me in a huff, startling me from my focus on Domari.

"Quit staring," Magnus's shoulder bumped mine. "It's rude." I rolled my eyes as his laugh rumbled through him. "We're setting up the bonfire soon, so we'll finish our," he paused, leaning over to check that Signe wasn't listening, "chore in the morning."

I nodded, happy with that plan after the long day. Magnus stood and tapped his brother on the shoulder. Following his lead, the men gathered the pile of stacked timber to light the bonfire for the evening.

Signe dozed, her hands delicately balanced on her belly. I couldn't get over how strong this woman was, both physically and in spirit. So much was handed to these people, between the elements, the raids, and the hard labor each day required. And yet, they were some of the most optimistic, happy bunch I'd ever met.

A gown rustled next to me as Astrid quietly came to my side. She offered a shy smile as I patted the ground next to me. She nodded and bent below the low-hanging branches to sit.

"I wanted to talk to you," I said as she settled herself on the ground.

Her voice was quiet but had a musical tone to it. "Likewise. I've been meaning to introduce myself. Magnus has talked about you incessantly since you arrived."

I glanced at her to ensure I didn't hear any hint of jealousy at her words, but this woman was at ease. I assumed, particularly after his display on the battlefield today, that she was secure in how much her young husband adored her.

"Don't worry," I grinned, "he talks non-stop of you as well."

A blush washed over Astrid's face, somehow making her already gorgeous face even prettier. It was unfair how stunning this girl was. "I am sorry for telling Magnus about the baby this morning."

"It's all right," she patted my hand. "I never wanted to keep it a secret from him but couldn't find the right way to say it." A loaded silence filled the air, as neither of us knew where to go from there.

"Our men take it very hard when their babes don't survive," Signe mumbled, eyes still closed. "Sometimes, it's easier to keep it a secret for longer than go place that worry on them as well. There is enough of that going around with Erik's health and all of this talk of Raud."

I wanted to ask more, but Signe had earned every second of rest she could steal. Plus, Astrid's eyes were full of worry, introspective as she thought of the journey ahead of her to bring this baby into the world. I squeezed her hand, offering what little support I could as the night passed quickly.

We eventually moved to the bonfire, perched on logs as the women took their spot next to their husbands. Domari slid behind me on a log after a while, pulling me into his chest as he laced his arms around my torso. It was nice, leaning against him and feeling his warmth at my back.

Silencing my mind, I took a sip of the honeyed mead and chose to live in the moment.

20

I woke with a smile, recognizing the weight across my middle as Domari's arm. We fell asleep wrapped together, had drifted apart in the night but found our way together again by sunrise.

I was content to lay there with my eyes closed, enjoying the heat radiating off of the delicious man next to me, when a figure loomed over the bed.

"Good morning, *elskan mín*," Magnus's voice whispered above us.

"*Knut*, I will wallop you until they revoke your win yesterday if you don't turn around and leave right now," Domari rasped, his morning voice even sexier than usual. I pulled the blankets over my head to hide the blush from the heat spreading through my body. As if sensing the change in me, Domari's arm pulled me further into him, and I could feel that he felt the same.

"I hate to break up this little moment, as I know how desperately Domari must need it. Maybe both of you, for that matter," he pondered, thoughts wandering, "but I do need to borrow Shelbie."

I sighed, my mind not ready for what might happen if I stayed in this bed any longer — what it might mean. My body, however, was willing to betray me. It was prepared for everything this man had to offer.

Throwing the blankets off, I rolled over and stood before I could change my mind. I waved Magnus off and told him I'd meet him at the door.

"Sorry, brother," Magnus said as he was leaving. Skin hit skin as I assumed Domari took a swing at Magnus. His laughter vibrated through the house like an alarm.

I washed quickly and gathered a new dress Yrsa had left for me. This was a traditional high-neck Viking style in a beautiful sapphire color. I admired the tiny runes embroidered along the neckline in gold embroidery that almost seemed to glow. Momentarily distracted by it, I ran my fingers over the intricate threads and marveled at the work that must have gone into such an elaborate garment. My ribs were healing, so I undid my bandages as I slipped into the dress.

That done, I left to meet Magnus outside. We stepped through the morning dew, fog lapping at our feet, and walked to Erik's longhouse.

"I've been soaking the berries," he said when we were out of earshot. "They should be ready."

I patted his arm, sharing in his excitement. "What are we making?"

"I don't know what to call them," he turned his grin back on me. "We'll put the berries in with some honey, mix eggs and cream for a base, and bake it into a bread crust. I've never actually made them, but the traders talk of them in Paris, and I'm dying to try one myself."

I was shocked to hear they traded as far as Paris, but Domari had spent ten years in Constantinople. We entered the quiet longhouse and tiptoed past a reclining Erik, still asleep on his platform. Astrid and Frida were nowhere to be seen, though. A large table was covered in ingredients—berries, honey, cream, flour, and more I didn't recognize near the hearth.

"Have you gone on many trading expeditions yet?" I asked him as we mixed ingredients.

"Not yet," he glanced around his father's longhouse before going on. "My father is… not well. Hasn't been for a while. When it should have been time for me to accompany Gunnar on expeditions, he asked me to remain here. I was to watch over our village if something happened while he was gone."

I could understand Gunnar's reasoning, but I could see its weight on Magnus's shoulders.

"Do you have raids here often?" I asked, curious about what went into the responsibility placed on Magnus's shoulders.

"Some," he shrugged. "Mostly at the end of the raiding season as men are returning. If it hasn't been a successful season, they raid closer to home." His face twisted into a frown, an expression I hated to see on him. "It's known how prosperous our village is, far and wide. With Erik's health failing, it's more of a risk. We're seen as weak."

I squinted my eyes, appraising him, before pinching his

flexed arm muscles as he whisked eggs. The pinch drew his attention, turning to me with a question in his eyes.

"You look pretty weak to me," I shrugged, returning to my task of mixing the berries in with honey. He shook with laughter as we continued to work in companionable silence.

We rolled the dough flat, folding it into a small pot. Magnus then layered it with the custard and berry mixtures before placing it in the hearth. He pulled himself up onto the table we'd been working on, sitting in the flour and sweets that coated the table. I started to mention it to him but decided to let it be; he'd been covered in flour multiple times when I'd seen him already.

Glancing around the longhouse, I took a moment to notice details of the large structure. It was made of rough timber but still seemed lived-in and homey. A broom leaned against the wall, explaining how the packed dirt floors stayed neat.

The tables from the feast were gone, and the platforms had returned to their use as beds built into the walls. I was surprised by the number of beds I counted — enough for a large family and visitors to share this welcoming and warm space.

Behind us, shelves were built into the rear wall. Food stores took up the entirety of the area, enough to provide for much more than the residents of this house. My gaze wandered back to Magnus, who was staring at me quizzically.

I sighed, knowing what was coming next.

"Are you going to stay?" he finally asked.

I paused, unsure how to answer. I wanted to stay,

which surprised me a little. But I couldn't leave my family and friends behind with no answers. And what about Thor?

"I don't think I can," I answered honestly. "But I have no idea how to get home."

He cocked his head, pausing before answering. "And where is home?"

I puffed my cheeks, trying to think through this. I couldn't decide how honest to be. Magnus had been by far the most easygoing, no questions asked about all of my eccentricities and odd inquiries.

"Magnus," I hesitated as my decision settled over me. "I don't know how to explain any of this," I paused again, "but I think I've time-traveled."

His eyes went wide as he stared at me before reaching for a nearby horn of ale. I watched his throat work as he took a long gulp. He passed it to me, and I did the same before saying anything else.

"When are you from?" he asked. *When*, not where. He was going right along with it, and my heart fluttered at the easy support he offered me.

"I was born in 1990," I began. "I'm from Denver, Colorado, which hasn't even been discovered yet. Right now, it's probably home to natives and no one else. It's not on any of your maps and won't be for centuries."

He took another large swig of ale, turning his face from mine as he stared off into nothing.

"Why do you think the Norns brought you here?" he asked, still taking it in stride.

"The Norns?"

He turned to me. "That's the only way I can think of that this would happen. Fate must be involved."

My mind couldn't follow his train of thought. "Who are the Norns?"

"Three sisters, Urd, Verandi, and Skuld. Past, Present, and Future. They weave the fates of mortals and gods alike, leading us towards our destiny."

His words sank in as my mind reeled. I thought back on the museum in Stockholm, the image of the three women bent over their runes sticking in my mind.

"The Norns were highly revered in Norse mythology, set to have spun the fates of mortals and gods alike…"

But none of this made sense. I'd thought they were myths?

"Why would they choose me?" I questioned, trying to comprehend this, sorting out what I believed and didn't.

"I don't know," he shrugged and dropped the subject. He hopped down, pulling the desserts from the hearth and placing them on the table. Steam rose off the pan, sending a delicious aroma through the air in whisps. His eyes were bright with excitement as he turned to me. "Let's go find our girls."

We left the longhouse, Magnus juggling the hot custard. Signe and Astrid sat nearby playing with the twins. Gunnar stood watch over his family, and Domari was never far from his side.

As we grew closer, Signe stood up, looking in our direction. I avoided eye contact with Domari as a blush crept up my face remembering how I'd left him this morning.

"What is that smell?" Signe asked, standing on her toes

to peer into the pot Magnus carried. "The cooking contest was yesterday."

Astrid's eyes lit as she inhaled the sweet scent of lingonberries wafting off our creation.

"Well," I decided on honesty, "where I'm from, we recognize birthdays. They're my favorite thing to celebrate."

Everyone's eyes shifted to me. Until this point, I hadn't realized how little I'd talked about my home and what memories had returned to me. I cleared my throat as nerves settled over me under everyone's watchful eyes.

"When I heard you were born during Winter Nights, Signe, I knew we needed to honor it." My gaze turned to my friend. Her eyes sparkled with unshed tears as she looked back and forth between the custard and me.

"You did this… for me?" her voice quaked, her heart in her throat.

"I had some help," I elbowed Magnus, who exaggerated the hit.

"We have lots to celebrate," a deep voice said behind us as Erik joined our party. All eyes turned to him. "New babies, new friends, and a birthday, it seems."

Gunnar grabbed a nearby stool and dragged it towards our gathered group, helping his frail father to sit. Frida joined us, standing at her husband's side, as the family passed the custard, sampling our creation.

Magnus grinned at me, blinding in the morning sun, happy to be surrounded by those he loved. It was hard not to feel the warmth radiating off these people, even with the fall chill in the air.

❋

Shortly after, villagers wandered into the area, breaking up the sweet family moment. The games were set to begin again soon.

"What's up next for today?"

"Ax throwing is the last of the land sports," Gunnar answered, "and then we finish at the water." Exhilaration shone on his face as he mentioned it, eyeing his wife.

"Are any of you competing again?"

"We all are," Magnus answered with his signature, smug grin. "I'm looking forward to beating you both this morning. Though, I'm sure Domari has already been beaten once this morning since—"

"Enough, *Knut*," Domari cut him off. Magnus chuckled at his joke, and my cheeks flamed at his insinuation.

"Men," Signe scoffed. She grabbed Astrid and me by the arms and dragged us to where the event would occur. "All they can think about is their dangly bits between their legs and when they'll get to use it next. They think it's their finest asset." She turned a devious smirk on us as we walked. "But we can never tell them that it's their backsides I admire most," she laughed. "I'd be happy to stand behind those men all day as they throw axes pointlessly at trees that don't deserve it."

Her smirk had me shaking with laughter. The thought of leering at these men was just fine in my book as well. All of them were shirtless, and there were so many muscles on display that it was hard to focus.

Targets were painted onto the trees, and the starting

points were staggered to measure an equal distance. Twelve contestants took their marks, our three in the group's center. Erik perched in his chair to the left of the field of gathered villagers, watchful as ever, as he waved his hand to begin.

I watched as the contestants stepped up to their mark, gripping their axes low at the base. Despite the crowd gathered around us, my eyes zeroed in on Domari, watching intently. He lined his right foot up with the target, holding the ax far more gently than I would have assumed, and brought it up to his shoulder. His entire body flexed, poised, as he took a moment to aim. On an exhale, his balance shifted, arm releasing the ax. It cut through the air, spinning end over end, until it landed with a smack in the center of the bullseye.

I erupted with a shout before I could stop myself, and he grinned at my reaction.

Seven of the twelve contestants, all men now, hit the targets and advanced. They each walked to retrieve their axes from the tree, prying them loose in a way that rippled muscles down their backs and into their legs.

I may have drooled a little. Signe let out a soft moan that had me chuckling again.

The men returned to their starting positions and took another seven steps back, waiting for Erik's direction. He nodded, and it began again.

The delicacy and precision that went into something so ruthless was an odd marriage, but I could not pry my eyes away from the sight. Signe elbowed me, smirking, "I told you so."

The competition progressed, our three men advancing

twice more until only four remained. Standing twenty-one paces behind where they started, the four men paused and threw one at a time.

Magnus was first launching his ax with a speed I could hardly comprehend. The metal and wood whirred as it sailed through the air but dipped right at the end, landing just below the target. He swore to himself in frustration but let it go when his eyes reached Astrid waiting for him.

Domari was next, followed by the auburn-haired man I didn't recognize. Each time, the blade was a blur as it soared towards the tree but landed just outside the target.

I held my breath as Gunnar stepped to the line, the last to throw. Signe gripped my hand tightly in anticipation. Breathing deeply, Gunnar took his time as he aimed, adjusting his footing and shoulder several times. Finally, he brought the ax back, touching the tip of his shoulder. He stood there for a moment more, and I didn't dare blink, afraid I'd miss it. Muscles rippled under the skin as he launched the ax, releasing the handle with a resounding roar. Time seemed to slow as we all focused on the tree, waiting to see where it would land. A thundering crack rent the air as the tree groaned, and the hit landed so deep the tree began to tilt, right along the bullseye.

The crowd whooped — their future chieftain a victor in this sport. I bounced on my feet, excitement spilling out of me as I clapped with the villagers.

Gunnar spun, beaming, but his reaction was far more humble than most I'd seen. He bowed to his father and turned to scoop his children up, kissing his wife and walking off the field towards the river's edge.

Domari grabbed my hand in an easy grip as we trailed Gunnar. Kissing noises followed us, Magnus a few steps behind, taunting Domari, as always.

"I left an annoying baby behind and returned to find that he was left to choose between advancing either his mind or body. Not both," Domari mumbled, glancing over his shoulder at Magnus.

Grinning as per usual, Magnus flexed his bicep. "We have you here to overthink enough for all of us," he threw the insult back at Domari.

Gunnar said nothing, only shook his head.

Boats lined the shores, rowers posed in each, ready to push off.

At my confused expression, Domari leaned down to me. "They will row out to the center of the river, and contestants will leap from one moving boat to another. To win, you have to make it to the opposite shore. Dry."

This was the event that Gunnar and Signe raced against each other, then. My eyes scanned the beach, watching as mostly younger contestants gathered on the shore. Several women lined up among the men, all stretching.

"Most years, no one makes it all the way across," Domari whispered, his arms laced around me to pin my back against him. Sure, it made it easier for him to whisper these explanations to me, but the hold felt more possessive than that.

The river was wide, seven boats fitting easily across, with several feet of water separating them. My eyes landed on Signe as a whole new appreciation for the woman's strength settled over me. Not only had she competed in this event, but she'd *won* it.

The crowd gathered here was the largest I'd seen so far. I scanned the contestants but only recognized Arne with his twin at his side again. While the black paint of yesterday's sword fight was gone, the girl looked no less intimidating. Her eyes scanned the water, calculating even already.

"My bet is on Bodil," Domari whispered again, following my line of sight. His whiskers brushed my cheek, tickling in a way I could get used to.

My heart lurched, aching at the thought of eventually leaving this man whenever I figured out how to return to my time. How had so much changed in so little time? His arms around me felt so natural, fated, destined to be. I pulled them around me, leaning into his tall frame, determined to make the most of what time I did have. His chin rested on me, standing in an easy embrace as the competition began.

Everything happened so fast. Twelve boats rowed at different speeds, both against the current and with it, as contestants picked their way across the river.

My eyes scanned the boats. Depending on each contestant's path, it would take at least seven jumps to cross. Splashes came every so often as, one by one, contestants were eliminated. Groans passed through the crowd as we watched them swim back to shore in the frigid water.

Arne and Bodil worked in tandem, not together but never out of sight. I watched keenly as they each inched their way across. Adrenaline pumped through my body as my eyes zeroed in on the girl.

Intensity was evident in her every move. She crouched low in the second to last boat standing between her and the shore, calculating her next move. It was a long jump she had remaining, but no one else had made it yet.

Her petite frame rocked back and forth, pushing the boat's momentum to her advantage. She soared through the air, feet skimming the water's surface as she made it to the last ship before the shore.

Arne had stopped, waiting for the right opportunity to follow her, and found it at the last moment. Their eyes connected for a split second as they made the final jump in tandem. I gasped as they rolled onto the shore and screamed in shared victory. The entire crowd erupted, thrilled to see such an exciting and one-of-a-kind finish.

"This has been sensational," I sighed, thinking not only of the games but of my entire time here. My smile of only a moment before faltered as reality crashed down on me. Admitting everything to Magnus this morning had reminded me of everything I had to return to. I had to go home, however that would be possible.

"Wait until tonight," Domari squeezed me tighter as if he could feel my melancholy thoughts. "The final feast is always the best."

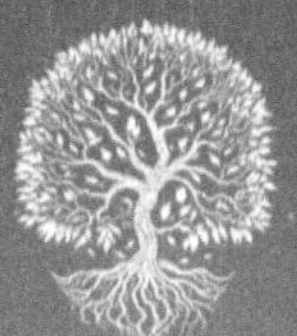

Several events took place on the water's edge, but none as riveting as Arne and Bodil's photo-finish.

Later that day, I followed Signe as she led me to where tables were set up near the platform. Erik was climbing the stairs there, taking his seat. As we milled about the area, villagers brought out trays of food, and barrels of ale were readily available. The sound of the events died down as more people moved towards the smell of the food.

Musicians took the stage carrying a drum, lyre, and what looked like a flute carved from a bone. The drummer began to beat a steady rhythm, resembling oars slicing through the water.

I was delighted to see Björn take the stage shortly after. His voice was sonorous as he crooned a haunting battle of war, victory, and grief at those lost. The crowd hushed, listening to the full notes of his music, luring the stragglers into joining around the tables.

The song ended, crowd silent, as Björn bowed low to

Erik. Applause didn't seem appropriate as tears gathered in the eyes of many of the onlookers, emotions high as the song lingered in the air. Erik stood shakily, bringing his friend into a tight embrace. Genuine happiness spread through me as the two old friends hugged on stage.

The sky faded to a slumbering amber in the setting sun as the musicians played a livelier tune, and a young woman I didn't recognize took the stage next. It went on like this for several songs, each different and mesmerizing.

Men and women alike rose to take turns, reciting poems and skits as the stars appeared and twinkled overhead. A tipsy Magnus gave a performance mooning over his pregnant wife's 'billowing bosom' that the men would never let him forget.

Music continued as the night grew dark. Several fires were lit, drawing people into smaller huddles. Signe pulled at my arm as she drew me into a circle near the stage, swaying with the beat of the drums. Gunnar stood behind her, hands on her hips as he moved with his woman.

It warmed my heart to see the two together, so in love. His calm presence was the perfect balance to her fiery, meddling, and demanding nature. Gunnar was a good man, and the two together would be wonderful leaders to these people when the time came.

I was lost in my thoughts when Domari slipped in behind me, placing a kiss on my shoulder. A smile spread across my face, heartwarming in his presence.

It was shocking how quickly my feelings towards this man changed, becoming something I'd never felt before.

The only thing holding me back was the unknowns that lurked just around the corner.

But those were worries for another time.

I pulled his arms around me and swayed to the music, content at the moment. One song gave way to another, and the evening passed joyfully.

"I'll go get us some drinks," Domari whispered after a while. I nodded, already missing the warmth at my back.

Suddenly, the wind shifted, and a shiver went up my spine. Villagers around me stopped, scanning the area for what had caused the disturbance.

Another gust came, sending the skirt of my dress up into the air. I slapped my hands down, holding the sapphire gown in place. Still, it came.

The wind seemed to herd me towards the stage as I fought to keep my balance. Several eyes tracked my movement as the fire's glowing embers caught and grew into dancing flames. Just as quickly, they almost flickered out as the music stopped, the silence only broken by the audience's collective gasp.

I brushed my windblown curls out of my face, seeking out the source of the crowd's reaction as three hooded figures approached. Even the wind seemed to pause to listen, the world silent as the three figures proceeded through the area. Everyone shuffled silently out of their way, but my feet moved *towards* them, magnetized. Mesmerized.

Who were they?

The trio ascended the stairs, cloaked in shadows and dark velvet hoods. Murmurs broke out around me, but nothing I could comprehend. My attention was gripped on the figures in front of me.

The dull fires did nothing to illuminate who these newcomers were. Inexplicably, they felt... familiar. How that could be possible in a world, in a time where everyone was a stranger to me, I didn't understand.

Promised, something whispered inside me. I rubbed at my chest as the trio all looked to their right, over the forest in the distance.

A cry rent the air, loud and terrifying, and screams of terror broke out across the yard. I followed their gaze but saw nothing of interest.

"*Quiet!*" Erik's voice boomed from the stage behind the figures, and the voices faded back to murmurs. The energy he spent on that one command seemed to drain him as he whispered, "Let them speak."

My feet moved of their own volition towards the stage, drawn to these three, still silent — waiting.

I glanced down as a hand slipped into mine, soft and warm. My eyes trailed up her arm to find Yrsa at my side, nodding with a sad smile. She squeezed my hand, comforting me in this strange moment, as I gazed back up at the stage.

The three stood, legs apart, arms outstretched, heads tilted back, but their cobalt cloaks still obscured their faces. Chanting began, and I watched with rapt attention.

After a heartbeat, silence washed back over the crowd. No one moved as we waited with anticipation.

"We have come with a warning," the raspy voice of an older woman came from the smallest of the trio. Murmurs broke out around me, and Erik raised his hand to silence them once again. "The tapestry of fate is ever-changing. The Eriksson clan will see much change, for better and for worse."

"Heroes have returned home," a clearer voice rang out over the crowd from the middle woman as her gaze slid to the back of the group. "And just in time."

Domari came to my side then, the crowd parting around him as his hand slipped into mine. I glanced up at him, but his gaze was fixated on the mysterious trio.

"Your journey is only beginning," the tallest one said, her voice melodic, rising into the evening sky even as I felt her hidden gaze zero in on Domari. "You had to return home to be on the right course, but home is more than a place, isn't it? From the look of things," her gaze drifted to our joined hands, "you've remembered that home is a *feeling.* To be ready for what is to come, you must remember what you are to protect."

His thumb brushed across my skin as I pondered the words, confused. Before I could ask anything, they continued.

"This clan has founded itself on compassion, wisdom, and acceptance," the oldest woman said. "But as with everything good, greed and jealousy follow. Against the rules of time, we have stepped in to weave together the fates of those most vital to what is coming." With that, all three women's gazes swung to me.

"Shelbie," I gasped, baffled how these women — these strangers — would know my name. The tallest woman lowered her hood, and my blood ran cold.

Before me stood a breathtaking woman with long platinum hair and skin so pale she seemed to glow.

This was the same woman who had known my name while she panhandled on the street. Her eyes found mine, full of empathy.

"My dearest. We have waited for you for so long…" her voice hitched as she glanced off to her right towards the forest. A loud crack drew the crowd's attention, now stirring around me, but I was locked in place.

"Your story is one I cannot foresee," she went on, her brow scrunched in confusion. "You have so much in front of you, but danger follows you everywhere, the last of your kind."

The older woman's hand shot out, gnarled and spotted with age but glowing just the same. "Enough, sister."

Her other hand rose to her hood, pulling it back as long, braided white hair tumbled over her elbow.

My breath caught, unable to escape me as I took in the woman from the park.

"You've followed the path we laid for you," her eyes turned to the forest to her right and then to Domari, gripping my hand in support. "And now it is time to return."

"But… how?" the words spilled out of me as Yrsa rubbed my hand. "How did I even get here? How is any of this possible?"

The middle woman's hood fell back, and the hands gripping mine were the only thing that kept me on my feet as I gazed upon the vendor who sold me my bracelet in town.

"I told you I'd find you," her eyes sparkled as she winked.

"I don't understand…" My mind was racing, trying to piece together so many things that didn't add up. "Why did you bring me here?"

"There are many strands at play. Your presence, Shelbie, is one we cannot understand. We set out to fix it, but you have changed this world, these people," her eyes turned sad as she looked at Domari and then me. "And you have much change still in front of you. However, the rules of time bend for no one. Your presence has—"

"We *cannot* say more," the oldest sister scolded. "There are too many unknowns. Too many dangers, sisters. We cannot say more."

Her gaze swung back to me, but screams rang out before she could go on. The wind whipped around me in a frenzy, blowing my hair as the ground shook. The sound of trees groaning in the distance mingled with footsteps stampeding away from the clearing, ringing in my ears.

I dropped Yrsa's grip to pull my curls from my face and saw it was only Erik's family left in the clearing. Gunnar and Magnus stood together whispering, alert, as their gazes tracked out over the treetops. Signe gathered the twins around her legs while Astrid gripped her arm tightly with a terrified expression plastered on her face.

"To send you back to your time," the middle sister said, and Signe gasped, "you must travel to the Sacred Tree. Danger lurks everywhere here, old enemies resurfacing and warring once again."

"So it's true…," Signe whispered, and I turned my

attention from the strange women in front of me to my friend at my side.

My heart lurched at the look on her face, and Magnus watched me close behind her. His smile was bittersweet, understanding dawning.

"*What's* true?" Domari questioned, drawing my eyes up to his handsome face.

Tears gathered, but I fought them back, cold resolution seeping into my veins. It was too good to be true — all of it — and my time was up.

"I'm not from here," I sighed, swiping at the single tear that escaped. "I'm not from *now.*"

I glanced up at the women on the stage, and they quietly nodded, urging me on. A loud exhale escaped me as I dipped my chin.

"I don't understand how…," I mumbled, fighting for the right words, "but I'm from the far future. I was born almost a thousand years from now."

His eyes searched mine, thinking through our many strange conversations, and I could do nothing. A loud *crack* rent the air, but nothing else mattered to me at that moment. Heck, it could have been the sound of my heart breaking, but several eyes shot back to the forest once more.

"You must go," the youngest sister interrupted urgently. "Leave tomorrow, and ride to the Sacred Tree. There, under the lights in the night, you'll find your fate."

We were all speechless as words couldn't seem to do everything that had just happened justice. So much had been revealed, and so many new questions had surfaced.

Erik broke the silence after a moment. "Thank you." After everything that transpired, that seemed a strange response, but he went on, "for returning my family to me. For weaving our fates. For warning us of what is to come."

"Anything for an old friend," the oldest woman said as she patted Erik's arm. "Your fate has been one of my favorites to watch. I am sad to see it end."

Erik's eyes lit with understanding as I watched their interaction closely. "Death is but a new beginning," he nodded, and my heart sank at his words. "I am forever in your debt, Urd."

Several of them exchanged looks at Erik's words, but I was tired of these revelations.

"Verandi. Skuld. It is always a pleasure," Erik bowed his head. "I will see you again in Hel."

In return, the three women bowed low. As one, they pulled their hoods back over their hair, joined hands, and disappeared in a cloud of smoke.

Everything seemed to fade away as my head spun, struggling to understand everything that had just happened. I was moving before I knew it, Domari pulling me towards Gunnar's longhouse.

Behind me, Erik called for Gunnar. I glanced back to see the younger son helping his frail father from the stage and back to his own house. Magnus followed closely behind his father and brother; their wives steps behind.

Domari led me past the house and towards the mostly finished barn. It was still empty as the animals slept in the pastures in the warmth of the evening. The women's words settled in as we entered, and sobs racked my body.

Domari pulled me into a hug, my tears soaking his shirt as my hands fisted in the fabric. He let me cry, stroking my hair patiently and waiting until my tears turned to gasping breaths.

"Who were those women?" I managed to choke out.

He sighed before answering. "The Norns, if what Erik said is to be believed." A long pause followed his words before he continued. "From your reaction, they visited you prior to this as well, but we'll get to that in a moment. First, I need you to explain what you mean when you say you're from the future."

I squinted my eyes shut, hating this conversation already. "I was born in the year 1990. I don't know how, exactly, but somehow when I fell — when you found me — I time-traveled to you."

Neither of us said anything for several moments, Domari still holding me against his now tear-soaked shirt. I pulled away enough to look up at him, finding his eyes searching mine.

"I didn't know how to tell you once I figured it out," but words failed to explain the gut-wrenching feelings racking my body. "And then so much had changed, I didn't know if I wanted to go home."

"Then stay," he whispered the words barely above a breath. "Don't go back."

I sighed, leaning my head against his chest, wishing that were indeed an option.

"You heard what they said. I have to leave," I choked, "and I have my own family I need to see. I can't leave them without any answers about what happened to me."

"The Norns are not an end-all, no matter how much they love to meddle in our lives," he replied, stroking my curls again. "They said I needed to return, to remember what home was, and Shelbie… you are part of that home. *My* home."

I squeezed my eyes shut as my heart pounded in my chest. How was it possible that I'd gone my whole life without feeling much of anything for a man, yet, here, now, in a matter of days, my heart began to sing?

And now I had to let him go?

It was beyond unfair, and my heart was breaking.

"But, Domari," my voice shook, "it's not just about us.

No matter how much I want to stay, to see where this goes… I can't."

We stood in silence, both of us feeling the truth in my words no matter how they hurt.

"Then I'll come with you," he whispered. "I'll follow you."

I gasped, my chest torn in two. "You can't. How can you? They need you here. You heard their words. Erik is dying, and soon from the sounds of it. Gunnar needs you. You can't leave him."

"I can't leave you either," he growled.

I was overflowing with emotion, heart racing, ears pounding. This was an impossible situation.

"Why?" I screamed, banging my fists on his chest.

Why did I have to come here and live this life that so vividly highlighted everything I was missing? Why did I have to meet this man, open my heart, and then leave him behind? Why did I have to leave a place that finally felt right — felt like home?

But no one answered.

There were no answers.

Domari's hand rested on the back of my head, providing the only comfort he could give to either one of us.

"We'll go together," his tone was final, "to the tree. We'll go together, and I'll steal as much of you as fate and time will allow."

My lashes lifted, vision fogged from the last of my tears, and I was startled by the fire in his eyes — the passion in his voice.

Before I could even catch my breath, his mouth

descended on mine, seizing my lips fiercely. My fingers fisted in his shirt for balance as hands slid to my waist, pulling me up into him. I arched my back, unable to stand even an inch remaining between us.

My heart pounded, pulsing in my head and lower as he kissed me with a passion I'd never felt before. I melted into him, taking everything he gave with greedy delight.

After several moments, he pulled back a fraction, and I gasped for air. He turned his head to scan the barn. I followed his gaze to a rack of furs neatly stacked for storage. Seizing my hand, he pulled me towards the back wall, only letting go of me long enough to grab a large pelt and lay it across the freshly swept dirt floor. I watched him carefully, his muscles flexing as he flicked the fur to straighten it. The care he took with the motion only fanned the flames of the fire in my veins.

He turned to me then, staring wordlessly as he removed his boots, then loosened his shirt, but stopped there. Heat settled low in my belly as I watched his every move, his gaze never leaving my face — an invitation but not a demand.

Any hesitation I might have felt left me as I stepped towards where he waited, hand outstretched. I followed his lead, removing my boots before stepping onto the fur with him. He pulled me into his body with a sly grin, leaning down to kiss me again. It was slow and languid this time, savoring as his hands roamed my back.

"I can't share you with the rest of the house tonight," he whispered with his lips against mine. I pulled back only enough to search his gaze, and my heart surged at the vulnerability there. I nodded, leaning up to kiss him again, and ran my palms under his shirt, across his chest.

Domari moaned against my mouth as my fingers grazed across his hot skin. His hands bunched my dress, gripping me tightly until I lifted my hands in the air. He pulled it over my head, and his shirt followed, a growing pile of discarded clothes on the floor.

No matter how many times I'd seen his bare chest, I couldn't help but be enthralled. I brushed over his skin lightly, feeling across the many scars running through the coarse hair on his chest. I traced the edge of the large shield tattooed across his hip, and his breath hitched as my fingers skimmed his waistband where the shield dipped below.

He grasped my wrist lightly, and I glanced up through my lashes, meeting his heated gaze. His breaths grew heavier as he fought hard to keep his control, and it sent molten heat through my veins. Seeing the power I had over this fierce man sent a ripple of confidence through me. Domari's hands reached towards my bra, and I helped him remove it, tossing it onto the pile as well.

"Perfect," he said, eyeing me, mostly naked now standing in front of him. He pulled me towards him, lips finding mine again as our bare skin touched, sizzling between us. His weight shifted, pushing lightly on me, urging me down onto the furs. My back hit the soft fabric, tickling across my sensitive skin as Domari's forearms landed on either side of my head, caging me in. My head tipped back as his lips trailed over my neck, collarbone, and lower.

"I've wanted to do this for days," he drew out the moment. "The peek I got in the hot springs wasn't nearly enough." He stopped talking as his hands and mouth went to work worshiping my body, kissing, licking, nipping — exploring every inch of skin I offered.

My hands tangled in his hair, loving the contrast of his soft kisses and rough beard scraping their way across my skin. My body writhed, shifting my hips below him, signaling for more. He kissed along my hip bone, running his hands across my waist, tongue leaving a wet trail across my skin.

I could hardly breathe with how slow he was moving, drawing out this sweet torture. My heart was racing as my blood pooled low in my abdomen, pulsing with my desperate desire to be touched.

His hands settled on my hips as he inched the fabric down, and my breathing hitched, waiting in eager anticipation. Every inch of skin he uncovered, his mouth was there to kiss. Lick. Savor.

I lifted my hips, helping him along, but he still took his time as his chest rumbled against my legs, chuckling at my distress. His tongue licked up the inside of my thighs, and I shifted my hips, begging for any friction.

His hands held me in place as he finally reached my apex. I gasped as his tongue licked up my center, tasting the wetness that was gathered there, waiting for him.

He moaned as he tasted me. I threw my head back, flooded with sensation, panting at the feel of him. My breath left me in short bursts, gripping his hair tightly in my hands, heart pounding. The feel of his beard scraping across my skin added to the friction.

But it wasn't enough.

Reaching down, I gripped his chin as he rose above me. I had never wanted anything as much as I wanted him at that moment. Tugging his face back to mine, I kissed him deeply, pouring everything I was feeling for him into it. Running my palms over his muscled torso, I found the waistband of his pants and set to work loosening the ties while Domari rolled to my left to give me better access. He lifted his hips as I got them undone, sliding them down and off.

Every inch of this man in front of me was perfect, from his now mussed brown hair, his chocolate eyes, down to his toes, but especially what my hands found in the middle. He groaned at my touch, closing his eyes, head falling back. My lips tipped up at how he reacted to me and needed more. Rising to my knees, I pushed him to his back and grazed my tongue up the column of his neck as I fisted him.

His hands reached up, yanking my face back to his. Heat pooled at my core. The feel of his rough hands across my skin, over my soft belly, and up to my breasts, palming their heavy weight, set my body on fire.

I broke our kiss, threw my leg over his hips, and settled my weight across his chest. Domari's chest rumbled again as my eyes found his, a feral grin on his face at my sudden surge of confidence. His fingers trailed down my back leisurely, but I had had enough with this teasing — I was ready to take what I needed most. I ducked my head down into his shoulder, eyes screwed shut, unable to comprehend what was happening — who was doing this to me. He gripped my chin, lifting it to his own as he settled along my entrance.

"Look at me," he said, drawing my eyes back open and onto his beautiful face.

I expected heat in his gaze, but what I found there was tender. Emotion brimmed in me, heart soaring as I paused. Before words found me, he thrust into me, stealing my breath as I was filled so completely. He steadied himself, waiting for my body to adjust. But I rose, running my hands across his chest, wiggling my hips in eagerness.

I moaned, and he chuckled. I pushed up, feeling the stretch as he slid through me, and lowered myself back down. His hands gripped my hips, helping me as our bodies found a rhythm easily, my hips working in time with his, until we were both left panting, on the cusp of release.

His leg twined around mine as my eyes shot open, suddenly flipped onto my back. Domari rose over me, hands running along my left leg, lifting it to his mouth and kissing along my calf as he thrust in me again.

I didn't recognize the sound of my own voice as I breathed his name. I was lost to sensation, never having felt this high before.

"That's it," he said as my body tightened around him, my pulse surging, ears ringing, limbs tightening. *"Ástin min."*

My body came undone at his words, quivering as I was hurled off a cliff. My shout of ecstasy had him following me over, body pulsing, as he dropped down on top of me, tangled together.

Our hearts pounded a speedy rhythm, coming down

from this high together, sticky skin touching everywhere. Eventually, he rolled us, pulling me into him. My head rested across his warm chest. His beard brushed across my shoulder in a kiss as I drifted off to sleep, warm and satisfied.

"I can't let you go," he whispered. "Not today."

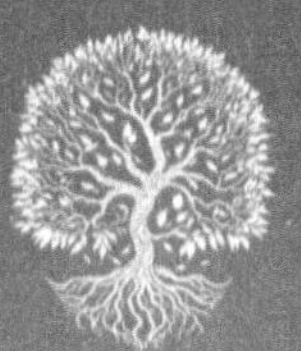

Our passion bled into the rest of the night, neither of us willing to voice that this could be our only chance. I woke to a rustle behind me the next morning, still groggy from a lack of sleep and body aching in all the right ways.

"Sleep," Domari whispered as I turned to see what he was doing. He kissed my forehead and stood, slipping on his pants and boots. I saw his chiseled bare chest for a moment more before he slid his shirt on and walked out of the barn.

I rested there for a moment longer, not ready to face the reality of everything that happened yesterday. Domari was speaking to someone outside, and when I fixed on the voice, I could tell it was Gunnar. Then, more voices joined.

Why was everyone gathered out here at the barn?

"Shelbie," Domari said as he walked towards me. "You need to get dressed."

I sat up, pulling on my clothes and boots quickly. "What's going on?"

Domari scrubbed a hand over his face, sighing loudly before answering. "Erik passed in the night."

I gasped, eyes wide as I stared up at him. The words of the Norns' visit yesterday echoed in my head.

"Is this because of me?" Guilt settled low in my stomach as I recalled their words. Had my presence here killed him?

"*No.*" Domari bent, kneeling at my side, gathering me into him. His hands ran over my tangled hair, soothing me when it was him who had just suffered a loss. "Don't even consider that. Erik has been sick for a long time. This has nothing to do with you."

I nodded, reassured by the words, but my heart still ached for everyone here who loved him.

"What do we do now?" I asked, eyes searching his.

He looked out the doors, then back at me, sighing, gathering himself. "Let's go talk to Gunnar before we make any decisions."

"I can't ask you to leave with me," and the words broke my heart. "I can't let you leave them when you're all mourning. And aren't Viking funerals a big deal?"

Domari rubbed at his face again before dropping his hand to his side. "Gunnar is in charge now," he said, nodding to himself. "He will decide."

I ran my fingers through my curls as we walked, knowing there was no hiding the evidence of last night but doing my best to tame my mane. Nervous energy filled me with every step. Mist rolled over the ground, painting an eerie picture in the early morning light. I heard voices as we rounded the house where several villagers had already gathered.

Signe spotted me and rushed to my side, throwing her arms around me. I pulled her into a tight embrace as sadness filled me for a man I hardly knew.

"I'm so sorry," I whispered into her hair, but the words felt inadequate.

"He was a good man," she sniffled.

The conversation turned to hushed whispers before us. Magnus, Gunnar, and Domari stood in a circle, and the expression Gunnar wore was more frustration than grief. Magnus's eyes brimmed with tears as he glanced at me with a sad smile. It was all I needed to see.

I needed to leave before my presence was blamed for the danger I'd brought to their door. Fear was a powerful emotion, especially when tangled with grief. So few of us had heard the Norns' final words, listening when Erik admitted he knew death was upon him.

What they had heard, though, was the warning about me. *"Danger follows you everywhere, the last of your kind..."* But what did that mean?

"I have to leave," I whispered to Signe, still hugging my friend.

"I know." She hugged me a little tighter, crushing her belly between us. "I didn't want it to end like this."

I was hollowed out at the thought of goodbye. There would be no coming back, no holiday visits, no birthday parties. This was it.

Tears pooled, but I was done crying, silently mourning

Erik's life and everything that would never be mine. Turning to hide my face, I forced the tears down, and I walked into Gunnar's home, straight to Domari's bed.

Pulling the sapphire and gold dress over my head, I quietly slipped out of the borrowed clothes and back into the ones I had arrived in. The polyester blend of my leggings scraped across my skin in an odd feeling after days spent in warm dresses. The swish of my down jacket seemed extraordinarily loud, the laces of my boots excessive. I grabbed what little else I had brought with me and headed towards the door, leaving no sign that I'd ever been here.

Magnus stopped me at the door, imposing as he took up the entire frame. "Do I not get a goodbye?"

A choked sound escaped me as I rushed into the big man's open arms. His hug was crushing but warm as he lifted me into the air.

"Thank you," I mumbled, pressed against his big chest. "For your fast friendship—your easy acceptance. It has meant more to me than you'll ever know. I'm sad I won't see you as a father, as I know how lucky that baby will be to be loved and protected by you."

He sniffed loudly before setting me down again. "Shine bright, Shelbie. Blind those who can't stand the light, but don't dull yourself for anyone." He leaned down, kissing the top of my head as his wet tears dripped down on me. "Goodbye, *eldr hjarta*."

I did my best not to run from that point, but my heart was splintering at a rate I couldn't stand. Domari stood with the horses, Gunnar and Björn at his side, deep in conversation.

Saddles were cinched, horses moving their feet in anticipation of a ride as I neared. The men turned to me as one, and Gunnar nodded.

"I am sorry it ends this way," his sad eyes settled on me, the weight of the day ahead of him resting on his shoulders.

"I understand," I attempted a smile, and my lip quivered, battling the emotions I tried to keep locked tight. "Thank you for everything."

The men continued discussing directions as I leaned onto Mjölnir.

"Yrsa packed you this," Björn said, approaching my side. He handed over a small bag. I opened it to see it was filled with tonics and other miscellaneous items. A heavy gold chain sat in the bottom of the bag and glowed in the dim light. My brow drew together in confusion as I looked back up at the big man.

"I can't take this," I pushed it towards him. "You have done plenty for me already, more than I can ever thank you for."

He shook his head, pushing the bag back into my chest. "She said you would know the right time for each item. I've learned after many moons not to question her."

His countenance was sad but genuine. I hugged him, unable to find the words to say how grateful I was for how he and his wife had cared for me.

"Thank you," I mumbled into his big chest, putting as much sincerity into my tone as I could.

Domari walked to my side, hands lingering on my waist for an extra moment before lifting me onto Mjölnir's back. He quickly mounted another horse next to me, taking the reins and spinning his horse to face the two men before him.

"Return to me this time, brother," Gunnar said fiercely. "I cannot lose you again, too."

Domari nodded but said nothing as he turned his horse around, Mjölnir following, and we rode off into the mist.

For most of the morning, we rode in silence as a numb feeling settled over me. The sun hid behind the low-hanging clouds fogging up the forest. It was cold, but the feeling spreading through me was frigid.

If I was going to make it through this, it seemed the only way. My mind ran in circles, reliving everything that had happened yesterday. Everything was too... much.

Domari motioned me to stop a little while later. I dismounted, stretched my legs and back, and bent down to touch my toes. As I stood, Domari walked towards me.

He stopped right in front of me, eyes searching mine, before pulling me into him. His arms laced around me, locking me tightly against his chest. After a moment, I reached up and returned the embrace, sighing into his strength. He leaned down, kissing me on the lips gently, before stepping away. No words passed between us, just a simple act to know he was right here with me, going through this with me, supporting me.

No more tears.

I chanted it to myself, but my eyes were too dry to muster any more. No matter what either of us wanted, whatever had started between us would end in two days. I had to go home, and so did he. Long-distance relationships were hard enough, but across time was impossible.

We watered and fed the horses while waiting for some of the fog to dissipate before beginning again.

"Tell me about your home," Domari said as he rode next to me, his voice startling as he broke the silence of the morning. "You've seen mine; tell me of yours."

I sat in silence for a minute, thinking of where to start.

"Well, I live in a large city in the mountains, not too different from here. They're called the Rocky Mountains because, apparently, no one could think of anything more clever." He smiled at my commentary, nodding for me to go on. "I grew up about two hours from there if you drive by car... which, I guess, is a whole topic we'll skip over for now. We still ride horses, but it's more for fun than a mode of transportation now."

His face turned to mine, skeptical but letting it go. "My mom and dad are wonderful, Janet and Steve. I have an older brother Jacob who is married to Lauren, and they have four kids — three girls and one boy. You'd love them; it's pure chaos." I laughed, thinking of my family fondly. "I should make more effort to be in their lives — I can see that now after watching you with yours. Family is important."

He nodded, agreeing with me at that. "Yes, it is."

"I have a best friend named Sabrina, and she's married with two little girls." I smiled at the thought of Sabrina, of what she'd think of the man riding next to me. "She is my polar opposite in about every way. We've been friends for the last sixteen years, and she is the best. She actually named her first daughter after me. Annie. My name is Shelbie Ann Smith."

My mood lifted, thinking of the wonderful people I would be returning home to.

"I love to ride horses and recently got back into it for fun after work," I went on. "I'm happy there, at the ranch. Partly because I love the horses and partly because the ranch owner is hysterical and makes me feel good about myself. Her name is Charlene, and words cannot describe her. I can't do her justice." I chuckled to myself for a minute, lost in my previous conversations with the woman.

"I'm going to ride more," I said to myself, adding it to my list of changes to make when I got home.

"But most importantly," I hesitated for a moment, unsure how to explain our bond, "is my dog, Thor. I'm obsessed with him, and he tolerates me at best." I smiled at my own commentary. "He's huge, black, and so furry. It gets everywhere. He's an elkhound mix. They're from around here, I think."

He nodded, confirming what I'd read. "Why did you name him Thor?"

"Honestly, I knew nothing of your culture. I knew that Thor had a famous hammer, and my Thor's tail is a weapon. He swings it with wild abandon, not a care in the world as to what he'll take out with it. Knees, drinks, small children — he doesn't care."

"Mjölnir," Domari said, and my brow wrinkled in

confusion. I looked down at his horse, trying to see what he was talking about. "Mjölnir is the name of Thor's hammer."

My eyes went wide, realizing that my beloved pet and his went together perfectly. "Well, that just figures." I was back to pouting over leaving the man next to me.

It had been a long time since I'd been in a meaningful relationship. I'd repeatedly been told I was "too much." To some extent, I understood.

I was highly independent. I had a demanding job that sucked away most of my free time. What free time I did have, I spent it with Thor or with my nose in a book. I wasn't interested in the bar scene and hadn't put myself out there much. I'd been waiting for fate to come and find me.

Be careful what you wish for, I thought far too late.

Saying all of the things my heart was yearning to would only make this worse, though. What difference did it make how I felt when I was with him, in his village, if I had to leave anyway?

"They all sound wonderful." He shot a bittersweet look at me, learning about people he would never meet, things he would never experience. My heart broke a little more with that thought. I was glad to know I had my people at home waiting to put me back together.

As the sun dipped, Domari found a small clearing in a copse of trees to make camp. He walked me through each step, explaining the poles and fabric used. Domari glanced at the sky before looking around the forest.

"Snow is coming, but not tonight," he thought aloud. "I'll make a fire so we can have a warm supper."

He went about the task quietly, preparing fish he had caught on one of our earlier stops and passing me bread and hard cheese he'd packed in his saddlebags. I pulled one of the packets out of my sack Yrsa had packed and brewed an herbal tea in the pot we'd brought along. We talked of nothing important the rest of the night, keeping our emotions in check.

As we settled into the tent later, he rolled me into his chest, leaning down to kiss me. I melted at the sweetness of it, savoring every moment. Clothes fell off much faster than yesterday, hands touching everywhere, exploring, memorizing the feel of each other. The heated passion of the night before still sizzled, but in an entirely different way. This was making love, and I could only look away to keep from crying.

"Not today," he said, echoing his words from the night before as I dozed off to sleep. "Not today."

24

The following day, breaking down the camp felt like an ending, another step towards returning home. My heart lurched as we saddled our horses and mounted for the day.

The fog from the day before had cleared, but the temperature had dropped significantly. Domari observed the clouds, reading the weather in a way I could not comprehend. The only thing I knew about the weather was how to check the forecast on my phone.

We filled our ride with idle chatter, Domari telling me of the many expeditions he'd gone on while serving in the Varangian Guard. My mind was boggled, listening to first-hand accounts of so many things that happened so far before my time — talk of Anglo-Saxons, Normans, popes, conquests — too much for my mind to wrap around.

The terrain rose as we passed by bogs starting to freeze, snow falling off of low-hanging branches from a previous storm. Trees surrounded us everywhere, making me lose any sense of direction I might have had. Later in the after-noon, clouds rolled in, and Domari scanned the sky.

"What do you think they meant?" I asked aloud, drawing his attention to me. "The Norns. What did they mean about me?"

"Which part?"

"Well, all of it. They said they'd been waiting for me for so long. But how can that be?"

"I don't know what it means, other than that fate had plans for you."

"She said I'm the last of my kind. *What* kind?"

A sudden breeze passed over us, sending a chill up my spine, and the horses became antsy.

"Easy, boy," I brushed my hands down Mjölnir's neck, soothing him. He hopped in place, snorting as he threw his mane. I caught a glimpse of Domari's horse doing the same, eyes wide, scanning for danger.

"What do you think is scaring them?" I asked Domari, still running my hands down Mjölnir's side.

"I'm not sure," he said in a whisper, stopping the horses for a moment. A whooshing sound flew overhead, sending the horses into a panic as I turned my face to the sky.

"What was that?" I asked Domari, panic rising in me.

"Stay in the trees," Domari's only answer.

We rode along for another hour, the horses settling but still uneasy. Our conversation seemed to falter, and I was completely fine with Domari's attention shifting to search for hidden predators lurking in the woods. Snow fell lightly, gathering on Mjölnir's black and white mane, dusting the trees and ground white.

The ground leveled out as we neared a clearing while Mjölnir snorted and tossed his head. Domari's horse began to stamp his feet, moving in place as Domari fought the animal for control.

A gust of wind sent the snow on the ground into the air, swirling, blocking our vision completely in a white-out. I inched out into the clearing, Domari behind me. Mjölnir let out a startled neigh, warning me right before he reared. A startled cry left my throat as I spun through the air and crashed to the ground in the center of the clearing.

I landed hard on my side, rolling out of the way to avoid being trampled by the panicked horse as he fled. Domari shouted my name as I rose to my knees, the snow settling around me.

A humongous black *thing* stood in the center of the snow, breathing hard.

"Don't move," Domari warned. I crouched low, eyes glancing up, wide in fright.

A cry filled the sky, shaking the trees as it echoed through the clouds. I squeezed my eyes shut, paralyzed in terror, as I attempted to sink into the ground.

The snow finally settled, and my vision cleared as I glanced up.

That was no *thing*.

That was a dragon.

.   .   .

My heart thundered in my chest at a breakneck pace, panic locking my every muscle in place. I battled between wanting to squeeze my eyes shut, flattening myself to the ground, and running for everything I was worth back to where Domari stood at the edge of the forest. I may have practiced hiking a lot lately, but under no circumstances did I think I could ever outrun a dragon.

Please be a dream. Please be a dream. Please be a dream.

The dragon reared its head into the air and let out a plume of fire that scorched the clouds. My hair was blown from my face, my eyes parched as the heatwave washed over me.

That felt pretty real. I don't think this is a dream.

My mind raced, trying to come up with any way I might survive this, and came up blank. I clutched my bag with a grip so tight that the seams groaned.

"Don't move," Domari repeated.

No shit, Sherlock.

Nostrils flared on the giant, black beast as I gazed into a mouth full of sharp, spiked teeth.

My, what big teeth you have.

A laugh stuttered out of me at the thought, my mind completely gone. The dragon stared in my direction at the sound, and our eyes locked. Green orbs with catlike pupils stared back at me, so immense even from a distance. Instinct took over, and my right hand went up, showing I had no weapons. Domari had all of those behind me, and one man against this gigantic dragon didn't seem like good odds, even as strong as Domari was.

"I come in peace," I said, rolling my eyes internally at my own line.

Really? That was the best I could do?

"We're not here to hurt you, only passing through."

Nice dragon, don't eat me. Please don't eat me.

The dragon huffed, smoke gathering at his nostrils as my heart continued to attempt to break free of my rib cage. I sorted through everything I'd ever read about dragons, which was all fiction, considering that I very much thought dragons were *not real* until that moment.

His heavy tail swished across the snow sending up a shower of white behind him, a stark contrast to his black and gold shiny scales. He thumped it hard, and the ground beneath my feet shook.

My mind suddenly jumped to Thor and his tail. The easiest way to calm Thor was treats. I racked my brain for anything I might have to bribe a creature twenty times my size not to eat me for an unsatisfying snack.

The necklace.

Dragons loved priceless items, right? I slowly reached into my bag with one hand raised still in the air. The dragon watched my movement, opening his mouth to let the smoke roll out as I stopped.

"I brought you something," I said to him, talking to dragons the same way I talk to dogs and horses. I was sane like that.

My hand scraped the bottom of the bag, searching until I felt the smooth, cold feel of the chain. I pulled my hand out, a large pendant taking up my palm, glittering in the snow. I spared only a moment to glance down at it, noticing the sizeable onyx stone set in the center with a golden dragon surrounding it. How Yrsa came to own such a necklace, I didn't know, but now was not the time to ponder such questions. Hand outstretched, I rose and somehow convinced my feet to take a step forward.

"It's shiny," I faked a smile, my body working overtime to keep pee from running down my leg in fright. "I bet you like shiny things. Dragons always love shiny things."

The dragon's eyes flicked down to my hand before rising back to mine.

"Would you like this necklace?" I asked the dragon, still over here, losing my mind. Black scales moved along his neck, revealing hints of gold underneath. "Look, it even has a dragon on it," I lifted it to show him. "You can have it. I brought it for you."

He raised his mouth, releasing fire over my head that had me ducking to save my curls. Any moisture in the air evaporated as my knees locked in place, unable to move. The fire died down, the heat still lingering in the air, as I looked up again.

"That wasn't very nice," I said, now plain brazen with this dragon. If I was about to die, I wasn't about to go down without a fight.

The dragon chuffed again loudly before lowering his front legs, belly on the ground. I kept my eyes on him as I squatted down and threw the necklace with everything I had. It landed a few feet in front of his face, and a large black wing dipped in gold swept over it, pulling the jewelry under his belly.

"See? We can be friends," I said with a nervous smile.

"It's a pretty necklace. I'm not here to take any of your treasures. I just need to go home."

The dragon glanced at Domari, weapons in both hands, before glancing back at me.

"He thought you were going to eat me," I sighed. "Can you blame him?"

The dragon made an odd purring sound I hadn't expected from a creature so enormous before laying his head down on the ground. Large spikes rose off his head in a crown, terrifying to behold. A part of me with a death wish wanted to continue forward and touch the dragon, to feel its black and gold scales beneath me.

"You're like Thor, aren't you? Scarier looking than you are."

"That's Hadriel," Domari finally said, sensing the worst was behind us. "He's not scarier looking than he is. The dragon before you, *The Dark One*, is the legendary scourge of these lands, and you bribed him to lay down for you."

I looked back at Domari, then at the dragon, before shrugging.

"I still think I'm right," I smiled at the dragon. "You're not so bad, are you, Hadriel? *Don't listen to the big, mean man,*" my voice turning into a baby-talk version I used on Thor. "He doesn't like anyone."

"You're challenging that statement with your every move lately," Domari said under his breath. I heard it, though, and my grin spread at his words.

I inched my way back, saying a silent prayer that my new dragon friend didn't change his mind on the whole wanting to devour me thing. As I came close to Domari, his hands wrapped around my arms, spinning me into him. His embrace was crushing, knocking the wind from me.

"I'm okay," I said finally. My heart was still pounding, a predator still behind me, but I did not end up as dinner. I called that a win in my book.

Domari's hands roamed my body, finally settling on my jaw as he pulled me in for a kiss. His forehead leaned into mine, still needing the contact as a gust of wind sent snow cascading around us like an eerie snow globe. Domari's eyes tracked the movement, up and over us, as Hadriel flew off.

"I cannot believe that happened," Domari sighed, still searching the skies for my new friend.

"Why didn't you tell me dragons were real?" I smacked his arm, insulted that no one had confirmed the existence of my favorite mythical character. "Do the trees talk too?" I glanced up excitedly, staring into the forest as I listened hard for creaks and rustles to make out words.

"Why... would trees talk?"

I sighed; dreams crushed a little that not every aspect of my favorite fantasy novels was real. "Never mind."

Domari went off searching for his horse, but Mjölnir had returned to his side like a well-trained mount after he fled. I stroked his mane, calming him as his panic eased. Hadriel must be gone.

My mind snagged on the contents of my bag, now wondering what else Yrsa had packed me and how else I may need it. The necklace came in pretty handy, that was for sure. Add me to the believers along with Signe — Yrsa was magic whether she admitted it or not.

A while later, Domari returned, horseless and frustrated. "We don't have much farther to go," he said, patting Mjölnir's neck. He glanced at the sky, darkening as clouds settled in, fluffy and full of snow. "There is a cave not too far from the tree. We'll head there for tonight, and tomorrow we can scope out how to best cross the water to the island. I would guess it's still another day before we see the lights."

A thought crossed my mind, and panic set in. "The Norns never told me how to get home, only to go to the tree. How am I getting home, Domari?"

Domari pulled me into his arms again, kissing my head, calming me as he had already done so many times since we met. "We've got time. We'll figure it out."

omari settled behind me on Mjölnir as we rode the rest of the day. His arm laced around my torso, his hand under my jacket, tracing small circles on my abdomen. The movement was reassuring, but his touch was maddening. My mind wandered to how those hands felt elsewhere. He leaned in, kissing my neck as if he could sense my train of thought.

The sky continued to darken as dusk neared but held steady, no snow falling yet. The clouds blocked out any trace of moonlight or stars, forcing us to find shelter soon.

The worn path we followed split; one pointed towards where the beginnings of blue showed — the river running into the lake surrounding the tree — and the other led into the hills. Domari pulled left on the reins, Mjölnir carrying us up the incline and towards a rocky cliff face above us. After a few minutes, Domari dismounted, and my skin instantly chilled at the loss of his body heat at my back. He lifted the reins over Mjölnir's head, leading him up the hill.

The horse's stout body seemed perfect for this terrain, low to the ground. I patted his neck, ever grateful for this horse.

Gazing out over the rising rock face, more blue showed in the last of the daylight as the lake came into view. There, in the center, rose a small island with a large tree, gnarled and barren of leaves. My heart sank at the view, nausea rolling through me. It was a glaring red exit sign, and I despaired at its sight.

We stopped at the entrance to a small cave, barely large enough for Mjölnir to join us. Domari made quick work of unpacking. Our tent was lost with the other runaway horse, but fortunately, our furs, blankets, and a cooking pot were still with Mjölnir.

Silence filled the cave, and I was at a loss for words for one of the first times in my life. Domari squatted, shrugging off his fur jacket as he began to arrange a small fire. His back and arms flexed with the work, and I couldn't help but stare.

He was so perfect. Even his forearms were stunning, laced with their tattooed bands. And not only was he a knockout, but he was so genuinely kind to me. I hadn't felt this way about a man in a long time. Maybe ever, if I was frank with myself.

Tears gathered in my eyes as I watched him, not ready to admit out loud the three words pounding inside my skull. What difference would it make? I had one more day.

Domari rose, the fire started, and turned back to me. My eyes found his as he cocked his head to the side. We stood there for a minute, a few feet apart, just staring. Memorizing. Remembering.

His gaze slid to the ceiling above him as he sighed and then pulled me into him. I wrapped my arms around his thick torso, fingers digging in for purchase, as I locked down the tears threatening to fall. This slow march to goodbye was killing me, and I didn't know how much longer I could take it.

After a moment, he let me go, walking me to the furs he'd laid out as he left the cave.

"I'm going to find our dinner," he nodded, grabbing his bow and arrow off Mjölnir's pack. "You stay here and keep warm."

I watched him retreat and then curled on my side, hands around my knees, as emotions flooded me.

Domari trudged through the woods as he watched the ominous clouds overhead, ready to unload their heavy burden.

He had to focus on something else. Something he was good at. His heart was breaking at the thought of losing Shelbie, and he could come up with no alternative to stop this.

He was falling in love with her; he knew it like he knew the constellations hiding in the clouds above. He'd known it from the moment she'd calmed his overwhelming guilt in the hot springs.

She was fierce, standing up for herself and what she

wanted, even in the face of a stranger.

She was loyal, immediately accepting, and helpful to all his people.

She was kind, generous with her time and emotions to all who needed it.

And she was beautiful. Watching her face down Hadriel today, her curly hair wild with the wind of his enormous wings, confidence pouring from her as she bribed the dragon, was an image that would be embedded in his mind until he crossed into Hel.

Legends were told of women in their culture who tamed the dragons, but he'd always dismissed it as a fable. To him, it felt more of a euphemism for calming the rage that flowed beneath the skin of every Viking he'd ever met. However, seeing her today made him question everything he'd ever known.

But it wasn't possible.

She wasn't Viking, and it was clear from her reaction that dragons no longer existed in her world.

"Danger follows you everywhere," the Norns had said to her. He chuckled at the thought. Danger had followed him his whole life, and he'd felt it the moment he'd seen her. *Hàski.*

However, she wasn't only dangerous to herself the way he'd initially used the term. She challenged everything he knew — all control he thought he had.

Domari wanted nothing more than to keep her forever, let her rule his world, listen to her talk until his ears bled, anything to be in her presence.

Shelbie glowed, illuminating the lives of those around

her, exuding warmth and happiness with every smile she gave.

He rubbed at his temples, bringing his focus back to his task, searching for dinner. A rustle in the bushes to his left drew his attention as a white hare, ready for the coming snow, hopped out of its burrow. Domari shot fast, the hare falling to its side where it stood. He leaned forward, grabbing it, as the seer's words in Constantinople returned to him.

"You have been running for too long. It's time to return home, as fate has written your destiny. A true warrior's heart is needed, and only you can answer the call. Go home, Domari."

The seer's glowing skin and blonde hair had stood out so vividly in Constantinople as he felt drawn to her that night in the tavern. She reminded him of home even before she uttered those words. Said his name.

Skuld. That's who the seer had been. *Future.*

Her words were the only thing locking Domari in place, not allowing him to trail Shelbie to wherever she was going. He would follow her to the ends of the earth, but the Norns had chosen them for a reason. He was needed here, for what purpose he didn't yet know, but he could not leave his people again — his family.

Domari stopped outside the cave, gathering himself before entering. This slow march to goodbye was killing him, and he didn't know how much longer he could take it.

❄

My mind was spinning; my body curled in on itself. I felt hopeless, forlorn, and all-over miserable. I needed a plan, to take action, to do *anything* to stop this pain from spreading through me.

I sat up, keeping my legs covered in the furs as I reached for my bag. I had two small pouches left and an odd brick-like green thing. I took it out, running my fingers over its slightly earthy feel before putting it back in the bag. I had no idea what to do with that yet, but I knew I should keep it close after how handy the necklace was.

The two small fabric bags sat in front of me on the blankets. I carefully untied them, bringing them to my face and sniffing.

The first smelled strongly of lavender, my eyes sagging at the scent.

The last was heavier, revealing not a tonic but a cracker-like bread, sealed and crisp. Good to know.

Footsteps outside drew my attention up. Domari stood at the cave entrance with a hare in hand and a heavy water skin. Our eyes locked for a moment, hesitating until he ducked to enter the cave.

The tension was palpable, both of us knowing this was coming to an end. There was so much left to say, and none of it helped at all.

We spoke of the weather, the horse, the dragon… anything but what mattered. After Domari roasted the hare, we ate, then cleaned up before reclining on the furs.

My chest ached, weighed down by all of my swirling thoughts.

This was awful; I couldn't bear it.

I stood after a minute, left the cave, and paced outside. Air escaped me; my breathing was entirely too shallow. My heartbeat was racing, pounding out a heavy rhythm.

I needed to leave. *Now.*

Domari would never allow that, so many unknowns still lying between me and that island. But I couldn't go on like this for another minute.

Cold resolution swept over me as I headed back inside and stooped to pick up my bag. Drawing out the pouches, I clutched them both in my hands, turned to the fire, and poured some water into our pot.

"Just making some tea to calm my nerves," I threw the words over my shoulder, unable to look at him as I dumped in the lavender pouch. I stirred, letting the aroma sweep over me, soothing me as my body relaxed. I knew why Yrsa had given me this one — it was to encourage deep sleep.

Removing the pot from the fire, I turned and set it on the ground, letting it cool.

"I made enough for both of us," I smiled at Domari, hoping my face didn't betray my plan.

He nodded, propped up, as I eventually rejoined him on the furs. I took a sip, so small that hardly any liquid passed my lips, before giving it to him. He took a large gulp, stopping to examine the contents.

"Yrsa sent it with me. It's delicious, isn't it?"

"Yes," Domari said, taking another sip before passing it to me. We passed it back and forth as I pretended to sip with him until the pot was empty.

I walked back to the fire, replaced the pot, and returned to Domari. He laid out on his back, arm out, as I curled into his side. His lips pushed against my forehead as I laid my hand across his chest, feeling his heartbeat under my palm.

"I wish there were another way," he whispered.

My heart collapsed at his words. "I know."

I fell asleep curled into his side, and a few hours passed before I jerked awake. Mjölnir stood at the cave's entrance, dozing, and the night was lightening behind him.

Domari's heartbeat was slow and relaxed from sleep and the tonic I'd given him. Rising to my knees, I nudged him to see if he'd wake. But he didn't move, still breathing deeply.

I leaned over him, tears in my eyes, as I kissed him on the lips.

"In another life, another time," a tear dropped off my cheek, landing on his, "you are all I'd ever want. All I've ever dreamed of."

I choked out the words, sobs threatening to rack my body, as I rose, grabbed my pack, and led a sleepy Mjölnir out of the cave.

26

I led Mjölnir by the reins down the hill as the sun attempted to rise. The clouds were thick, blocking all but the slightest light, as snow heavily dusted the ground. I glanced into the sky, trying to read anything as I'd seen Domari do so many times — it didn't look good; that's all I knew.

But I had to go.

I couldn't sit there, staring at everything I'd ever wanted and everything I'd never have for another moment.

My will turned to steel in my bones, and with every step, I channeled each ounce of strength I had into putting one foot in front of the other.

The world around me seemed to fade as my mind went to all of the powerful women in my life. Charlene's face came to mind, sparkly and vibrant with all of her sass and independence. My steps became a little surer.

No one could soothe my broken heart quite like my

mother, ready to hold me in my worst moments. Another step forward.

Sabrina's supportive, but no-nonsense attitude came next, willing to push me on when I was ready.

I might crumble again later but now was not the time. Now was the time to prove that I could make these women proud. I could stand on my own two feet, write my own story, and seize all that lay before me, no matter what dangers lay ahead.

"Your story is one I cannot foresee. You have so much in front of you. Danger follows you everywhere, the last of your kind…" The Norns' words rang in my ears.

I didn't understand what they meant by the last of my kind, but I did know why they couldn't see my story. I *did* have so much in front of me, and I would write my own fate: no more waiting, no more sitting back and watching what unfolds, no more sidelines of everyone else's stories.

I would return home and face whatever came with the strength of a Viking.

Trees passed as we descended, and I recognized where the paths crossed. With a final glance up the hill behind me — to everything I was leaving behind — I turned Mjölnir to the left and headed to the water's edge as the snow fell around me.

"We can do this, can't we, buddy?" I leaned into Mjölnir, hugging his chest, before reaching up and grabbing his mane. I shoved hard off the ground and climbed up, riding bareback through the woods.

I let Mjölnir pick his way through the rising snow, trusting his instincts more than my own. He skirted the trees, walking close to their trunks where the snow hadn't accumulated. I leaned into him to duck below the low branches and pulled my hood down over my head. Even with my face tucked into the neck of my jacket and my hands buried in my pockets, the wind was biting. The storm brewing around me matched the one in my heart.

We made slow time, but I had all day. The snow continued to fall, now in large sheets, as vision became obscured.

Suddenly, the sky lit up. A bright light flashed about me as a booming clap of thunder sounded. Startled by the sound, two ravens flew overhead as they fought to find another perch in the storm.

Mjölnir nickered, shaking his head and stomping his feet at the coming snow as I fought to keep my balance.

"Easy boy," I stroked his neck. "We'll stop."

He snorted, nodding his head at my words. The snow was coming down too hard for us to continue. Thunder clapped loudly again, and a split second later, the sky lit — the storm was close. My heart was racing, realizing how alone and unprepared I was for this.

I tried to calm my racing heart and mind, taking deep breaths. I turned, scanning the forest, looking for anywhere to provide even a little cover. Snow was falling so densely that it was hard to see, but I squinted into the white.

There, to our right, was a large copse of evergreens. It was farther into the woods, but the tightly clustered foliage seemed to be blocking the worst of the snow.

I hopped down, the snow piling well above my ankles now, as I pulled Mjölnir towards the measly shelter. We maneuvered under the trees as another clap of thunder sounded overhead, illuminating the bright white sky for a moment. I urged Mjölnir to lay down, as far under the boughs as possible. Sandwiching myself between him and the trees, I huddled against his big body for warmth.

I had no idea how much time had passed as the odd thunderstorm mingled with the blizzard around me. My hands mindlessly ran across the horse's shoulder, calming both him and me as we waited out the storm raging around us. My world had become an intense and terrifying snow globe, tilted end over end as the snow poured down around us.

Hands tucked as tight into my pockets as I could get them, I leaned forward across Mjölnir's warm back. My fur hood created a barrier to block out as much of the blowing snow as possible, with my face buried in his warm side. His steady heartbeat underneath me was lulling, calming my own until I finally dozed off, Mjölnir and I as snug as was achievable.

I woke sometime later with my face smashed into Mjölnir's body, warm and fuzzy with his winter coat. Snow covered the ground, piled halfway up Mjölnir's big back as he lay on the ground. A dry circle of earth surrounded me, the trees and this remarkable horse blocking me from the worst of the storm.

I grabbed my pack, pulling it open to munch on the

crackers left in there. They were delicious, seasoned with herbs, and perfect for this moment. I fed one to Mjölnir, more than worthy of my food after he sheltered me from the storm.

The sun peeked through the clouds now, lower in the sky than I would have anticipated. It was sunrise, I realized after a moment, and I gasped as I took in the implications of that. An entire day had passed since I left Domari in the cave.

My hands and feet were frozen despite the shared warmth of the big horse in front of me. I needed a fire, quickly, before frostbite set in. Glancing around, I stood and grabbed several branches that still laid relatively dry in the same thicket I'd sheltered in, looking for anything I thought I could even attempt to start a fire with. My mind snagged on that earthy brick in my pack. Could I light it?

One of the brighter ideas Sabrina had ever had was insisting I bring a lighter in my bag. Fortunately, I still had it. I grabbed the brick from Yrsa and all the branches I could gather and arranged them in a small pile. Squatting in front of the sad sight, I flicked my finger over the lighter and sent up a prayer.

Mjölnir rose, shaking snow from his coat, before stepping away. I handed him another cracker as smoke rose from the pile with a bright red glow. As a flame licked the top of the pile, I let out a loud whoop, thrilled that I'd done this on my own. I hopped to my feet, dancing around in a circle to an imaginary beat, celebrating my victory.

I squatted back down, rubbing my hands together over

the small fire as a hint of warmth spread through me. I could survive this.

My life at home needed lots of changes, but I could do it. If I'd learned anything from my time here, it was that life was meant for the living. I'd been letting it slip by me for too long, waiting on something unknown around the corner.

I fed every branch I could to the small fire, but it died out sometime later as the sun rose higher in the sky, dawn giving way to the morning. The snow glittered, a fresh blanket laid over the earth, sparkly and new.

My pack from Yrsa was now empty, so I folded it into my own small bag, and grabbed Mjölnir's mane, climbing on again. I smiled, remembering when I couldn't even do this much. I'd already come so far since I booked this trip — just a little more.

Mjölnir made his way through the deep snow, leaving tracks through the woods that would be easy to follow. I had no idea how far Mjölnir and I had made it yesterday before the storm set in, but I was sure that Domari was awake and moving now, too. Hopefully, the storm was enough to trap him in the cave yesterday, and I could outpace him as he'd be on foot in the snow. I couldn't endure repeating goodbye.

Water came into view, a river growing wider as we rode along its edge. Up ahead lay a shoreline.

I'd done it.

Voices to my right drew my attention, startled to hear others in the quiet of the morning so deep in the wilderness.

Men.

Several of them from the sound of it.

My heartbeat sped up, nervous about being alone out here. While I was acutely aware that the Vikings I had encountered so far were all honorable, moral men, I wasn't naive enough to think history had gotten it entirely wrong. The men could be violent and aggressive, loud, brash, and dominating.

"Danger follows you everywhere..." I didn't need the Norns' words clanging around in my head to add to my sense of panic — something about this situation felt ominous.

But Mjölnir and I would make too much noise retreating through the forest, and I needed to keep moving forward. Time was running out, and I still didn't know how to get home. I glanced around, but there was nowhere to hide both the horse and me.

I did my best to stand still and silent, rubbing my hands up and down Mjölnir's side as I sent out a silent plea for him to be quiet. But he snorted, and the voices stopped. Panic rose in me as the moments of silence went by, lingering, and I scanned the tall evergreens around me.

"Well, what have we here?" a gruff voice said from my left. My head whipped in his direction to find a man standing before me in knee-deep snow. Furs were draped across his ample chest, mingling with his enormous black beard. However, it wasn't his clothes or beard that drew my eye.

His head was clean-shaven, uncovered even in the storm, and showcased black tattoos covering his scalp and neck. Dragons, skulls, and weapons were mixed into so

many runes that I couldn't focus. On his neck was a knot —
one I'd recognize anywhere, as it was the same as Domari's.
This man was a terrifying Viking if I had ever seen one.

"What did you find, Raud?" a second voice came from
behind the man.

Raud.

My heart galloped at a breakneck pace, pounding out
of my chest as I remembered the hushed words I'd heard
passing his name around.

Slave-trader. Murderer. Rapist. *Barbarian.*

"A present from the Gods, that's what I found." A sneer
spread across his face as his eyes flicked over me, sucking on
his teeth.

"Hello, Mjölnir. I'd recognize you anywhere." His
glance went down to the horse below me as a sinking
feeling set in. "Where is Domari? And who is this delicious
creature on your back?"

My heart thundered in my chest as I stared at the man in
front of me. Even if I hadn't heard about him, everything
about this man screamed *bad*.

He sucked on his teeth again, the sound sending a
shiver down my spine as I observed him. His eyes traveled
over Mjölnir and up my legs, entirely too slowly, until he
reached my face. Studying.

"Please tell me you stole his horse," he said after a
minute as his sneer spread to a smirk. "What a fitting story

it would be if you did," he laughed to himself, but the punchline was lost on me.

His hand reached forward faster than I could track as he ripped the reins from my hands. Mjölnir started at the motion, retreating as his feet shuffled in the snow. I gripped with my legs and wound my fingers tightly in his mane, preparing for him to rear. Raud's hand came up gently, stroking Mjölnir's face as he whispered something to the horse I couldn't make out, and my mount immediately calmed underneath me.

No! I thought to myself. *Kick him in the face! Send me flying, but don't give in to this man!*

Raud glanced around in a circle, searching the ground, before looking back at me. "I see no signs of Domari with you. Or anyone, for that matter." His eyes crinkled in delight as a shiver racked my body.

"I'd heard he returned after all these years," he stroked Mjölnir's big face, and the betraying horse allowed him to.

"Tell me, how is Gunnar? Settling into leadership well?" His head tilted at his words. I was shocked he'd already heard of Erik's passing, as it had been only days ago. This man was tracking their clan closely, and apprehension ran through me at what he might do.

"I hope so, as victory will be that much sweeter when I steal it all. Maybe I'll even murder his wife in front of him. And she's carrying a baby, isn't she? It'd only be fair."

I reared at his words, how casually he spoke of murdering a pregnant woman. My mind reeled as I thought through everything I knew about this man.

Hadn't Domari said Raud had been in love with Tove? But Gunnar hadn't killed his sister…

But that's not what mattered here. The thought of any harm coming to Signe turned my backbone to steel. Under no circumstances would I be willing to let anything happen to that woman. Or any of them.

My thoughts raced for any actions I could take as Raud pulled me towards the shore on Mjölnir's back. Nine more men waited on the beach, each more terrifying than the next. My heart raced as we stopped. Raud ripped me from the horse, dragging me to the ground. I stood on shaky feet, eyes scanning.

Two large rowboats waited on the shore as the men stood near them. Several fresh kills lay around the beach, horses tied to the trees on the far side.

Raud followed my line of sight as I tried to comprehend what was happening here.

"Sacrifice," he sneered at me, yanking my arm hard as he pulled me to the boats. "I have been waiting for ten long years to seek out my vengeance, and it will be *mine.*" He growled out the word, flashing his teeth at me as panic took over.

My breathing came fast and shallow as I tried and failed to rip my arm from his grip. Raud's tattoos seemed to darken, shifting under his skin as he leaned into me and laughed. "So fiesty. Why, you'll make the most delicious sacrifice of all, won't you?"

His nose grazed my neck, and it took every ounce of strength in me not to shudder at the touch. "You even smell like him."

The touch of his wet tongue as it drug across my skin right over my pulse made me want to scream. "To spill fresh blood on the tree — yours and Mjölnir's both, I think — will surely draw the giants' attention."

My heart dropped to my feet. Black spots formed on the outside of my vision, panic taking over. I shifted in his grip, but his fingers dug into me, pressing harder every time I tried to break free. I lifted my boot to stomp on his foot but was pushed off balance as I fell to the ground. Glaring up at him, a mixture of anger and terror filled me.

"Your story is not one I can foresee… the last of your kind…"

This is *not* how my story would end.

This was *not* my fate.

Pulse racing, I pushed my chest off the ground, eyes full of fury as I spat.

"Your words don't scare me. Your *name* doesn't scare me. But I should scare you…," I stood in front of the man.

The men all laughed at my comment. Raud chuckled, his smile spreading wide.

Untapped power wove through my veins, a fire I'd never felt before surfacing as I stood straighter.

Yes, the deep and raspy voice inside me said, purring in approval of my actions.

"I am far more than you've bargained for."

"…the last of your kind…"

Before I could go on, a gust swept off the lake, wind whipping my hood back as my hair flew free and wild, and several men looked up. Clouds filled the sky, hovering over the lake.

Whoosh.

The sound came from our left, and everyone's heads snapped in that direction. The horses neighed frantically, throwing their heads as they yanked at their ropes to break free, hooves kicking up snow.

"Something is up there," a man whispered by me as their eyes all scanned the sky.

Whoosh.

"HADRIEL!"

My gaze shot to the sky as enormous black wings broke through the clouds, leaving a dragon-shaped hole, the sun peeking through for a moment.

Raud's furious gaze flew to me, and the grin that spread across my face was victorious. I had no idea how Hadriel found me or how he knew I needed him, but he was *here.*

An ear-splitting roar filled the air as rage spilled off the man in front of me.

"Load the boats *now!*" Raud shouted furiously. Men were yelling back and forth, actions hurried. They did as he said, but attention was scattered at the sight of the terrifying dragon so close. He disappeared behind a cloud, gone from view again as the men became frantic.

A piercing shriek shook my bones, terrifying, as I looked out over the water. There, hovering just above the water's surface, floating on air, was Hadriel. His eyes glowed as his mouth gaped open, searching the shore.

A crazed laugh escaped me as the most blood-curdling creature I'd ever seen flew straight for us. Terror gave way to sheer delight at the sight of the black and gold dragon coming to my rescue.

Fire lit the air, catching several men as screams and the

smell of burning flesh overpowered my senses. Raud dropped my arm and grabbed his sword, defending himself.

"FIGHT BACK!" he shouted to his men.

But they didn't.

His men fled into the woods, sprinting away from the dragon. The snowy beach had turned to chaos, boats forgotten. Mjölnir stomped a hole into the keel of the ship he had been loaded onto before jumping ashore and fleeing into the woods as well.

Raud turned his furious gaze on me, eyes alight with anger.

"What did you do, *witch*?"

I cackled, because I was insane. "Befriended a dragon."

Something at the edge of the forest caught his eye, and he glanced away from me. Hadriel landed hard on the shore behind me at the same moment, smoke curling out of his nostrils. I looked over at him, his mouth open, displaying many teeth, and smiled.

"Good boy," I said, grinning like the maniac I was. "You're a good boy."

Raud roared, anger pouring off of him, as he yanked me up and into him, a knife at my throat. He turned, holding me there as blood trickled down my skin.

I did my best to calm my breathing, putting as little pressure as possible on the knife. This seemed surreal, something straight out of a book and couldn't possibly be my life. Raud spun me and stepped back, forcing me towards the only boat left on the shore as I followed his line of sight.

There, under the trees, stood Domari, ax in one hand, sword in the other. He glared at Raud, then glanced in my direction.

"Step away from my woman," Domari said in a voice so low my knees quaked. "Lay a hand on her again, and I'll happily remove it from your body."

Raud breathed heavily against my back as the two men stared each other down, waiting for the other to cave. Hadriel let out another shriek, my curls shifting in the gust. Raud stilled, standing straighter, as Hadriel prowled across the beach towards us.

"This is your last chance," Domari said. "Drop your knife, or the dragon and I will take you down. I don't want to kill you, friend. But I will if you so much as glance in her direction again."

Heat spread through my body at the look on his face, the tone of his words. Leave it to me to be turned on as I was about to be sacrificed.

Raud finally took a step away from me, dropping his knife as he raised his hands in the air. Domari nodded as Raud grabbed another knife from his belt and threw it at Domari faster than I could even track the movement.

I screamed, time slowing as I watched the knife spin end over end. But I'd seen Domari in battle — I should have known the man would not be caught off-guard by such a move. Domari brought up his sword, sending the knife clattering off to his left as he deflected it. The clang of metal on metal rang in my ears as the two men eyed each other.

"Another day, Domari," Raud hissed. "Another day that you have everything and I have *nothing*. I will see it all taken from you before I enter Valhalla." He spat on the snow as Hadriel let out a hot plume of steam, growling in his direction.

His gaze snapped to the dragon behind us, seeming to have forgotten his enormous presence. Raud's hand raised, finger shaking in my direction.

"I'll be back for you," he growled. "Your days are numbered, girl. I will relish your ending, bathe in your blood, and feed you to the wolves. On that, I promise."

I gulped, suddenly far more ready to go home than I'd been earlier. My eyes glanced up to Domari, now halfway down the shore to me, as Raud jogged off into the forest following his men.

27

As Domari ran towards me, my feet staggered forwards on their own, sinking in the snow. Breath rushed out of me as he crushed me into his chest, hands searching everywhere, ensuring I was still whole. A sob escaped me as the adrenaline rush wore off, leaving behind cold terror as I thought through everything that had just happened.

"You're okay," Domari whispered, kissing my temple as he hugged me to him. "You're okay." He gripped my arms, looking me over to ensure his words were accurate, as he pulled up his shirt. My eyes followed his movement, watching as the fabric peeled away from his torso, and my fingers trailed across his hot skin exposed there.

I felt his chuckle rumble through his skin under my hand as I drew my eyes back to his face. He gently took the edge of his shirt and wiped away the blood on my neck, cleaning it as best he could.

"A small scratch," he mumbled, nodding. I watched his

lips move, unable to focus, as his pout turned into a smirk. My eyes continued up, finally finding his and the fire they contained.

"You drugged me," he whispered. I gulped, glancing down at his lips again as my tears dried. "I am not happy about that. Not at all."

"I couldn't stand another goodbye," I replied shakily, my breaths uneven as I ogled him. My heart lurched, craving this man in front of me.

"It's not time for that yet." His face lowered to mine, beard brushing my cheek as he leaned in impossibly close yet still too far away.

My breathing hitched, eyes scanning his face as his lips finally descended on mine. I moaned into his mouth, the sound sensuous, as my arms made their way around his neck.

Our tongues tangled, the embrace urgent as blood rushed lower in my body. Heat pooled between my legs as I rubbed my thighs together, seeking friction. Domari's arms circled my hips as he lifted me, my legs coming up around his waist as he walked us into the forest.

"This will only make it harder," I gasped, coming up for air, as he pushed my back up against a nearby tree, pinning me with his large body.

His chest rumbled as he leaned down to my neck, sucking and kissing his way down my throat, careful of the fresh cut on my skin.

"It's entirely too late for that." He ground his hips into me, letting me feel exactly what he meant as my head fell back against the tree, eyes shutting — soaking in this moment, searing it into my memory, as it would be our last.

My hands made their way under his shirt, reaching for any skin I could touch as he placed me down on my feet and spun me around.

Breath whooshed out of my lungs as I grappled against the tree for balance, feeling his heavy weight leaning into me.

"You left me," his mouth moved against my ear as he ground into my backside. "I woke, and you were gone."

With those words, he yanked down my leggings, exposing me to the cold air around us. I gasped, hands digging into the bark as his fingers trailed over my naked skin.

"Then I tore myself apart with worry, unable to get to you in the storm," he growled as his hands slid towards my core. I moaned at the feel, ready for him, but he held out.

"But of course, you were okay, *háski*. Danger is nothing new to you, hmm?"

His fingers slid through me, slick and waiting for him. I moved, breathing heavily, needing him more than I'd ever needed anything.

"And then I find you here," his fingers slid across my apex, circling as I gasped, nerves overloaded. "Standing in front of a man who promised to bathe in your blood. And yet, you still did not cower."

Then, a finger pierced me, and my mouth fell open, gasping for air. My body was glowing; I was so on fire.

"You have no idea what you do to me," Domari growled as another finger joined the first. I pushed my hips back against his hand, grinding into him with over-whelming need.

"I need you," I moaned as his hand stroked down my spine. The sound of his laces coming undone had me turning my head, eager to watch, as a hand landed on my hip again.

"Say it again," he snarled, eyes alight with molten fire. His hardness brushed against me, and I shifted my hips.

"*I need you,*" I hissed. I wasn't even sure that I meant physically, but at that moment, my mind could only comprehend the emptiness in me that he needed to fill.

His eyes lit with satisfaction at my words as he thrust into me in one sharp motion. My head dropped forward as he pounded into me, his hands grabbing my hips as skin slapped on skin, the sound echoing through the forest.

I moaned his name as my eyes rolled back in my head.

"There has never been a better sound than my name from your lips," he groaned, breathing hard.

I couldn't take it much longer; my body was coiled so tight I was ready to explode. My breathing stuttered, rising high, as a wave crashed over me, plunging me into depths I'd never experienced before. Domari moaned, a deep and resonating sound, as his body twitched along with mine.

Shivers racked my body, both from the cold around us and my nerves short-circuiting. After a moment, Domari pulled out, leaning down to fix our clothing with careful attention, before rising again.

I turned, and his eyes found mine, full of unspoken words neither of us could voice, as he leaned in and kissed me. It was tender and soft, unlike everything else that had just happened.

By the time my breathing calmed down, the sun had lowered to the tops of the mountains surrounding the lake. Domari's gaze followed mine, staring out over the water.

We sighed in unison, then laughed at the sound. His forehead leaned against mine, one last kiss before he stood and strode towards the beach.

"It's time," he said.

I nodded and followed.

Hadriel was gone as we approached the boats. One had been demolished between the damage Mjölnir had done and the flames Hadriel had sent licking across the shore. Domari spent a moment inspecting the last remaining vessel, checking it to ensure it was still intact. I watched silently, but my mind was solely fixed on the tree across the lake.

The sun was setting, dropping into the tops of the trees, as he pushed the boat out into the water. He braced one hand on the edge as he reached back with his other and grabbed my hand, helping me into the ship. I settled, hands in my lap, as he climbed in after.

Water sloshed around us, waves rippling across the glassy top as he dipped the oars into the water, propelling us towards the tree. I faced away from the island, unable to handle seeing it inch closer with every push. Domari's arms flexed as he rowed, leaning forward and then back. My eyes ate him up, taking in every last glimpse I could steal as we paddled across the lake.

Wings flapped overhead, sending birds scattering in the trees as Hadriel flew over us, watching. It was odd that I didn't feel threatened by his massive presence. Instead, a warm feeling of rightness settled into my bones at his sight. I had made a dragon-friend, and the thought made me smile.

"Beautiful," Domari whispered. "Your smile lights my world on fire. It illuminates my every moment. I will die happy knowing I stole those smiles, put them there, even for such a short time."

I said nothing, only smiled back at him, trying to show him how happy I'd been here with him.

The scuffing of the boat hitting rocks below us as we settled onto the island was a sound I would hear for the rest of my life. The creaking wood seemed final, the scratching an end.

It took every ounce of my willpower to throw my legs over the side of the boat, letting my feet sink into the pebbles below. Domari made his way to my side, and his hand reached out, seizing mine as he brought it to his lips.

Roots broke the island's surface, visible even amongst the fresh snow covering the ground. They were large, tangled tentacles clawing to the water's edge. My eyes followed them, rising to the tree in front of me.

It was immense, wider than Domari and I standing shoulder to shoulder at the base, and it ascended into dozens of limbs thick with age. A lone leaf clung to the tree, ready to fall as winter descended upon the land.

Hadriel landed behind us with a *thwack* as the final leaf rippled through the air, touching down on the glittering snow beneath. The sun dipped below the treeline as the clouds began to clear. I glanced up, taking in the limbs rising high into the sky, and noticed the stars appearing overhead.

"Tell me about the tree. This is the Sacred Tree?"

Domari nodded as we paused, staring up at it. "*Yggdrasil.* It is said to be the gateway to the Nine Worlds, home to gods, giants, dwarves, elves, and mortals alike."

Before he could go on, I gasped as purple and green wisps lit the sky. They flew like the wings of the dragon behind me, showering the island in light. The colors danced, swirling together and apart, in a beautiful motion my eyes could hardly track. Arms laced around my torso as Domari stepped into my back. His chin rested on my head as we watched the lights weave a story.

Eventually, my eyes drifted down to the tree, searching for answers among the branches and roots.

"I don't know what to do," I whispered, and my heart sank at the words.

Domari untangled himself from my arms before walking in front of me. He pulled me closer to the trunk, stepping lightly between the tangled roots. My eyes tracked them, glancing from one to the next, as I noticed bones, gold, jewels, furs… everything that had been sacrificed at this spot. My breath hitched, remembering the words Raud had said, realizing how close I'd come to lying among these very roots.

As we moved closer to the tree's heart, I spied small carvings etched into the wood. I knelt in front of one of the more extensive roots, tracing my fingers over the engraving — runes. Leaning back, I glanced at the other roots nearby and noticed they were everywhere, different runes and combinations engraved in other spots.

"What do they mean?" I glimpsed up at Domari.

He stooped next to me and then leaned to his left. "They're each different," he confirmed my earlier thought. He pointed at a root that held the most precious items, a vast pile holding helms, weapons, chalices, crosses, and jewelry, and explained, "This one here is for Victory."

He rose to his feet, walking around the roots, taking in the others. "This one is for love and family." Clothes and food items were piled in and around the roots.

We stepped around the tree, looking at all of the forgotten items, as my eyes caught on a thick root at the base of the trunk. The root rose from the ground, leaving an exposed area underneath. I leaned closer, inspecting it, and noticed the rune carved above it.

ᚲ

I gasped, glancing down at my hand. Domari's brow scrunched in confusion.

"My bracelet," I said after a moment. "That is the same rune as my bracelet." I pried my hand free of Domari's, lifting it to show him the red leather strap wrapped around my arm.

"Verandi said this one chose me in the market before I met you," I explained. "This has to be it."

I squatted down, inspecting the root, and ran my fingers over the rune. "This has to be it," I repeated. "What does it mean?"

Domari's hands pulled me up and into him as his arms laced around my back. A loud huff sounded behind us, Hadriel watching our every move as he roamed closer.

"That," he sighed, "is the rune for fate. The Norns."

"Why would this have been the one they chose for me?"

He looked back over his shoulder towards Hadriel and the water. The dragon huffed, a plume of smoke rising from his nostrils at Domari's attention. It almost seemed as if Hadriel had nodded, but I also loved to imagine talking animals. "I wish I knew."

"Thank you," I said, and his face turned back to mine, "for everything. For showing me kindness in my weakest moments. For making me laugh. For drying my tears. For all of it."

Peering up through my lashes, I watched so many emotions flash across Domari's face. Without a single word, I knew they echoed the own that I felt deep in my heart. Given time, I would love this man. I knew it, and yet it changed nothing.

"It was the pleasure of my life," Domari whispered, his voice raspy as he choked back his feelings. He silenced us both as his lips descended on mine in one final kiss.

"And you," I turned to the dragon behind us as a single

tear dripped down my chin, "I will never forget you. You're the goodest boy."

Hadriel nuzzled his head into us, and Domari went stiff at the motion. I reached out my hand and ran them over his scales, softer than I'd imagined, as a smile lit my face. *Promised,* the voice inside me said again.

"Thank you, too."

With that, I turned, loosening my bracelet to slide it from my wrist. I smiled one last time as I knelt to the roots in front of me and dropped my bracelet into the hole beneath the tree.

28

Domari watched as Shelbie knelt to the ground in front of him, removing her bracelet, and lingered for a moment. Then, the red leather slipped from her hand as it fell to the ground, dropping under the roots of the tree.

Before he could comprehend what had happened, she collapsed; her form went limp as she sank to the ground.

He howled, dropping to his knees, throwing his body over hers. Sobs racked his body as he held her to his chest, running his fingers through her blonde curls, tracing the side of her face. Her head tipped back, eyes closed, as he put his ear to her chest and listened for a heartbeat.

None came.

"Thank you," he said, tears falling from his face onto her lifeless body, "for everything."

A screech sounded behind, Hadriel mourning her right alongside him.

His body was bent over her, arms draped across her

chest, clinging to any remnant of the light she'd brought into his life. Suddenly, his hands began to sink to the ground, drawing his eyes open. A gasp escaped him as he watched her body fade into mist, rising into the night sky.

"No. *NO!*"

He clawed with his hands, trying to grab onto any bit of her, but it was no use. Far too soon, her body disappeared, the mist joining the green and purple wisps overhead.

Shelbie was gone.

I awoke with a gasp, sitting bolt upright as my eyes fought to clear my vision of sleep. Where was I?

My fingers ran over the soft cotton sheets underneath me, covering the downy bed I sat on. Beautiful watercolors depicting the wildlife of Sweden hung on the walls, matching the light tones of the birchwood furniture in the room. A small fireplace sat in the corner with a white, pileous rug. My mind spun, trying to catch up with my surroundings.

This was the inn.

How did I get there? The last thing I remembered was the island with Domari and Hadriel. I ripped off the blankets, peering down at my outfit to see a matching pajama set Sabrina had given me for my birthday last year.

Where had my leggings and jacket gone?

I stood on shaky legs, my head and heart competing for

which would break first. Somehow, I forced my legs to cooperate as I walked to the sink along the wall, turned on the faucet, and watched it fill the glass. My mind was numb as I fought to remember what was real.

Turning around, I noticed my backpack was perched at the foot of the bed. The zipper screamed through the room as I slid it open and peered in — everything I'd started the trip with and left behind in the barn before my fall was right there. And there, on the wall, hung my jacket.

My brow scrunched in confusion as my thoughts rattled in my head. How was this possible? Had I never even left? Had I dreamt the entire thing?

Was *any of it* real?

I rubbed my hand across my chest, heart aching at the questions running through me as I silently dressed for the day.

My jeans were stiff and uncomfortable, the sweater itchy as my senses were overloaded. Pulling my curls off my face and into a messy bun on the top of my head, I sighed, ready to find some answers.

The steps seemed to echo as I descended, loud and pounding with each footfall. I turned the corner to see Hans and Annika behind the desk.

"How did you sleep, dear?" Annika asked warmly. "I am sure you needed the rest."

My hand rose to my temple, rubbing across the skin as I tried to process everything. "When did I get back?"

A few beats of silence went by as the two exchanged a look, and then Hans answered, "You arrived after dark last night."

"And," I had difficulty even getting the words out, "what day is it?"

"It's Monday," Annika answered slowly, questions filling her expression. "October 11. Is everything okay?"

I smiled, rubbing my head again, as I nodded. "Yes, I'm fine. I slept hard, that's all. It's been a long trip."

She reached across the desk, patting my hand as she rubbed her thumb across my skin.

October 11.

I had been gone for thirteen days, yet I had no idea how I ended up back here. I stepped out of the inn a few moments later, inhaling the salty sea air. It was colder now, but I'd left my jacket in the room. Rather than retrieving it, I pulled my hands up into my sweater sleeves as I turned and walked into the street, scanning the area.

There was no market set up today, but I wandered, looking for any sign of a woman, neither short nor tall, with brown hair greying at her temples. *Verandi.*

I stopped at several stores, asking about a woman who made rune jewelry, showing them the bracelet still tied to my wrist, but no one had ever heard of such a vendor.

I rubbed at the bracelet absently as I walked. After an hour of fruitless searching, I headed for the cafe where I'd met Gustav and my gang of travelers.

His salt-and-pepper hair stood out as he sipped a giant pint of ale with a group of men. I approached him, not even sure what to ask.

"Gustav?"

He turned in his seat, gaze passing over me as his scowl took over. "Gustav. It's me. Shelbie."

Recognition sparked in his eyes. "You missed the trip," he said after a moment, taking a long sip of his ale again. "We don't offer refunds. Sorry."

He turned back to his companions, conversation over, as my mind spun.

I *missed* the trip?

But I'd left with him.

I'd hiked through Hell's Gap, sat around a campfire, gone to the horse barns with the dreaded English saddles. All of that had happened, and yet... had it?

I was so confused. The small coastal town blurred around me, details fading away as my mind tried to sort fact from fiction. Nothing made sense, not time-travel nor Norns. Not the missing days I'd been gone — none of it.

"Did you find what you were looking for?" Annika asked, kind eyes crinkling at the edges as I pushed open the door of the inn. "Any last-minute souvenirs?"

I smiled weakly, shaking my head. "No, I don't need anything else. Just taking a last stroll."

She nodded in understanding. "I'm sure you're ready to be home."

H*ome.* The word echoed in my head the entire flight to Denver.

Home.

What did it even mean? My mind was numb as I went through customs, found my bag, and walked outside the airport.

Home.

Was home my apartment? My bed? My things?

Home.

Sabrina's blue SUV pulled up to the curb as she hopped out, pulling me into a hug.

. . .

This was home.

Warmth radiated off her as she hugged me fiercely, not letting go. "I've missed you so much," she said in my ear, still embracing me. I gripped her tighter, needing the contact as I sighed.

"Look who came along for the ride!" She had the back window rolled down, and an enormous, fuzzy black head stuck out, panting. I leaned into Thor, running my hands through his fur.

This was home.

His wet tongue slid across my face, drenching me in slobber, as he nuzzled into me. "I missed you too," I hugged him to me. Sabrina rounded the car, eyeing me as she took my backpack. I turned my face, not ready to answer any of the questions I knew were coming.

"Did everything go okay?" she asked tentatively, reading my body language the way she always did.

"Yes," I said, avoiding her eyes. "It was life-changing."

Days blurred into weeks as I went through the motions. My life had never seemed so empty, so lifeless, so grey. I was depressed, and I knew it.

Everything in my life that made me unhappy seemed glaringly obvious now. I was sick of this apartment with my whiny neighbors hating on Thor. I was bored with my job, writing about things I wasn't passionate about. I was tired of my commute and hours lost every day in maddening Denver traffic.

I slept terribly. Some nights, I lay in bed awake for hours, unable to turn my mind off, remembering every stolen moment of my time in Sweden. Others, I woke gasping, tears streaming down my face at dreams I couldn't remember but haunted me for hours after waking.

All that had happened on my trip felt entirely too real. The memories of Magnus's easy smile, his booming laugh, came quickly to mind. Signe's strength, her smirk, her commentary — a ghost of a hand pulling me into the center of everything. Astrid's quiet company. Yrsa and Björn's thoughtfulness. Gunnar's heart was as golden as his hair. I even missed Hadriel. Who wouldn't miss an oversized, terrifying cuddler who may or may not want to eat you? And Domari…

I missed his warmth in the dead of night. I missed his hands, secure on my waist, always watching over me. I missed his smile, rare but saved just for me. I even missed how he rolled his eyes when I talked too much.

My heart hurt too much for it to have not been real. I ached, longing for a place, a people, a person who no longer existed. Who may never have lived at all?

I needed a change.

It was a Saturday in early December that I found myself driving to Charlene's on autopilot, needing an escape. I'd spent many days here since I'd returned from Sweden, avoiding the searching eyes of Sabrina and my family, looking for an explanation for the change in me. Since my return, I'd needed the solitude of the mountains around me to clear my head. Horses didn't ask questions, and Charlene was usually an excellent distraction.

I honked as I pulled up to the gates, heart easing at the sight of the mismatched barns and buildings on the property. Charlene emerged from her house, standing out on the porch with a coffee cup in hand, as she waved me through. The gate creaked open, and I parked my Jeep near her house.

"Come have a coffee before we get started," she said, walking inside. I followed, only one of a handful of times I'd gone inside her home. The air was chilly, but the warmth of her home seemed fitting as her very presence warmed my soul, too.

The living room was exactly what you'd expect; turquoise everywhere with beautiful paintings of wild horses on the walls. Crosses of different sizes, materials, and textures lined the hallway, just as shiny as their owner.

Charlene poured me a cup of coffee and then added something else. "Hot chocolate," she smirked. "Have you ever mixed the two? It's *divine.*"

I smiled as she handed me the mug, the sweet smell wafting into the air. It was hot, burning my tongue as I swallowed, but delicious.

"We have a lot to do before it snows this week," she said

after a minute. "I need full-time help out here, but it's hard to come by."

My head popped up at her words — the silence felt loaded, and her eyes were on me. "What?"

"Well," she sighed, "I'm just wondering when you're going to stop moping around and quit that dumb job of yours."

I was startled at her words, trying to remember what I'd even told her about my job. "And then what would I do?"

"Come work for me," her eyes sparkled with her idea. "And, I don't know. Read. Write a book, maybe. Something that makes you happy instead of the shit you spend your days doing."

I sighed, raising my mug to my mouth again. "That sounds wonderful, in theory, but it takes me over an hour to get here. The thought of the commute alone makes me want to vomit."

She laughed at that, nodding. "I don't blame you even a little for that. But who said anything about a commute?"

My brow scrunched at her words, trying to follow along. "What are you suggesting?"

"My sister's house behind the barn has been empty for twenty years," she jerked her head in the direction of the house. I glanced out the window, trying to see what she was talking about. "Marlene has no interest in coming back here unless it's to taunt me and leave again. The property's not *technically* hers since she made me buy her out of Daddy's inheritance. Why don't you go take a look, and you let me know if you and Thor could be happy there."

She leaned down, rummaging through a drawer, before

pulling out a leopard-print key on a pink rhinestone keychain. "I think this is the one." She reached across the counter and dropped them into my palm.

I looked down at the key in my hand as a chuckle shook me. This was the most Charlene-looking key of all time, and I didn't even know that was a *thing*. She shooed me out the door as Thor and I walked across the property towards the house.

It was small — simple, with two windows perched on either side of the coral-painted door. The white shutters needed a new coat of paint but would contrast nicely with the rich red brick of the house once I painted them. A shiny metal roof reflected the last of the autumn sun as it snuck through the trees and mountains surrounding the property. Thor followed me onto the porch and plopped down between two oversized wooden rocking chairs.

I turned to the house, put the key in the lock, and twisted the handle. Musty, stale air greeted me as dust drifted through the sun's rays. My hand raked along the wall as I reached for the light switch. A fan and light flickered on overhead, revealing a quaint living room, perfect for a couch and a chair. The walls were covered in a floral wallpaper that wasn't my style but didn't make me want to burn the house down either. I could probably figure out how to remove it.

There was room for a table and two chairs between the living room and the kitchen, a cute L-shaped layout surrounding a small island. Pans hung from the ceiling over the island, shifting in the wind coming through the open front door. The cabinets were painted white and had crystal knobs, making me chuckle again. But I loved the butcher-block countertops. I glanced around, taking in the small space and imagining what life would be like here.

I drifted down a narrow hallway leading to a spacious bathroom with a large vanity and two small bedrooms.

The smaller of the two would be perfect for an office. A window framed the spectacular view of the mountains behind the ranch, with a thin space on either side. My mind immediately imagined bookshelves placed on either side of the window and a small desk in the center. This could be the perfect place to write.

The larger bedroom was painted a pretty pale blue, shockingly serene knowing the taste in decor Charlene and her sister favored. It was about the same size as my apartment, but I was used to small, so it would be fine.

Was I truly contemplating this?

I wandered from room to room for a while longer before making my way back out. Charlene stood close by, brushing her horse tied to a hitching post as I locked the front door behind me.

"So," she said, not even glancing in my direction. "What did you think?"

"I'm surprised it wasn't decorated more."

She laughed at that. "I burned all her shit years ago." Her smile was devilish and not the least bit remorseful.

I laughed at that and picked up a brush to help her.

We worked in companionable silence for a while; the topic dropped for now before she spoke again.

"I'm still waiting for you to tell me what happened in Sweden. But I'll wait until you're ready."

I stopped what I was doing, hands falling to my sides as I thought through how to answer.

What had happened? I wasn't even sure.

"Does he have a name?" she said after another moment. My eyes found hers as she leaned against her horse, petting him softly.

"This here is Bryan," she stroked her horse, "And he's the only man for me." She kissed him on the bridge of his nose with a grin. She was content in her life, I realized. Charlene was happy with what she had even though life hadn't turned out quite as planned.

I needed to find my way to that place, too.

My eyes drifted down to my hands, fiddling with the brush rather than looking at her. "His name was Domari," I said finally.

Hearing his name out loud brought tears to my eyes. I hadn't spoken it since I'd been home. How could I even begin to tell anyone what had happened? Had it even happened at all?

I had no recollection of any other portion of my trip — no memories of hiking or riding other than before my fall. And time had passed as if I'd been gone.

But time-travel? The Norns? How was that possible?

"Well, I can tell he was a hottie by how you said his name. *Domari,*" she purred. I laughed, glancing up at her at last.

"You have no idea."

The day passed as we chatted idly, not touching on Domari again. By the time the sun set, my eyes seemed to catch on the tiny house at the back of the property.

"Just think about it," Charlene said as she patted the hood of my Jeep. I smiled at her, nodding, as I backed out.

The following week, every day in the office was a beating. One thing after the next seemed to go wrong, and I was sick of it. By Wednesday, my mind was absorbed in daydreams to escape the never-ending pressure of this unfulfilling job.

"When can we expect to see the final draft?" a voice said to my right, drawing my attention from the doodles I'd been drawing in my notebook.

Not doodles, I noticed. *Runes.*

I'd been drawing runes.

"Oh. Um," my mind tried to play catch-up to remember what we'd been talking about. "I'll get it to you by Friday."

My client nodded at that as Jordan's face lingered on mine. Everyone was dismissed from the meeting as he motioned to stay in my seat.

"Let's chat for a moment," Jordan said. I nodded, closing my notebook. The last attendees left the conference room, shutting the door behind her as she glanced back at me. I watched them walk away through the glass hall window, unsure what to expect next.

"Shelbie," he said after a minute. "I'm worried about you."

My eyes came up, reading his unspoken words, as I exhaled. I knew what my heart wanted me to do, but my mind was more than a little hesitant about what was coming next.

"I think...," my pulse pounded in my ears, decision made, "I think it's time for me to move on. I don't think I'm the right fit for this company anymore, and it's time I find something that sparks passion in me."

Jordan sighed, tapping his pen on his notebook as he nodded. "I agree. I hate to see you go, as you're one of our best writers, but I can tell you aren't happy here. And I want that for you. We all do."

I nodded, my mind playing catch-up to this conversation. *Had I just quit my job?*

"With the holidays around the corner, why don't we make this an easy transition, and you leave before the winter break?"

"Oh...kay."

"Does that sound fair to you?"

"Yes," I fought to put more strength in my words. "Yes. That would be great."

I returned to my desk a few minutes later, shock rippling through me at what had just happened. What now?

I shot a text off to Charlene, letting her know I'd quit.

"Yeehaw! Time to move!" she replied quickly.

Should I move? Lord knows I wouldn't be able to afford my apartment for much longer without getting another job, and that was something I wasn't quite ready for yet. I needed time, and that was what Charlene was offering me.

The rest of the day passed by quickly as my mind turned to thoughts of redecorating, painting, and furniture placements. I pulled into my apartment complex's front office space later, and my car door slammed as I practically skipped into the lobby to turn in my notice. My heart felt lighter than it had in weeks — *months* — as I took Thor for a walk that night.

That weekend, I purchased some boxes from the local hardware store and began to pack my belongings. On Sunday, I drove out to Charlene's with a trunk full of clothes.

"Are you sure about this?" I asked as I popped the trunk.

"Yes, girl!" she smiled. "It'll be fun to have someone else out here with me."

She grabbed a stack of clothes off the top and walked down to the little house. I smiled as she pushed open the coral door, knob glistening in the sunlight, and walked down the hall, hanging my clothes in the closet.

Home.

I stopped inside the door, clothes in hand, and looked around the space, waiting to become mine.

This could be home.

The following two weeks passed in a whirlwind, and I had three days until my lease was up. Friday had been my last day at work, and I drove into the mountains to see my parents after saying my goodbyes. My company had thrown me a thoughtful farewell luncheon, and everyone wanted to know what was next.

Honestly, I didn't have the answer yet.

To be determined.

My Jeep was packed tight, full of presents for my nieces and nephew. Thor sprawled across the backseat, lounging, as I waited in the holiday ski traffic. The roads were clear, which was a good thing as I would easily make it across Vail Pass. I channel-surfed the radio, unable to settle on anything in particular, but I was sick of Christmas music non-stop. I gave up after a while, switching it to a classic rock station I listened to often. The sound of Fleetwood Mac carried through the car as I sang along.

Two hours later, the sound of giggles filled the air as I

drove up to a snowball fight in my parents' front yard. Thor barked loudly when I rolled down the window, tail wagging as he was ready to join the fun. Jacob's daughters squealed in excitement, one climbing him like a tree to get away from big, bad Thor.

My car rolled to a stop, and I turned off the engine, parking for the weekend. Jacob waved to me as I hopped out of the car, opening the door for Thor. He jumped down and dove straight into the closest pile of snow, spinning as he shoved his face into the white powdery surface. His nose flicked the snow into the air and sent it showering down over the kids as his tongue hung out the side of his mouth.

He was smiling. My big, grumpy puppy was smiling as he played in the snow. I laughed at the sight, feeling lighter already.

"Let's get this stuff inside," Jacob said as he grabbed bags from my car.

"Can I open my present now, Aunt Shelbie?" my niece tugged on my pants.

"Yes!" I answered excitedly with a grin that would have made Magnus proud. "Why not?"

Jacob glared at me over the heads of his screaming children, now running to the front door in excitement.

"Thanks for that," he said in a flat tone.

I chuckled, smiling down at Thor, now rolling in the snow. His entire black body was covered in white.

Wrapping paper covered the floor a few minutes later, obscuring the rug underneath completely as they tore into their presents. Evening came quickly as the girls played happily on my mom's kitchen floor, under the table, and anywhere they could find an open surface. Lauren sat in my father's oversized leather chair, dozing with a baby on her chest as Jacob eyed me.

"You quit your job?"

"I did," I said confidently for the first time. "And I'm moving this week."

"To be a… ranch hand?"

"For now," I nodded, happy with the thought of spending my days with the horses. "I think I may try to write a book."

"About what?"

I thought about that for a while, silence spreading between us. "A girl who goes on a trip and her life is changed forever."

He eyed me at that, unspoken words in his gaze.

I rose after a few minutes, carrying dinner dishes to the sink, and settled in with a book by the fire. Thor sprawled across my feet, and I glanced around the room. Everyone was chatting happily around me, and I was happy to be there.

The smell of bacon woke me the next morning as I made my way to the kitchen. My dad was on the porch, steaming coffee in hand as he was every morning. I poured myself a cup and grabbed a strip of bacon before joining him.

Sliding the doors open, a cold gust of wind hit my face, and I pulled my robe tighter around me. "Elk tracks in the valley back here," my dad nodded in the direction he was looking. "Come take a look."

I stood silently at his side, sipping our coffee as we

watched the peaceful view. Today was my first day unemployed, and I already felt a little better. One step forward towards finding what made *me* happy.

We went inside after a while as the sounds of little voices reached us. Everyone was awake, and the house was busy. My mom bounced a baby on a hip as she poured orange juice into sippy cups, handing them out with a smile on her face. I grinned at the chaotic scene. This house was full of love.

After some begging, I caved and made cookies with my nieces, preparing for Santa's arrival later that week. We measured the oats, chocolate chips, brown sugar, and other ingredients needed for my favorite oatmeal chocolate chip cookies. To be extra special, we added some M&Ms to the top, ensuring our house stood out among the others in the area so Santa would remember my nieces.

"I hate to be the bearer of bad news, especially right after you've just arrived," my dad said as I was washing dishes later. He leaned on the counter next to me, holding up his phone. "Look at this, though." I glanced at his outstretched hand and saw a weather radar map with a large shape moving closer.

"This storm is supposed to hit late tomorrow morning, and they'll close the pass again. Don't you need to move out on Monday?"

I sighed, thinking through everything that this meant. I did have to be out on Monday, and if I was snowed in here, that would be a problem.

"I'll leave in the morning, I guess," I decided. "It was

good to have a little time with the girls anyway. I'm sure you'll have lots on your plate this week."

"Come back up in a few days after you're settled if you'd like," my dad leaned in, kissing me on the forehead. "You know you're always welcome here, Bumble Bee."

I smiled at the use of my childhood nickname. "I know."

The sky was still dark when I awoke the next morning. Something felt different, maybe the pressure in the air from the coming storm, but I wasn't sure.

I packed quietly, snagging a bagel and a coffee as I made my way out to the Jeep. Dad had already turned it on for me, so it was defrosted and ready to go.

"Drive safe, okay?" he said as he helped me up into my car. "Call me when you get home."

Thor jumped up into the backseat, and we pulled out of the driveway. Dark clouds blocked out the last of the moonlight threatening the snow still off in the distance.

Everything about the morning drew my mind back to my final days in Sweden. Spending the day sandwiched between a tree and a warm horse surviving on my own had changed something in me, even if it was only a dream.

That day, I'd promised to myself that I would face whatever came next with the heart of a Viking, and I would.

"You have so much in front of you...," the Norns had said, and I did. I wasn't sure what that looked like yet, but I was

going to forge a life for myself that centered around my happiness.

As those thoughts and memories circled, I found myself driving towards the hill we'd hiked this summer. I had my snow gear in the car with me, planning on playing in the snow today with my nieces anyway, and I was yearning for one last feeling of home…

"Wanna go for a walk?" I said, glancing in the rearview mirror at Thor. I turned off the car at the base of the hill and pulled on my hat, jacket, and mittens. We climbed out as I clipped his leash onto him and worked our way up the snow-dusted trail.

Fresh air bit into my skin, cold and brisk but full of life as it mixed with the pungent smell of pine. The trees around me blocked most of the wind, and the silence of the early morning was as peaceful as anything I'd ever felt. The sun was rising now, peeking over the mountains, glittering off the fallen snow. I smiled as we walked into the forest to Thor's favorite pouting spot.

As we approached the clearing ahead, the very same one Thor and I had spent so much time in before, a low growl escaped his throat. I stopped in my tracks, glancing around the woods for predators. Bears would be hibernating by now, but mountain lions could still be about. My senses were on high alert as branches crunched ahead of us.

"What is it, bud?" I whispered, leaning into Thor.

I glanced up, searching for the source of the sound, as Thor continued to growl. My eyes caught on movement in the trees, headed towards us, but what was there was far taller than a mountain lion.

As the sun peeked through the trees, my breath caught, held tight inside me.

Walking towards me was a mountain of a man. He had warm brown hair, longer on the top and shaved closely on the side, mingled with a beard equal parts massive and neatly kept, not a hair out of place. His deep brown eyes pierced me, searching my face and body. He was dressed in a combination of furs, draped casually over his shoulders, and I knew exactly who he was.

Domari.

To Be Continued
In Book Two: Fates Promised

EPILOGUE

Long ago, the three sisters paced along the shore of the lake, staring up into the sky as shrieking filled the air. The green and purple wisps floating in the air turned blood red with flashes of green as hatred and anger rained down on the water below.

"We must stop him," Skuld said, her voice shaking in distress as she wrung her hands together.

"Nidhoggr is an Unpromised," Urd answered, "He cannot bring down the Tree alone."

While her words were reassuring, doubt showed on Urd's face, as if even she didn't feel the truth in them. Verandi broke her trance on the skies above for a moment, glancing back at the hut only paces behind them. There, inside, safe and protected, lay their last hope.

A pulse rent the air, and the furious cries above them paused as even the nightmarish creature above sensed the change coming. The three sisters spun as one, rushing into their home.

The wood of the front porch squeaked under their hurried steps. They pushed inside the warm space, lit dimly by the hearth in the center. A faint light shone on the tapestry filling the room, still and lifeless behind them. But the loom and textile that demanded so much of the sisters' time were not their intended target.

Stopping next to the fire, the three paused. There, kept warm by the flames, sat a large, golden egg. The priceless object had laid dormant for years — never moving, never cracking.

The sisters had protected it, keeping it hidden in their hut as they watched the great White Dragon wreak havoc on the Tree. This golden egg was precious, for it was the last of its kind.

Inside the golden shell, the last dragon waited.

Dragons' fates were different than mortals and gods — a blind spot in the sisters' ever-seeing eyes. They had done everything to protect this egg, hoping that a new Promised would be revealed when it hatched. For a dragon at full power with a Promised at its side would be the only way to defeat the dragon flying above their hut even now.

Heatwaves wavered in the air, tangible in the warm summer night as the sisters huddled over the egg.

CRACK

The sound was so sudden that all three sisters jumped, gripping each other's hands tightly as they waited.

Prayed.

Wished.

CRACK, the sound rang out again.

A chip broke apart from the golden egg, falling to the floor as a tiny black head emerged. Its scales sparkled in the firelight as hints of gold shone through. His tail was wrapped around his already large frame and slammed against the shell. It splintered, more pieces falling to the side as the dragon unfurled.

"Hadriel," Verandi whispered. *Dark One.*

At the sound of his name, the baby dragon released a plume of fire, flames licking the chair in front of the hearth. Skuld quickly stamped it out and bent to scoop up the tiny reptile. Unafraid, she ran her hands over his smooth scales, and the dragon purred, leaning in.

"Shelbie," a raspy voice said in her head. *"She is not here. I will wait."*

Skuld's face shot up, her brow creased as she looked to her sisters. "He has a Promised, but she is not here."

"Hand him over," Verandi demanded, taking the small dragon from her sister and walking outside towards the water's edge.

This had never happened before. A dragon and his Promised were always born on the same day. Fate foretold the two were meant to be together from their origin, Promised even before their first breath.

"I will wait," the small dragon projected again.

Verandi spared only a glance into the sky, waiting to see if Nidhoggr would appear, but the White Dragon had fled.

Someday, the battle would come. Once Nidhoggr discovered that Hadriel, the last-born dragon, was a Promised, but without his mate, he would return.

The sisters could only pray that they could find the missing thread and restore the bond before that day.

For if they didn't, the Tree would fall.

If Nidhoggr were left unchecked, Ragnarok would begin.

ACKNOWLEDGMENTS

It is surreal to know that anyone has read this far even to see these words, so thank you. It means the world to me. So many of you have helped make this dream come true.

Before I go any further, though, I have to pour praises over my husband, Chris. None of this would have happened without you pushing me and encouraging me every step of the way. The hours we've spent standing in our kitchen, going over every plot detail, are ones I'll cherish always. I love you forever.

To my girls: I am so proud to be your mama. Every time you told random strangers excitedly that your mom wrote a book, you have no idea how much that meant to me. Thank you for being my biggest cheerleaders.

To B: it probably would have taken me years to get this far without you. In fact, without you demanding to know what came next, I don't know if I ever would have finished. If all that happens with this book is that it brought you into my life, it was still worth it.

To the Catherines, Kaitlin, Amanda, Karen, Melissa, and Mom: thank you for bearing with me through this from the beginning, sharing all of your advice and feedback, and lastly, for making sure I understood that this was a story worth telling.

To Bryan: Thank you for the most jaw-dropping, laugh-out-loud, memorable line of my book. You and your horse babies are the absolute best.

To all of the new friends I found along the way, especially Lex and Brit: I never could have guessed how much this book would change my life for the better. I'm so glad this world brought us together!

Last, but most certainly not least, to the entire Bookstagram Community: Keep cheering each other on. You have no idea how much power you have, holding the ability to build each other up in this long and challenging journey. I feel so blessed to have stumbled across this little pocket of the internet.

THANK YOU!

ABOUT THE AUTHOR

Fueled by peach tea and chaos, Aimee Vance believes that life doesn't end for romantic heroines in their early twenties and that everything would be better if magic was real, both of which are prominent themes in the stories she tells.

Outside of writing happily-ever-after endings for hot-mess heroines, she spends her days with her husband and two young daughters in Texas.

Fates Illuminated was her debut novel and the first in the series, The Call of the Norns.

instagram.com/aimeevancebooks

ALSO BY AIMEE VANCE

Call of the Norns

Fates Illuminated

Fates Promised

Fates Defied - Coming Spring 2024

Deadlights Cove
Cowritten with B. Perkins

Smoke Show

Deja Brew

A Very Merry Christmoose (Novella)

Wing and a Miss

Pier Pressure

Karma is a Witch